PRAISE FOR *THE NATURE BOOK*

"Symphonic, both in its structure—four movements, the third of which is the most distinct and the last of which references the first and goes out in a brilliant burst—and in the way language echoes, builds, works its accretive magic. . . . Seeing the world like this, without us, traversed in a way we could never traverse it in our human bodies, is a powerful and exhilarating experience."
—**Cara Blue Adams**, *The New Yorker*

"A meditative, lush narrative on the relationship between time and nature. . . . Like Proust, Comitta centers you in the reading experience, not just demanding your labor of comprehension at the languorous, long sentence level, but also requiring your attention and patience. . . . You'll be hard-pressed to find another book with as verdant an archive of beautiful descriptive sentences as the one contained in *The Nature Book*."
—**Darina Sikmashvili**, *Los Angeles Review of Books*

"An epic journey—visual, textural and musical—that illustrates the vastness of our environment and its representation in literature."
—**Joseph Holt**, *Star Tribune*

"[Comitta's] authorial vision weaves together a wild variety of styles with a steady eye on the land, sky, and water, as well as on the plants and animals living in each. Comitta approaches assembly with a conceptual rigor, but they do not sacrifice polish or readability. The novel flows beautifully. . . . An optimistic critique of the form, made entirely of the form."
—**Crow Jonah Norlander**, *BOMB Magazine*

THE NATURE BOOK

THE NATURE BOOK

Tom Comitta

COFFEE HOUSE PRESS
Minneapolis
2023

Coffee House Press books are available to the trade through our primary distributor, Consortium Book Sales & Distribution, cbsd.com or (800) 283-3572. For personal orders, catalogs, or other information, write to info@coffeehousepress.org.

Coffee House Press is a nonprofit literary publishing house. Support from private foundations, corporate giving programs, government programs, and generous individuals helps make the publication of our books possible. We gratefully acknowledge their support in detail in the back of this book.

LIBRARY OF CONGRESS CATALOGING-IN-PUBLICATION DATA

Names: Comitta, Tom, 1985– author.
Title: The nature book / [compiled by] Tom Comitta.
Description: Minneapolis : Coffee House Press, 2023.
Identifiers: LCCN 2022034761 (print) | LCCN 2022034762
    (ebook) | ISBN 9781566896634 (paperback) | ISBN
    9781566896641 (ebook)
Subjects: LCSH: Ecofiction. | LCGFT: Experimental fiction. |
    Novels.
Classification: LCC PS3603.O4776 .N38 2023 (print) |
    LCC PS3603.O4776 (ebook) | DDC 813/.6—dc23
LC record available at https://lccn.loc.gov/2022034761
LC ebook record available at https://lccn.loc.gov/2022034762

PRINTED IN THE UNITED STATES OF AMERICA

30 29 28 27 26 25 24 23   2 3 4 5 6 7 8 9

for Daya

CONTENTS

PREFACE

This novel contains no words of my own. Through a process of collage and constraint, I have gathered nature descriptions from over three hundred novels and arranged them into a single book.

What you hold in your hands is a story, but also an archive. In examining language from hundreds of texts, it searches for commonalities and reveals patterns—from the humorous to the banal to the troubling—in how we think and write about nature. It also attempts something atypical of collage: it avoids disjunction in favor of cohesion. In this way *The Nature Book* is closer to a YouTube supercut than a Burroughsian collage novel. I call it a literary supercut.

The Nature Book challenges what we might see as a more "natural" reading experience by including only what many readers skim over. As Mark Twain put it, "Nothing breaks up the author's progress like having to stop every few pages to fuss-up the weather. . . . Persistent intrusions of weather are bad for both reader and author." Many would say the same about nature descriptions in general, making *The Nature Book* likely the worst perpetrator of this offense yet.

More interesting to me is the book-object itself: an excess of nature language now printed and bound, removed from and yet inextricably linked to the natural world around it. On one hand, this book is just letters and words on a page, black shapes impressed onto tree pulp, a record of how hundreds of writers have rearranged these shapes over three hundred years. On the other, it's the story of three hundred years of rendition, how authors have distorted, praised, belittled, anthropomorphized, projected onto, and spoken through countless animals, landforms, and weather patterns. As such, there is no nature in this book; it's all illusion and distortion. Entirely human.

The Nature Book is also a story of our ecological past. The natural world described by Austen and Dickens is different from that of Plath and Baldwin and still farther from the early works of DeLillo and Atwood. It's even more removed from the time of this writing, when climate change is devastating the planet. In these ways, *The Nature Book* is time-stamped, a time capsule even, or, as Edward Abbey described his book *Desert Solitaire,* "a tombstone . . . a bloody rock."

Whichever way you look at it, *The Nature Book* operates inside several contradictions—somewhere between past and present, human and nature, narrative and archive, lyrical excess and data analysis. It's a puzzle I pieced together from fragments of literary history, and now, sitting in your hands, or on a table or a shelf, an awkward cousin to the books around it, alien to and yet entirely of them.

THE NATURE BOOK

I. THE FOUR SEASONS

I

SINCE THE BEGINNING, TIME WAS A FORM OF SUSTENANCE, pleasant as the spring, comfortable as the summer, fruitful as autumn, dreadful as winter. Weeks, months, seasons passed with dream-like slowness, and the Earth moved in its diurnal course.

To a waiting horse, perhaps time passed with torturous languor. To a tree, this phenomenon was common enough; much more unusual was the fact that years passed, and by some accident another tree arrived, and flowers and birds and insects.

On earth time was marked by the sun and moon, by rotations that distinguished day from night. The present was a speck that kept blinking, brightening and diminishing, something neither alive nor dead. How long did it last? One second? Less? It was always in flux; in the time it took to consider it, it slipped away.

There were times, though, especially towards the end of a long, cold, dark winter, when time slowed to an operatic present, a pure present. Sun was all shrouded over with mist, and could no longer shine brightly, and the snow began to fall straight and steadily from a sky without wind, in a soft universal diffusion, a continuous symphony.

At such a moment it seemed that time stopped. The day and the scene harmonized in a chord. Words. Was it the shifting colors? The snow fell so thick that it was only by peering closely that such heavy flakes blended like the elements of color, elements that, somewhere in the grid of time, would recede and show that, amid the prostration of the larger animal species—the few nearby trees and plants buried under amorphous white cloaks and winter storms—time disappeared, and it was like seeing all time as you might see a stretch of Mountains.

All time. The slow passage of years! The constant alterations! It was all ephemeral, filmy, dreamy. It was the mystery of creation, the stupendous miracle of recreation; the vast rhythm of the seasons, measured, alternative, the sun and the stars keeping time as the eternal symphony of reproduction swung in its tremendous cadences like the colossal pendulum of an almighty machine—primordial energy flung out from the hand of the Lord God himself, immortal, calm, infinitely strong.

The earth was at work, as it is always at work, and it moved slowly. A thousand times in the future this irresistible movement would change the aspect of the earth's surface. The mountains continued to push upward. New-forming land would rise from the sea to be weathered by storm and wind. Sometimes the sea would wash in bits of animal calcium, or a thundering storm would rip away a cliff face and throw its remnants over the shore. At other intervals, flowers would bloom—spectral substance vibrating in silent winds of accelerated Time . . .

Time-lapse of a million billion flowers opening their heads, of a million billion flowers bowing, closing their heads again, of a million billion new flowers opening instead, of a million billion buds becoming leaves then the leaves falling off and rotting into earth, of a million billion twigs splitting into a million billion brand new buds. The grass would be growing and dying back to nothingness in much the same fashion.

Wherever sun sunned and rain rained and snow snowed, wherever life sprouted and decayed, places were alike. Winter was long. Spring was a very flame of green. On certain spring days, there was a hint of summer in the air—in the shadows it was cool, but the sun was warm, which meant good times coming.

When the days were longer, when summer afternoons were spacious, laughter was on the earth. Primroses were broad, and full of pale abandon. The lush, dark green of hyacinths was a sea, with buds rising like pale corn. The rich odour of roses and the light summer wind stirred amidst the trees. Flowers, acre after acre, bloomed side by side, each bathed in the sun, each held in the wind's sway, each deeply rooted in the rich, dark soil. Poppies, sunflowers, daffodils, dogwoods, tigerflowers waved in the sun, and days were bright with the colored balls of song as the birds tossed back and forth, small unspeckled birds. These were the realities of the external world.

But here, the summer before last, as time went on and each day it became hotter, the soil became dryer, and much of the earth lay dried and cracked while water which had accumulated during the rainy season remained in deeper ditches and craters. Flowers slumped and grasses bent. The ground bred all manner of insects, and the mosquitos in particular seemed everywhere. Day after day was hotter than the day before, day after day the west wind blew and began to be regarded in a different light.

At first nothing had been outwardly altered here, but while the summer had gradually advanced over the western fields, beyond the elms and lindens, a sluggish stream, fed from snows in the mountains two hundred miles to the north, vanished completely. The land dried up, and the cloudless sky, the haze of heat, rather betokened a continued drought. All day long, every day, the blazing midsummer sun beat down, and there was no escape behind the boughs, in the shade of hazel bushes. The sunlight, filtering through innumerable leaves, was still hot.

Then one day the wind picked up—some southern wind of passion swept over, bringing with it the tang of verbena, and soon the sky was painted with a small number of flat clouds that looked like sandbars. The wind had freshened, and it grew, and grew, till soon, the air was crystalline as it sometimes is when rain is coming. The temperature dropped, and late that afternoon there was more activity overhead, clouds forming and moving. The blue cloud-shadows chased themselves across the grass like swallows. Real animals came along, flying a yard or two at a time, and lighting. And then the light rain began to blow on the wind although the sky was not properly covered with cloud. A mist of silver radiance kissed the earth. Nature smiled once more.

Thereafter the summer passed with routine contentment. Routine contentment was: In the mornings the meadow larks rose singing into the sky. All day the curlews and killdeers and sandpipers chirped and sang in the creek bottoms. Often in the early evening the mockingbirds were singing. And the days were bright. Trees, rich and voluptuous, waved in the sun, roses were in bloom. The night was luminous with moonlight.

Every hour, every day, was a good one. If it was going to rain, enormous clouds glowed like archangels. If the sun were shining through a mist, its light and glamour spread in all directions. It seemed as if a lull was here, the one solid reality. There were young colts and meadows. There were little hollows of water that caught the light and looked like precious stones scattered over the landscape. There were other comforting things.

As the end of summer came near, the weather remained unusually calm, but two events, two things, saddened. One. The air was very still. Some days not a leaf stirred on the green appletree. Not a single closed flower of the morning-glories trembled on the vine-stalk. Two. The martins were now coming and going elsewhere. Other birds in the valley were flying homeward to the south. It was strange how everything had been so full of life and funny and in a way sad. It didn't make sense.

It was during those same weeks of change, flux and reflux, that the sunsets had become almost unbearably beautiful. Watching the sky go from yellow to pink, watching flights of martins sweep low over the Hills, was very pleasant. One evening, on the last day of summer, tall trees sent their shadows across the grass. The sky, as often on those summer evenings, had become a pale purple colour. The few clouds glowed blue and red and mauve. By the time the sun was low on the horizon, the amphitheatre of round hills glowed with sunset, the meadows golden, the woods dark and yet luminous, tree-tops folded over tree-tops, distinct in the distance. And soon the edge of the earth trembled in a darkish haze. Upon it lay the sun, going down like a ship in a burning sea, turning the western sky to flaming copper and gold. Wisps of cloud hung low like smoke rising from the trees. Other clouds, under an altered dispensation, were purely ornamental.*

While the sun dipped lower and lower, the trees were silent, drawing together to sleep. An occasional yellow sunbeam would slant through the leaves and cling passionately to the orange clusters of mountain-ash berries. Only a few pink orchids stood palely by, looking wistfully out at the ranks of red-purple bugle, whose last flowers, glowing from the top of the bronze column, yearned darkly for the sun.

Just before the coming of complete night, the sky overhead throbbed and pulsed with light. The glow sank quickly off the field; the earth and the hedges smoked dusk. The sun had gone down, but the sky was still blue, a very pale blue, with a few high clouds still golden with sunlight. Soon four stars were visible in the place where the sun used to be.

As it grew dark, there was something . . . about the river and the good meadow land and the timber, about the clouds grinding against the mountains and the trees sticking out of the ground . . . something. Something to do with watching the sun set, watching the night build itself, dome-like, from horizon to zenith. Something special in the wind, the crickets and the birds, the stars swimming in schools through the night sky. Something special at the end of summer, a grand finale . . .

---

* Another postmodern sunset, rich in romantic imagery. Why try to describe it? It's enough to say that everything seemed to exist in order to gather the light of this event. Not that this was one of the stronger sunsets. There had been more dynamic colors, a deeper sense of narrative sweep. But this day was a good one and, taking some secondary appearances into consideration, it was likely to be interesting and a more affecting thing than other days, that was sure.

2

BUT THAT NIGHT, AS ALL THE LOWER WOOD WAS IN
shadow, almost darkness, night came and nothing happened.
Lightning bugs were still about; the night crawlers and flying insects had not gone wherever they go when autumn comes.
Summer ended, and within a few hours the autumnal moon had
risen, but not a trace of cool weather with it.

At dawn, when the light summer wind stirred amidst the trees,
it was the same. Trees and flowers lived under the same sky as
the day before yesterday. In the grass, the faint hum of the insect,
the mellow complainings of the pigeons, the contented clucking
of the hens—all of these noises mingled together to form a faint,
drowsy bourdon, prolonged, stupefying, suggestive of an infinite
quiet, of a calm summer.

By the morning of the next day, it was clear what had happened. Nature had used no subtlety at all: It was the period
between seasons, when nothing was being done, when the natural
forces seemed to hang suspended. There was no rain, there was no
wind, there was no growth. The sun alone moved.

With the same result, well, the days went along. Whole days
suspended in air. Every event was measured by the emotions of
the mind, not by its actual existence, for existence it had none. It
was the best of times, it was the worst of times, it was the season
of Light, it was the season of Darkness, it was the spring of hope,
it was the winter of despair. Gone the reasons, gone the seasons, in
the land of lost of time.

It was a peculiar thing, but as the hours passed and the days
passed, the nothing place began to settle. This nuisance flattened
out. The light, full and smooth, lay like a gold rind over the furze

and yew bushes. The trees were gorgeous in their leafiness—the warm odors of flower and herb came sweet upon the sense.*

At about the same time, the days grew short and the nights grew long. The light a little less each time. Dark at half past seven. Dark at quarter past seven, dark at seven. The temperature dropping, the water turning cooler. Gold and crystal moons rose over. Blue horizons waved in the distance. Between sunrise and sunset, those autumn suns seemed to shine out somewhat brighter: a ray gleamed any morning, every morning; fertile plains matured under the level beams.

In this light the leaves were changing, and the golds and purples of autumn mingled with the predominating green, breaking up the green monotony of summer, touching the beech-trees with russet, willows with coppers and ochers. Each day and each night the track of the golden autumn wound its bright way visibly through the green summer of the trees. Oak trees with their leaves going burgundy, leaves that were big and floppy, a few gold or ruby-red around the edges. Ashes and plane trees whose red, brown, and yellow leaves were merging again into a flow of colour. Some leaves were falling, flickering in the sunlight as they drifted downwards.

As the golden summer changed into the deep golden autumn, the spirit of youth dwelt in it. All that was gracious triumphed, all red and gold, with mellow mornings when the valleys were filled with delicate mists as if the spirit of autumn had poured them in for the sun to drain—amethyst, pearl, silver, rose, and smoke-blue morphing gently from one shade to the next. And in the mornings the dews were so heavy that the fields glistened like cloth of silver, and there were such heaps of rustling leaves in the hollows

---

* All these objects under the quiet light of a sky marbled with high clouds would have made a sort of picture: a sun in a platinum haze pervading the upper edge of a two-dimensional, dove-gray cloud fusing with the distant mist, a line of trees silhouetted against the horizon, and clouds inscribed remotely into misty azure with only their cumulus part conspicuous against the neutral swoon of the background.

of many-stemmed woods. There was a tang in the very air that inspired the wind, scattering the red and yellow leaves in a whirl-wind of confetti.

On such a morning, nothing else would be stirring—or so it would seem. But as the dawn came on and the leaves moved overhead, gradually ears would pick out tiny rustlings in the vines nearby, where a mourning dove would call unseen—a round, clear, bouncing note, as though a soft ball had been dropped on the lowest key of a xylophone: "Tuuu . . . tuu tu tu." Another dove would answer a distance away. They would call again, closer to each other each time; then they would emerge together from the mist, of the mist, gray, graceful, and be off together wing to wing like reflections of each other in a looking-glass sky. The red-winged blackbirds would wake all at once, like soldiers to Reveille. They would shake themselves from the grove and swing in a glistening pack to settle in the nearby bunchberry vines, where they waited for the mist to lift from the cattails, singing incessantly or draw-ing the black feathers of their wings and tails slowly through their bills. Then the blue grouse would drum away its kin, the flickers and sapsuckers would begin knocking the trunks of hemlocks for breakfast . . . And after all the other birds were up and about their affairs—even after the jay, who would burst each morning from the mist, screeching in a blue rage at these damned early birds who never let a fellow finish his rest—the crows would make their stately entrance. Overhead very high and very faint they could hear the calls of birds moving south.

On serene afternoons, the procession was constant. Squirrels were chattering, birds were singing, and huge amber-brown Monarch butterflies lazily drifted south, their incompletely retracted black legs hanging rather low beneath their polka-dotted bodies. And birds of course, blackbird and thrush, their song sadly dying with the daylight. From the tops of the firs they would swoop and circle away.

As the days shortened, it grew colder. Air crisp in the morn-ings and cold at night. In the afternoons the sunshine was like life itself, warm and full. Its light cast shadows and reflections from the trees and the clearing to the hill, over babbling brooks, soil, grass, mud, leaves. The light was as bright as ever, but the brightness had changed its sign.

Now the stars were out every night. The moon rose late, and when it did, it had the hardness of rock, but the color of a pumpkin, low on the horizon, brother of the Sun. Under its light the white mist glimmered, and chevrons of brant geese came over, sounding quite close. These phantom birds, thousands and thousands of them, wafting through the night. Sailing over lakes and rivers. Over dense heads of trees. Past the low moo of cows calling across the meadows. Under the full moon . . .

3

ONE FINE MORNING JUST BEFORE DAWN, THE HONKING
faded off. A few spindled clouds smoldered and glowed a most
unfiery pink. Widgeons came in low, in scrambling clusters of six
or seven. Other birds arrived, made a sound, but of all upland birds
and all the waterfowl and all their numerous sounds of migrating,
nothing even came near to a feeling approaching the soaring, pure,
lonely sensation from hearing a honker . . . *Wild geese flying through
the air, through the sky of blue-oo . . .*

The morning was cold and crisp and the air smelled clean and
the fields were drenched with dew. The hedges were covered in
a network of spider web that caught the dew in beads so that it
glistened white as frost. There was a filmy veil of soft, dull mist
obscuring, but not hiding, all objects, giving them a lilac hue, for
the sun had not yet fully risen.

A robin was singing in a tree, and then another. One bird chirped
high up; there was a pause; another chirped lower down. And then
the sun flung a long shaft over the mountain, and in that brief instant
everything was newly washed into being, in a flood of new, golden
creation. It was so perfect with promise, the golden-lighted, distinct
land, that all that world of cloud and valley and ridge quickened
with the soul of day, while it colored with the fire of sun.

A few minutes passed. Radiant, glorious, the sun rose higher,
and the sky grew bright. The power of each day spilled over the
hills, visionary, stretching into the moist, translucent vista of trees
and meadows. The valley was full of a lustrous haze, through
which the meadows shimmered, and the leaves were more gorgeous than ever. One or two kept constantly floating down, amber
and golden in the slanting sun-rays.

As the sun rose, vast mists were rising, soft, silvery mists clearing off before the sunbeams that bring out all the gorgeous beauty of colouring. The place was a wilderness of autumn gold and purple and violet blue and flaming scarlet. The sunshine deepening the hue of the yellowing trees made one feel that one stood in an embowered temple of gold. Across the fields it was as if the world had opened its softest purest flower, its chicory flower, its meadow saffron. It was like a painting too vivid to be real—every pebble, every blade of grass, every leaf that the wind lifted, every rustle of a pheasant hen sharply defined.

The sun was past its zenith when at length the advanced parties of the deer began to show themselves. At the foot of each sloping, grey old tree stood a family: the hind led her fawn from the covert of high fern, and the stately hart paced at the head of the antler'd herd. Soon the entire herd appeared at the head of the glen. The stragglers came bounding out into the clearing by two or three at a time. The deer were reddish brown, the hair short and shining. Their antlers appeared at a distance like a leafless grove.

While they browsed the meadows, they moved down the valley and reached the bubbling and glistening stream at the bottom of a hollow. The animals drank. They lifted their heads and looked out downstream, watching where young deer were sporting in meadows: a hundred yards ahead, the little fawns and their mothers kept starting up and dashing off. The tallest of the red-deer stags, deer of extraordinary size, were grazing where the fallen leaves lay like golden disclets.

At first, the only animate objects that appeared were the deer—with their pretty antlers and their pretty, skinny legs—grazing under the shade of the woods or in the light. The deers would still be drinking out of that water for the rest of the day. But in a short time, other animals had gathered, joining these groups of deer. The squirrels woke up and chattered. Wild turkey came out on a small, stony edge of the field, sunning themselves among yellow pumpkins, the big yellow pumpkins that lay about unprotected by their withering vines. Then, from a long way off, came the sound of a woodpecker pecking with his ivory bill.

Other sounds began to rise, but the sound of the stream was crystal to the ears, far more delicate than the rest of the earth. The bubbling and glistening stream was capable but never turbulent, quiet but never totally disappeared. The water flowed full, greengoldenly through the grass, past all of the wild deer, past the mounds of leafcovered stones, past the meadows that sloped golden in the light. It smelled of damp roots and mud, and all along the creek banks, the deer's tracks were thick, and every hoof-print held water. Along one section of the bank, the grass had grown very tall, deer tracks disappearing into bramble and the shadow of a forest glade. Here also were some of the oldest things: a sprawling wood composed of oaks, willows and chestnuts, yews and sycamores, the beech and the birch; ground felted with fallen leaves; a pond; a brook bubbling cold over its stony bed. The running water murmured down its stone-bedded channel that led to the forest, unlike the animals who remained in place, breathing the dank air.

4

IN THE FOREST, IT WAS PEACEFUL AND DESERTED, JUST THE silvery patter of tree leaves moving in the breeze with the trickle of the brook. The same trees lined the banks on both sides—oaks and chestnuts, yews and sycamores. There was one fir tree, too, that wasn't molting. A reciduous tree. Beside it, the beech and the birch flickered with yellow leaves like bright blossoms. In light, dry gusts, the air riffled the leaves, and a few floated softly downward into the water, following the course of the brook, floating and sinking, sinking and floating.

The water flowed west through the falling coloured leaves. Following its course were old and new gnawed circles around the treestems, a thread of woodland broadening into a spinney and ending at several beaver lodges shaped like dilapidated beehives or wooden haystacks. Beaver had dammed the stream, forming a small lake. Sure, the lake was a mud-hole, but it was a wonderful home of wonderful animals.

The beavers were busy. Two beavers were tying branches and tree lengths into the bottom, weighting them with rocks and mud and other trees as they whisked by. Other beavers emerged to swim with logs and pat mud walls with their paddle-like tails and to go on with their strange, persistent industry. They were the builders jumping up and down in a state of great ferment.

Suddenly, a young female beaver splashed into the water. Moving to all the prominent places on the shore and to the ledges in the creek, she stopped at each and grabbed a handful of mud. With her other hand she reached to the opening of her body where two large sacs protruded, and from these she extracted a viscous yellow liquid, one of the most gratifying odors in the natural world. She was at work marking the corners of her estate and soon began teaching her children how to start erecting a higher and better dam.

Her mate flared past and away. He was great on starting things, but when it came time for doing the hard, backbreaking work, he was usually absent. He halted at the edge of her territory and watched as his mate proceeded with her engineering. He snapped at the kits when they placed branches carelessly, indicating that if he were in charge, he would not accept such sloppy workmanship. Occasionally, the big male emitted a monumental burp of contentment.

All afternoon the mother and father beavers and the noisy companionship of the five kits went about the job of gathering food, stripping bark and storing it for the winter. Once they saw a large herd of elk, and twice, small groups of flapping turkey. They saw no bears, but bears were seldom far from their thoughts.

Like rabbits, the beavers had become shy, day and night. This was why beavers made their clever dams and always they remained near. The great toothed animal could choose to descend on the pond at any time.

Now, there was a time when the beavers were busy building their dams that afternoon, and a stray breeze came through the arbor, a little gust over the water. Thus a scent of leaves, of something else—the rooks? What? Something came with the breeze. The mother of the little kits and one-year-olds sensed peril. She was roused by something incongruous, went to each of the compass points and to the salient ridges in between, and at each she scooped up a handful of mud and mixed it with grass and kneaded in a copious supply of castoreum, and when the job was done she swam back to the middle of her lake and smelled the air.

This was her home, and nothing would drive her from it, neither loneliness nor the attack of otters nor the preying of wolves nor the flooding of the river. For the home of any living thing is important, both for itself and for the larger society of which it is a part.

Amid these thoughts the wind had come up, the clouds floating silently along the blue expanse, now veiling the sun and stretching their shadows along the scene. Because the clouds were in the way, the forest was dark and cold. The beaver saw something move from beneath one of the boulders that lay across the water: a dark form, no more than that, like the shadow a cloud casts when it scuds over the sea.

As it slouched along, and its appearance was fearsome, that hallucination, or whatever it was, was suddenly more disquieting than it had been since the first shock of its appearance, too rash, too unadvised, too sudden; too like lightning. As it grew closer it began to take shape.

5

THE BEAVER WAS CERTAIN IT MUST BE AN OTTER, THE most fearful of her enemies. She dived deep and headed for any cranny within the bank that might afford protection, and as she flattened herself against the mud, she saw flashing through the waters not far distant the sleek, compacted form of an otter on the prowl.

She hoped that, with the wind coming up from the east, his first sweep would carry him downstream, but his sharp eye had detected something, so he turned in a graceful dipping circle and started back. She was trapped, and in her anxiety, fought for any avenue of escape. She went deep into the water, and since she could stay submerged for eight or nine minutes, this gave her time to swim far.

The Otter showed itself above the edge of the bank where she had been and found that she had left her food. An errant May-fly swerved unsteadily athwart the current. A swirl of water and a "cloop!" and the May-fly was visible no more. The Otter showed a gleaming set of strong white teeth as he laughed.

As she probed along the bottom of the bank, the beaver came upon an opening which led upward. It could well be some dead end from which there was no escape. But whatever it was, it could be no worse than what she now faced, for the otter was returning and she could not swim fast enough to escape him. She ducked into the tunnel and with one powerful kick sent herself upward. She moved so swiftly that she catapulted through the surface and saw the secret cave that had formed in the limestone, with a chimney which admitted air and a security that few animals ever found. Soon her eyes became accustomed to the dim light that filtered in

from above and she perceived what a marvelous spot this was, safe
from otters and bears and prowling wolves.

But outside a great storm was coming, this one heading right
toward the woods. The sky had clouded over ominously, and the
wind was picking up. Shadow was flung over the trees creaking
with apples—cloud shadow on the tops of bushes and a real tree, a
giant tree, a magnificent golden ash tree towering high above.

As the clouds came sweeping on, the tops of the mountains stood
like sentinels protecting it, the entire forest. In some places there
were clumps and stretches of fir trees, whose notched tips appeared
like battlemented towers crowning black-fronted castles. Behind
these Fortresses of the trees, the sky stood framed in the branches.
Armies of cloud marched in rank, almost brushing the darkness
of these towering forests.*

The light of the day had begun to fail. Cold breaths of wind
came, and overhead there was an unfamiliar sky through frightening leaves, a new world, material without being real, where poor
ghosts, breathing dreams like air, drifted about . . . Down here
the trees had begun to shiver. The wind blew cold, and strewed
leaves about, and whistled dismally among the great old chestnut trees. A leaf, violently agitated, danced past. Other leaves lay
motionless.

That the earth was hastening to re-enter darkness was apparent. That the weather forecast was in error was clear. It would
be at least three hours before the thunder and lightning had come
together. For now, though, the clouds hovered in the air above
the tremulous world; the wind-pressures changed and blew directly
into the trees.

---

* Soon the trees against the gray sky seemed to be marching up and down the
ridge, marching everywhere in uniform gloom, watching the stormclouds build.
Bluish and hard-edged, the massed armies of forest trees encamped on all sides,
the mountain wall above bristling with trees like guns. Then a horrible develop-
ment took place: clouds lowered and huge blasts of frightening gale-like wind
came pouring in, making all the trees roar with a really frightening intensity
that sometimes built up to a booming war of trees.

In this lacy leafage, amidst the continuous and increasing bombardment of the heavens, fluttered a number of gray birds with black and white stripes and long tails. They were mocking-birds, and they were singing cheerily in contrast to the gray cold changed autumn weather. Leaves were falling, ever flying in the superb upward rise (like the beak of a ship up a wave) of the elm branches as the wind raised them. Now and again a whitened and hollow straw was blown from an old nest and fell into the dark grasses among the rotten apples. One long, silver-tipped branch dropped, and upon it sat one of the graceful birds, swelling and quivering its throat in song.

As the birds were whistling, the keen wind was cutting its way in all directions. The yellow leaves chittered round, making a keen, poignant, almost unbearable music among the shadows. The deer pricked their ears nervously. A worm sucked itself back into its narrow hole.

The woods were wilder every minute, as if angered by the approach of the storm. There had been a wind all day, but never so close; it was rising then, with an extraordinary great sound, and overhead there was an anger of entangled wind caught among the twigs. It, too, was caught and trying to tear itself free, the wind.

High over the trees was spread an unvarying sombreness of vapour. The sky was the color of television, tuned to a dead chan-nel. Clouds brooded. Nothing prospered but the wind, which chased a crow in a swift melodrama of the air. It was a wild scene: The crow was circling overhead, soaring on the evening blast. The wind was howling. The male swerved and sailed. The wind dipped, struck, and rose, groaning with the effort of the chase, but the crow hurtled frenziedly through the air and wrote a fast, jagged, exuberant message with its sharp-pointed wings across the sky. The wind continued its assault, gusting and then swirling around him one moment and gone the next. Then the bird dove under the can-opy of the woods, down through the trees, lost, so small amid that dark mess of leaves, the fragmented image fading down corridors of television sky.

The crow looked down into the darkening foliage, flying through the air with dizzying swiftness. He saw a wolf loping along, a pack of beavers swimming around the margin of their pond, and his ears rang with innumerable melodies from full-throated mockingbirds. As he went farther and farther through the woods, the wind whipped the boughs, ruffling the shiny black feathers. Ke ke ke, said the crow, scolding the wind, but the wind couldn't hear over the din, and so it didn't answer, and the bird, now dropping, alighted on a branch sixty feet above ground. Two more crows whirled down the sky like black maple leaves caught up aloft, laughing with a sort of pitiless amusement at the lesser birds.

When the last of the crows swept down and clung hold of the trees, here one bird cocked its head. The bird looked up and cawed. Somewhere to the left of where they were, the rain was coming. It was moving slowly across the landscape like someone was shading in the sky with a pencil.

It became only a matter of time until darkness had to a great extent arrived. The wind was growing stronger, and the bird called and called and then fell silent. The wind continued. A few moments passed, maybe a minute. Another cry, longer this time. Silence followed, some wind, and then the dull sky began to tell its meaning by sending down herald-drops of rain to these curled twigs.

The crow lifted up its slick black shoulders and shuddered, which was the corvine equivalent of a shrug. It flapped its feathery wings once, twice, thrice, and then rose up from its perch, flying through the heavy boughs. The rising wind whistled and moaned, and the branches of the trees crashed together, the rain pelting down in big, scattered drops. Down below, a ragged line of wolves ran silently, in single file, following a deer trail through the salal. The crow cawed out a warning, in case anyone was listening, and then flew higher, away, until finally it cleared the canopy of the forest.

Soaring now above the treetops, it could see valleys thick with autumn, the rain all the way to the Sea. The sky was heavy, almost black. The shades were deepened by thick and heavy clouds that enveloped the horizon, anvils, ominous hammerheads. Circling higher still, up and up, the mountains of the Island Range came into view. On the far side stretched the open ocean and beyond, but the crow could not fly high enough to see its way home.

6

LIFE HAD NEVER BROUGHT A GLOOMIER HOUR. WITH THE coming of the night, the crow was going between branches and the rain-clouds of the skies, trespassing and wayfaring over peaks and summits, and visiting in dark mountains, ruminating and searching in cavities and narrow crags and slag-slits in rocky hidings, and lodging in the clump of tall ivies and in the cracks of hill-stones, from summit to summit and from glen to glen and from river-mouth to river, over the boulders and red stones, till it arrived at a small opening in the forest, in the centre of which grew an oak-tree of enormous magnitude, throwing its twisted branches in every direction.

When the bird landed, it found rocks and mud and other trees—a grove of gigantic live oaks, whose lower branches all but swept the ground. Here only cold currents came down below; the roaring and swaying was overhead in the tops of the huge trees. Before the bird flew off, a long roll of thunder sounded from across the valley beyond.

Rain was falling heavily by that time, and the accumulated clouds grew darker. As the night was fast falling, the trees overhead deepened the gloom of the hour, and they dripped sadly upon rotten stumps. Some rather large bats were flitting around over the rocks. And the air was cold and smelled of wet stone. Sad!

It was getting quite dark. Thunder trundled away in the distance. The forest was obscure and creaked with a blast that was passing through it. The boughs were tossing heavily above while one solemn old tree groaned dolefully to another, as if telling the sad story of the rain, or constrained to forebode evil to come.

As the night advanced, it kept getting darker and darker and spookier and spookier, the trees roaring and soughing in gusts of wind. All the mystery and witchery of the night seemed to have gathered there amid the perfumes and the dusky and tortuous outlines of foliage. Soon the only light came from when the lightning struck in the distance. Then the sky would be bathed for a second in white light. Then darkness, layer after layer, deeper than before. The thunder rolled. The echoes blended in one fearful, deafening crash. Nothing was heard save the melancholy shriekings of the night-bird and the storm. An owl flitted from tree to tree with a sobbing intensity. It was difficult not to think of it as meaningful. It scolded, screeched in the thunder.

Now was really a little like all the meaner things—the rat, and the owl, and the bat, the moth, and the fox, and the wailing of wolves—all these things had gathered under an oak tree, knotting their awful, blind, triumphing flanks together, and waiting, waiting. They were waiting for tandem storms blowing down-country from the north. Even the river's babbling sounded like the call of a liquid throat waiting, just waiting for the world to end. The brook in the gully, a trembling trickle most of the time, was tonight a loud torrent that tumbled over itself in its avid truckling to gravity, as it carried through corridors of beech and spruce last year's leaves, and some leafless twigs. As the lightning came closer, thunder came with it—the sound seemed to roll over like giant boulders. The rain increased to a torrent.

Soon lightning was crashing all around and the thunder came in big, flat cracks.* All at once a violent, rapid, incisive flash of lightning pierced the gloom, and the rent it made had not closed ere a frightful clap of thunder shook the celestial depths. And now

---

* Merciful heavens! The lightning uncurls and begins to flutter in the fir trees, white-orange and black . . . as far as the eye can see. The whole sky, from right to left, blazes up with a fierce light, and next instant, the earth reels and quivers with the awful shock of ten thousand batteries of artillery. It is the signal for the Fury to spring—for a thousand demons to scream and shriek—for innumerable serpents of fire to writhe and light up the blackness. The rain falls—the wind is let loose with a terrible shriek—now the lightning is so constant that the

more sound, more motion: the thunder was loud and metallic, like the rattle of sheet iron, and the lightning broke in great zigzags across the heavens, making everything stand out and come close for a moment.

With the lightning, such force and violence arose: The winds in fury rent up rocks and trees: The sky was now black with clouds, now sheeted with fire: The rain fell in torrents; it swelled the stream; the waves overflowed their banks; the river produced a flood which washed away the beaver dam, and most of the lodge. All earthly things were crashing and things hurtling and dashing with unbelievable velocity: the groaning trunks, even the grasses. Each tree had its own cry. There was nothing that did not utter its cry as the winds moved through it.

Then suddenly a big burst of thunder and lightning trampled over—again the same noise was repeated. It was a unique and horrific situation. The crashing thunder rattled madly above, the lightnings flashed a larger curve, and at intervals, through the surrounding gloom, showed a scathed larch, which, blasted by frequent storms, reared its bare head on a height above. Every few seconds the thunder burst with a terrific crash, and the rain would thrash along so thick that the trees off a little ways looked dim and spider-webby; and here would come a blast of wind that would bend the trees down and turn up the pale underside of the leaves; and then a perfect ripper of a gust would follow along and set the branches to tossing their arms as if they was just wild; and next, when it was just about the bluest and blackest—*FST!* It was as bright as glory, and you'd have a little glimpse of tree-tops a-plunging about away off yonder in the storm, hundreds of yards

---

eyes burn, and the thunder-claps merge into an awful roar. Bababadalgharagh-takamminarronnkonnbronntonnerronntuonnthunntrovarrhounawnskawn-toohoohoordenenthurnuk! Crash! Crash! Crash! It is the trees falling to earth. Shriek! Shriek! Shriek! It is the Demon racing along and uprooting even the blades of grass. Shock! Shock! Shock! Perkodhuskurunbarggruauyagokgorlay-orgromgremmitghundhurthrumathunaradidillifaititillibumullunukkunun! It is the Fury flinging his fiery bolts into the bosom of the earth.

further than you could see before; dark as sin again in a second, and now you'd hear the thunder let go with an awful crash, and then go rumbling, grumbling, tumbling down the sky towards the under side of the world, like rolling empty barrels down stairs— where it's long stairs and they bounce a good deal, you know.

The echoes crashed and crashed, and the wind whipped and slashed past obtrusive branches and stones. The wind was really howling, whipping the rain in circles, causing the stoutest trees to bend and groan, breaking the boughs, tossing the bushes, lashing the ferns to fury, flattening the grass, and whirling leaves far away. Shifts in the wind changed the direction of the rain so that, coming from the darkness beyond, it made a hissing sound, as if at the centre of a great nest of angry snakes.

Suddenly there was a movement, a shout of light in the dark vapours overhead—rather, the wind and the rain of heaven burst in a shock of whiteness. And that's when it hit with the force of a hurricane, and the thunder burst at once with frightful loudness from various quarters of the heavens as if a building had fallen down. A stream of fire issued from an old and beautiful oak, and so soon as the dazzling light vanished, the oak had disappeared, and nothing remained but a blasted stump. The tree shattered in a singular manner. It was not splintered by the shock, but entirely reduced to thin ribbons of wood. No more.

Now the battling elements, in wild confusion, seemed to threaten nature's dissolution; a livid flash and a crash came together; the ferocious thunderbolt, with impetuous violence, danced upon the mountains, and, collecting more terrific strength, severed gigantic rocks from their else eternal basements; the masses, with sound more frightful than the bursting thunder-peal, dashed towards the valley below. Horror and desolation marked their track. A smash, floods, falling trees. The mountain-rills, swoln by the waters of the sky, dashed with direr impetuosity from the summits; their foaming waters were hidden in the darkness of midnight, or only became visible when the momentary scintillations of the lightning rested on their whitened waves.

Down washed the rain, deep lowered the welkin; the clouds had now, through all their blackness, turned deadly pale, as if in terror. Then the gleams of lightning were very fierce, the thunder crashed very near; this storm burst at the zenith; it rushed down prone; the forked, slant bolts pierced athwart vertical torrents; red zigzags interlaced a descent blanched as white metal; and all broke from a sky heavily black in its swollen abundance, the spectacle of clouds, split and pierced by white and blinding bolts.

7

FOR HOURS THE FURY OF THE STORM CONTINUED WITHOUT surcease. Now and again some ancient patriarch of the woods, rent by a flashing bolt, would crash in a thousand pieces among the surrounding trees, carrying down numberless branches and many smaller neighbors to add to the tangled confusion. The gale blew on, and the steady swishing of the rain flooded spear-fields of cattail and skunk cabbage where loons and widgeon breed. It seemed that there was no life anywhere that was not storm-ridden.

Several times that night the wind began to change slightly for the better, but it did no good. At one point the rain had let up, and it seemed likely that the weather would "milden," until the wind came back with triple fury, thunder split the air, and lightning bursts illuminated the churning tempest. Another time, the wind had dropped and the rain turned soft, but the thunder crashed nearer and louder. Now the wind grew strong and hard, now dropped, now stung with rain, now not. It moved and sported like this for ever. The round-headed clouds never dwindled as they bowled along, but kept every atom of their rotundity. The rain fell harder and poured. There was no way to draw any beauty from it.

Real change appeared sometime after midnight. The wind shifted, descending for good, and the violence of the storm which so lately had raged was passed. The keen wind still jostled the clouds along, but its oncoming force was no more than a little brook compared to the roarings that had been raging up out of the west. The lightning was moving, and before long, the thunder, in low and indistinct echoes, sounded through the chain of rocky mountains, which stretched far into the distance.

Soon the clouds had run out of water and the rain had ceased.

The pealing thunders died away in indistinct murmurs, and the lightning was too faint to be visible. With the change in the weather, the moon was still completely obscured by a dense veil of high cloud, but there was a sullen, grey light over the landscape.

Before lay a scene of panoramic disorder. Here the trees, laden heavily with their humid leaves, were now suffering more damage than during the highest winds of winter, when the boughs are especially disencumbered to do battle with the storm. The wet young beeches were undergoing amputations, bruises, cripplings, and harsh lacerations, from which the wasting sap would bleed for many a day to come, and which would leave scars visible till the day of their burning. Each stem was wrenched at the root, where it moved like a bone in its socket, and at every onset of the wind, convulsive sounds came from the branches, as if pain were felt. In a neighbouring brake, a finch was trying to sing, but the wind blew under his feathers till they stood on end, twisted round his little tail, and made him give up his song.

The gloom of the night was funereal; all nature seemed clothed in crape. The spiky points of the trees rose into the sky like the turrets and pinnacles of an abbey. Nothing below the horizon was happy. In the wet hillside, never did cypress, or yew, or juniper so seem the embodiment of funeral gloom. Never did tree or grass wave or rustle so ominously. Never did bough creak so mysteriously and never did the far-away howling of wolves send such a woeful sound through the night.

8

NEXT DAY THE LAND WAS THE SAME, THE SKY WAS THE same. By the time the first light of dawn appeared, the dead moon hung in the west and the long flat shapes of the nightclouds passed before it like a phantom fleet. These clouds, as they changed in shape and tints, were continually assuming new forms of sublimity. Their effects on the lower world were few; trees now cold as the night, sad as the fog on the peaks.

As the weird light increased, the weather was comfortless. Day appeared, dropping out of the sky at dawn after the longest night in the world. The bank of clouds was the color of wet cement— graveyard clouds. A worn-out land lay below them. In the graying light, the Objects now appearing and vanishing were ill-calculated to inspire that calm, of which this land stood so much in need. The disorder of imagination was increased by the wildness of the surrounding scenery: by the gloomy Caverns and steep rocks, rising above each other, and dividing the passing clouds; solitary clusters of Trees scattered here and there, among whose thick-twined branches the wind sighed hoarsely and mournfully; the shrill cry of mountain Eagles, who had built their nests among these lonely Desarts; the stunning roar of torrents as, swelled by late rains, they rushed violently down tremendous precipices.

And as the light increased, flocks of shadow were driven before it and conglomerated and hung in many-pleated folds. Fog spilled from the heights like the liquid it almost was. Where it encountered woods, the most local of rains fell. Where it found open space, its weightless pale passage seemed both endless and like the end of all things. It was a temporary sadness, the more beautiful for being sad, the more precious for being temporary. It was the slow song in minor that combined with the gray of the morning to give a ghastly and unsubstantial appearance to every object.

Poor mountains! Poor landscape! Under the trees several pheasants lay about, their rich plumage dabbled with blood; some were dead, some feebly twitching a wing, some staring up at the sky, some pulsating quickly, some contorted, some stretched out—all of them writhing in agony, except the fortunate ones whose tortures had ended during the night by the inability of nature to bear more. The plants were scraggly but alive. The little creeping bushes were still green among the fleshier shoots of a bitter weed and brushwood. Every here and there, a broken tree lay on the ground, fallen trees, dead, smooth gray, swirlinggrainoftreelikefrozensmoke.

The rainy night had ushered in a misty morning—half frost, half drizzle—and temporary brooks crossed over the ground, gurgling from the uplands. One stream was full, swirling along, hurrying, talking to itself in absorbed intent tones. One stream behind ran zig-zag through the varied shades. Away on the bank on t'other side of the stream, hazels and stunted oaks, with their roots half exposed, held uncertain tenure: the soil was too loose for the latter, and strong winds had blown some nearly horizontal. A little farther on, gently upward to the nearest hills, the grass was turning yellow, full of dead leaves. In places the grass was gone altogether, and everywhere there were large puddles and patches of mud. The ground felt soft, almost marshy. The ground sobbed.*

Above, the trees caught the wind, and the young morning wind moaned at its captivity. The wet, grey wind shook the half naked trees, whose leaves dripped and shone sullenly. Black bars striped the grey tree-trunks, where water trickled down. A spider hovered. But how still it was on the ground. The smell was foul, but not a breath stirred among the saddened bracken. The leaves

---

* The tuft of ferns and grasses could do with a little TLC. It's always sad to see the leaves and nuts getting crushed and turning into yellow smears that look and smell like dog shit or vomit. There's something elementally horrific about the ground being in such a way as to cry out the deep things of the world.

lay plastered like little gilded fans, the bracken fallen face-down in
defeat. The discarded oak-leaves and the bracken uttered their last
sharp gasps.

There would have been something especially rough, unutter-
ably dreary, in all this, had strange shapes of rounded outline not
disturbed all perspective. Sight flowing ahead over the ground,
eyes filtering the shapes, the names of things fading but their forms
remaining, it was hard to see it at first, but creatures made a moving patch of thick shadow at the foot of the hill. Down there, there
was an odor of grass and roots and damp earth. Down there,
ferns of horror and slippery logs, mosses. There were rocks scattered here and there, and under the rough stone, a pool of water,
stagnating round an island of draggled weeds. The shallow pool lay
silent, deserted save for furtive little shapes that darted nervously
out of the leaves. Roaches and other things? Rats, maybe?

It was moving with rats. Two rats ran into the nearby rock
forms. The rats came out again, ran a little way, stopped, ran again,
listened, were reassured, and slid about freely, dragging their long
naked tails into the pool. Soon six or seven grey beasts were playing round in the gloom. They sat and wiped their sharp faces,
stroking their whiskers. Then one would give a little rush and a
little squirm of excitement and would jump vertically into the
air, alighting on four feet, running, sliding into the shadow. One
dropped with an ugly plop into the water, and swam, the hoary
imp, his sharp snout and his wicked little eyes moving at the edge
of the pool.

In the minute that had elapsed since the first shock of appearance, the number of rats had vastly increased. They seemed to
swarm over the place all at once and followed the shadows of the
great rats who butted right through the bracken, its yellow ranks
broken.

Beyond the bracken, the rats were multiplying and went running across the hillside. Indeed, the creatures, a whole mass of
phosphorescence, twinkled like stars through the dim medium of
the forest gloom. They ran alongside each other up the hill, over

the rocky terrain, and past the mounds of gawky dead trees among bushes so dense, and up to ground God knows how deep with hidden caves. At the top of the hill, three great rats half rushed at the entrance of a cave which smelled of urine perhaps. Something unusual. The rest of the rats followed them as they curved up the steep slope.

The whole place was becoming alive with rats in the foreground, and above them, in a dead tree, split in two by lightning, were perched three huge black birds, too big for crows. Ravens. One of them hopped clumsily to the end of a branch, which squeaked and bobbed under its weight and sent it squawking into the air. The other two followed, with a battery of flaps. They sailed over the meadow in a triangle formation, past the neck of arching rock, the rats racing in a pack through their own droppings, and flew cawing into the depressing wet sky.

In the open air, the weather was raw, cheerless. The clouds against the sky were the gray of rats, and the air was not damp but dank, the sun perpetually hidden from view. Vast mists were rising from the rivers and curling in thick wreaths around the opposite mountains, whose summits were hid in the uniform clouds. The scudding shadows of high cirrus seemed to smoke down from the ghostly ridges. A gray nervous cloud was scurrying eastward, searching for trees on which to rain.

9

AND SO THE DAYS WENT BY, SO THE WEEKS PASSED. Nothing, in that big land, appreciably changed. The winds blew and brought storm and cloud. Sometimes the stormclouds eddied for days, approaching but never striking. Some days a big storm, with a power of thunder and lightning, appeared to approach rapidly and the rain poured down in a solid sheet. Every day was cloudy, the drizzle of rain like a veil over the world, mysterious, hushed.

Gradually fading and fading away from its first sparkling intensity, autumn had brought in definition, a sense of gravity returning to a place where it had been chased out by the sun. The gold of the summer picture was now gray, the colours mean, the rich soil mud. The leaves fell about from the groaning branches, and the earthy decay in the atmosphere chilled, the mountains and naked rock appearing almost flat, two-dimensional like a photograph, and scratched slantwise by the rain as if the photo had been scoured diagonally with a stiff wire brush.

One afternoon there was a pause in this weather—a fresh, watery afternoon, when the turfs were rustling with moist, withered leaves, and the cold blue sky was half hidden by clouds; the sinking sun shot through layers of grey. But this time was soon dispersed by the wind in a most stomach-sickening way. In less than two hours, the clouds looked as if they were stumbling along before the wind: frightened, dark grey streamers, rapidly mounting from the west, and boding abundant rain. The wet, grey wind shook the half naked trees. The air throbbed with the thunderous crash of billows over the distant peaks. The Haunted Woods was full of the groans of mighty trees. Soon the rain was beating down over the shivering fields, cold and gray, and the storm went on, watching the pitchy wind bully the leaves to the ground.

After this season of congealed dampness came a spell of dry frost,* when strange birds from behind the North Pole began to arrive silently on the upland; gaunt, spectral creatures with tragical eyes—eyes which had witnessed scenes of cataclysmal horror in inaccessible polar regions; which had beheld the crash of icebergs and the slide of snow-hills by the shooting light of the Aurora; been half blinded by the whirl of colossal storms and terraqueous distortions; and retained the expression of feature that such scenes had engendered. These nameless birds came quite near till they dropped exhausted out of the sky, a shower of dead birds.

---

* In advance of the snow itself, the Arm of the Lord puts a stranglehold of frost on the woods so tight it freezes all the way. There's nothing else except the wind blowing . . . like a tumbling hill, accompanied by the sweeping sound of a whole mass of leaves and fine branches whipping the moving air. The autumn trees, ravaged as they are, take on the flash of tattered flags.

10

WITH THE LAST OF THE LEAVES HAVING FALLEN FROM THE trees during the previous week, the cold that followed was of an aggravated kind, and it now brought with it the worst consequence: the scene was presently stripped of all its leaves and colour in such a radical fashion it was difficult to imagine any of it growing green again. In summer it was alive with quivering flowers, but now through its nakedness an icy wind blew, and all of the trees were dead. There were dead skunks and even an occasional deer. There were no fish, no birds, no animals, and had there been, there would have been nothing for them to eat.

The hard bedrock contour of the mountain landscape was now nakedly exposed, its joints and striations etched in the fine hatched lines of an old engraving, and those mammoth rocks all tumbled sideways, crushed together and yet hugely intact. The no-nonsense organization of the earth's surface, to be admired and deferred to now for the first time in months, was a reminder of the terrific abrasive force of the glacier onslaught that had scoured these mountains.

Here winter came early. Water jeweled itself to a clear, frozen dribble. That grave of dead leaves and the sere brown refuse of the cedars wound vanishing slowly back into the earth. Already it was terribly cold, and if it snowed, which it might any day, these serrated mountains would suddenly vanish as great skiffs of snow came rolling across. For now, though, the clouds tilted all day, and a cold wind blew down from the mountains.

Then one day a peculiar quality invaded the air of this open country. There had been another black frost the night before, and the air was heady as wine. The rain had let up and leveled out . . .

not so much a rain as a dreamy smear of blue-gray that wipes over the land instead of falling on it, making patient spectral shades of the tree trunks, and a pathic sighing sound all along the broad mountain range.

That morning there was a shiver of winter in the air. Dew turned to ice on the tips of grass blades. The winds wailed as if they were looking for something they could not find. They looked down into the valley and throughout the insane shivering canyon. Among those thousand hiding-places it was easy to be lost. And anyway, the woods were full of treetops pointing everywhere: north? east? south?

About three o'clock, the sky was darkening even though it was still afternoon; clouds were purple and black, undecided if they should snow or not. The wind moving those trees sent an exhilarating loneliness through the mountains and onto the flatlands, a dark valley between three mighty, heaven-abiding peaks—the Trinity, in some faint earthly symbol.

In this vale of Death, the sense of loneliness was far more intense than it had been under the dreaming silence of autumn. No living creature was visible or audible. No rustling of the leaves—no bird's note in the wood—no cry of water-fowl from the hidden lake. The silence was horrible. Everything was cold and quiet.

The minutes passed—then the hours. Darkness fell, the knobby branches of the hundred-year-old trees, copses and solitary pines, all deepening to the nightscape latent across them all day. For the second time that day there came a moisture which was not of rain, and a cold which was not of frost. It chilled the eyeballs.

As night fell dark as slate, there was pressure in the air. A wind swayed through a clump of birches. The bare trees drummed and whistled. The sun no more than took a peek at things and then ducked behind the mountain.

II

IT STARTED SNOWING THAT NIGHT, JUST BEFORE DAWN.
The air was cold and dark. The bare trees stood up against the
frosty night. After hours of waiting, the weather broke: the wind
shifted from south to north-east and brought a peculiar mist,
which changed into a luminous haze. In this air, or this mist, there
was some quality—electrical, perhaps—which acted in strange
sort upon this mountain and its ravines. When the wind increased
slightly, the first lonely flakes of snow came drifting through the
trees, branches floating up and down with slow, wild elegance.

The first snow! *Will it settle? Will it melt? Is it sleet? Is it hail?*
This was just snow, period—big silent petals drifting through the
woods, white bouquets segueing into snowy dark: a topsy-turvy
land, something from a story book—the bewitched forest of fairy
tales, where talking wolves trot upright in bonnets.

By morning, snow was falling in earnest. In the east the sky
was pale, and through the gray woods there was thin snow on the
ground. It weighed down the black, ragged branches of the yews.
Then the wind blew again, shook down crystals of snow. Down
came the dry flakes, fat enough and heavy enough to crash like
nickels on stone. It always surprised, how quiet it was. Not like
rain, but like a secret.

With every tree around, the distant snow began to grow. The
big white flakes wafted through the leafless branches, the snow
really beginning to stick. Could have been a movie about the early
winter nights, when the sky riots with stars and the earth seems
doubly dark because of them. When the clouds roll by into the
darkness and the snow goes whirling, invisible tattooing needles
against the sky. The wind whips around, cold. Snowy birds fly and

hover with wings spread, low enough to touch. Time creeps and no light comes. Then it grows; snow gathers like light. Light narrows, grows brighter, shows fog pouring through from another bend of the mountains, over the river and the plain, and again across the crests of the mountains. Look before the snow blots it all out! Bloody *hell.* It's like movie snow!

The snow did not stop falling all day, or during the night that followed. It snowed steadily and long, three days. Piling itself, burying itself. Higher. Deeper. While the snow fell, the wind was blowing. The air was hoary silver. Trees stood vaguely at the distance, as if waiting like heralds. The snow came and fastened itself upon the earth.

In the following days, when the snow finally ceased falling, the pause was only long enough for the old clouds to leave and new ones to move in freely. Some days had very little wind—the snow wasn't swirling or pummeling as much, the sky was lightening. Sometimes the sun would burn a gold-edged rent in the clouds and then be swallowed by them. These brief moments of immemorial expiation threw golden shadows on the glistening fields. It was a beautiful thing. Fields got back a little of their colour under the dazzling light, and stood the palest possible gold; all about the snow was crusted in shallow terraces with tracings like ripplemarks at the edges, curly waves that were the actual impression of the wind. In this clear climate of fantasy, the snow appeared to be a firm substance of joy now coloured an exquisite cream or pink, soft, sunny, like a dream. When the sun slipped behind the clouds, a mournful peace hung on the fields and woods as though they felt the relaxing grasp of the cold and stretched themselves in their long winter sleep.

12

ONE COLD WINTER MORNING, WHEN TWO FEET OF SNOW lay white and crisp and even on the ground, the sun returned for good. The landscape had disappeared, and the whole world was changed. Every stream was now only a cleft between snowdrifts—very blue. The few little cedars, which were so dull and dingy before, now stood out strong, dusky and grey.

It was early morning and growing gradually lighter. Inlaid upon the darkness, a chill, icy wind; shadow of a feeble sun; a tree on a mountain-plain. The sky was all astir with little white clouds as white and light as snowflakes, some clear, some grading into luminous mist. The whole imperceptibly lightening scene of the vistas had a stillness about it that suggested photography.

The morning light, now glimmering in the horizon, shewed faintly, at a little distance, upon the brow of a hill, which seemed to peep from "under the opening eye-lids of the morn." The light illumined the rocks and tinged the snowy summits with a roseate hue, touched their lower points with various colouring, while the blueish tint that pervaded their shadowy recesses gave the strength of contrast to the splendour of light.

At last a red sun climbed steeply out of his hiding and was now standing benignly in the lower sky, pouring down floods of enchanting light to every point of the compass, hill after pale hill. All things shone magically in this light: tall, silver, and pearl-grey trees rose pale against a dim-blue sky, like trees in some rare, pale Paradise; the holly-leaves and long leaves of the rhododendron were rimmed and spangled with delicate tracery. The snowy landscape—peppered with toylike figures—was as smooth as sugar frosting on a birthday cake.

When the clouds cleared, the view of the mountains was unobstructed, picture-postcard beautiful in the twinkling brightness of morning. In front was a valley, huge slopes of snow and black rock, a plain of fields and trees, and at the end, like the navel of the earth, a white-folded wall, and two peaks glimmering in the light. A blazing blue sky poured down torrents of light and air on the white landscape, which gave them back in an intenser glitter. It was snow everywhere, a white, perfect cradle of snow, new and frozen, sweeping up at either side, black crags and white sweeps of silver towards the blue pale heavens.

From here a fine view was to be obtained of the plain. Fields glistening under the pale sun. The first pines about a mile distant, . a pine-wood with boles reddening in the sun and delicate blue shadows on the snow. There in the navel of the mystic world, these trees sheltered the land from the wind, which swept down from postcard mountains. The light breeze carried the snow granules away to fresh resting places. In the misty white light, they sailed across the fields and blew directly into the forest.

Within the forest, the trees were larger and pleasanter. The snow was so pure, and the bluish cones caught in its surface stood out like ornaments of bronze. The soft wind passed through the branches of the trees, seeming to encircle with peace and security. It blew all around the wood, reached a part of the wood where the pines were more widely spaced. Then the breeze fell and a warm stillness seemed to drop from the branches with the dropping needles.

Here the snow was in perfect condition, all glittering and snowy and delighted with sunshine. The shadows of the massed black pines were lavender in that bright light. It would have made an excellent spot from which to see the sky or take in long draughts of mountain air had squeaking and monotonous chirping not erupted at a pond nearby.

13

LIFE CAN TAKE THE MOST SURPRISING TURNS. THAT silence and placidity of the winter dawn was broken by a tiny sound. Sometimes it stopped for a few seconds, then it grew stronger. It was a rising and a moving sound. The noise came and went like a flock of birds, at times very loud, then rapidly dying off.

How was this possible after the storms and death, and stillness, and inaction? This seemed like the end of all things. The spirit of autumn had all too quickly eroded; the thunder and lightning had come together into the mountains where the storms had their lairs; ball lightning had run upon the ground; then the rain had ceased, and a deep, a gloomy, silence reigned (imperceptible hours had gone thus); and snow had laid its cold hand on the aspect of a world's death. Now there were no more events. There were no animals and nothing, no animal markings. No animals were in the fields or mountains.

The thing is this. Animals died, it was true. The snow covered them with a white blanket, their muzzles and hands still testifying to the agony in which they had died. It has happened before. It will happen again. Meanwhile, some of these forms were well adapted for life.* Ordinary cows could not have survived this ordeal, but a multitude of weeds, all kinds of insects, and a colony of birds, struggled on doggedly. Certain creatures laid eggs that

---

* It has to do with change. And with evolution. Look at this scarred mountain-side, how confused and senseless the upheavals seem which have given it its grandeur! It is continually wearing down. Erosion is diminishing it; that river is denuding it. Eternal change is the only law, and species are subject to the laws of evolution like the mountain peaks. So it goes.

were able to endure. Others survived by burying themselves in mud. Life went on. In fact, precisely at this transitional point, at the beginning of winter, many animals survived the sky's attack and were now lying becalmed about a half a mile in any direction, surveying the snowy landscape and sweet sunny sky, inhaling the pure, bracing air. And so, as Nature forgot, her children forgot also. Life went on as it had been before the darkness and the fright. The noises of the ordinary world were replaced by those straight in front and not far off, in fact so near that there was a ceaseless noise in the air. It was squeaking, chirping, twittering. The volume of sound was startling, but nothing appeared there save the verge of the hillock stretching against the sky, woods-woods-woods, and frozen ground.

That sound came from the pond-side over the hill, through aromatic trunks, over the rocky terrain, and past the small mounds of snow: a small sheet of water with steep wooded sides. It was a shy secret spot where frog and horn-pout dreamed in a sheath of ice. Across its frozen surface, from the farther bank, there was a big tree with a thick trunk twisted with ivy; it hung alone almost horizontal over the pond. Some ivy leaves were like green spears held out and tipped with snow.

Suddenly, the scene was startled by swishing black shadows that swept just above: an elliptic flock of pigeons, in circular volitation, soaring grey, flapping white, and then grey again, wheeled across the limpid, pale sky. A bright flock of pigeons swept over, a kind of wild pigeons, which build not in a tree, but rather in the holes of the rocks. At one moment the whole flock caught the light in such a way that they all became invisible at once, dissolved in light and disappeared as salt dissolves in water. The next moment they flashed around black and silver against the sun, the schools of pigeons all swirling round and round in a great squawking endlessly ejaculative anguish.

Below them, in their holes in the sandstone, more birds preened themselves and cooed softly. Further down, upon the ground, an indistinct gray figure, a certain beautiful, pale, winter-squirrel fur, having a bluish, or better say *sizily,* columbine, shade, was holding a reddish object in its front paws, its cheeks puffed out. It chewed and swallowed and, in one sinuous tendril-like movement, the skimpy squirrel dashed over a patch of sunlit snow where a tree trunk's shadow became greyish blue for a stretch. The intelligent animal climbed up into the tree, where he lay flat along the bough and listened to the wood-pigeons call among the trees.

The squirrel, invisible now in a crotch, chattered, scolding the delinquents who would pot him out of his tree, but the pigeons, dashing by, flew around and settled again simultaneously on two neighboring bare-branched trees; white pigeons and blue pigeons and grays, with iridescent wings. The squirrel departed, climbing down the trunk, and hid under a snow-drift, and a wood-pigeon began to coo roo-hoo hoo! roo-hoo hoo! To be sure, the same sound was that very moment perhaps being heard all over the forest.

Suddenly another sound sounded sweetly from afar, but this time from the direction of the face of the mountain: the bugle of an elk possessed by lust or a cold bed. Those high skirling notes marshaled birds and other animated elk forward like a tune from a satyr's pipe. A sudden snort. The sound of flight from a thicket. Elk every here and there peeping forth from among the trees formed a scene of singular beauty. But it was augmented and rendered sublime by the mighty mountains, whose white and shining pyramids and domes towered above all, as belonging to another earth.

14

THROUGHOUT THE DAY, THE SAME THING: THE SOUND WAS comforting; the view was glorious. The wind blew through the country, through the woods, over the snow. The sighing of the pines was heard, rising now and then to a noble requiem with the calling of birds.

In the afternoon, there were a few clouds, big lazy chryselephantine clouds that loafed around over the mountains. The breeze blew harder. There was no fall, but what had already descended was torn up from the earth, whirled round by the brief gusts, and cast into a hundred fantastic forms—more like sculpture than anything else.

At some point the wind dropped and there was an absolute stillness of the air. The unstained snowy mountaintop, the glittering pinnacle, the pine woods, and ragged bare ravine, the eagle, soaring amidst the clouds—they all gathered round. A maple tree, a frozen river, woods and winter chickadees. The stillness in the air, the glory of the light, the feeling of comparative safety—all had gradually sunk into a pleasing and complacent melancholy.

It was within half-an-hour of sunset when the wind came again, stronger now. The sun was brilliant, but it held no warmth over the cradle of snow and over the great pallid slopes. Here and there, color was materializing out of the white now, snow-clotted orange. The peaks of snow were rosy, glistening like transcendent, radiant spikes of blossom in the heavenly upper-world, so lovely.

And beyond, as the evening sun was shining on the remote heights of snow, there were other sensations, less definable but more exquisite. At the base of the mountains, the light was starting to fade—the ashes and yews casting long shadows—and high above this grew forests of dark fir, cleaving the wintry snow-drift, wedge-like, and stemming the avalanche. Dotted here and there on the mountains were sliding shadows, the shadows of cloud-flocks over slopes of golden stubble. As one bright evening cloud floated midway along a mountain, all at once, in this great serenity, great Nature spoke to a thread of gold in the soft mist. Hill after hill made beauty of distance, and there was simply no saying what miracle might happen.

Away the sun sank, and the pine-boles turned from red to grey. The snow grew bluer and bluer, and the sky now showed itself of a reddish-yellow, like a slice of some semilucent stone behind which a lamp burnt. And the sky, as it paled, saw the quiet evening cloud grow dim, and all the colours in the valley fade, and the golden snow upon the mountain-tops become a remote part of the pale night sky.

The trees grew darker and darker, the snow made only a dimness in an unreal world. The twilight spread a weird, unearthly light overhead, bluish-rose in colour. And like a shadow, the day had gone into a faintly luminous evening.

Up in the mountains, visibility was unlimited. An hour after sunset, when a pause obtains in the world, this was when the sun's photons weren't breaking up molecules in the ionosphere. When positive and negative particles in the air quickly recombined. The thinness of the atmosphere, through which every object came so distinctly to the eye, surprised and deluded. The snow-capped peaks rising with immortal and changeful beauty into the purple heavens. The eternal closing-in, where the walls of snow and rock rose impenetrable. The cradle of silent snow.*

---

* All these views revealed the mere shapes and patterns of things becoming, as it were, refined in the twilight, and gaining a kind of symbolical value, as though they were themselves patterns of some other and more perfect form whose shadow they made real. How strange it all was: patterns very difficult to imagine were made together by everything the eye could see, merging into a supernal harmony their unexceptionable varieties—drowsy patterns so beautiful that they drugged the eye.

Soon the darkness had come on. There was no moon, but the starlight was clear among the clouds. On the snow, cloud shadows passed back and forth, and the trees in the distance moved. It was by grace of this dark, the coming of complete night, that the conspicuous grandeur lay, for there the mountains rose in such splendor, and the most attractive, most curious scene came into view. In the valley below, in the great bed of snow, were two small figures. Some deer. Or caribou.

The caribou stood in the bluish darkness: they were standing leg-deep in the snow, giant deer with huge palmate antlers a sort of yellow-brown. They had heavy dark-gray coats, and their breath snorted out in white plumes and carried away in tatters by the wind.

The winds drove them on in silence through the comparative clearness of the fields. Sometimes their way led them under the shade of an overhanging bank or through the thin obscurity of a clump of leafless trees. At other times—and especially when following a level stretch—the night was so still that they heard the frozen snow crackle. At one point the crash of a loaded branch falling far off in the woods reverberated like a musket-shot, and once a fox barked. But all this was nothing. Time and time again nothing distracted the wild caribou. Here and there one of the swift and noiseless birds of the winter's night seemed to follow them, circling a few feet in front of them, disappearing and returning again and again. The deer turned their heads, but they did not notice.

As the deer moved, a new light began to spread in the sky. Distant objects, until now hidden, came into view. In front was the faint shadow of the mountain-knot, a slope sheered down from a peak, with many black rock-slides. Over the broken ground, the peak reached up, blotting out the stars, like a ghost.

When the caribou came down from the northeast, as they so often did when making their rounds of the north, the light grew. They saw in rapid succession a moose, a pair of red foxes. And something else: another line of caribou appeared on the horizon in great quantity, came right down a hill. On the farther side of the hemlock belt, the country rolled away before them, grey and lonely under the stars and clouds dipping low and trailing across the mountains.

As the light grew, all the sky seemed to get brighter. Enormous shadows began to shift over the face of the deep cradle of snow. The deer turned their heads, watched the growth of the faint radiance appearing in the sky. The light increased among the shadows till presently the moon burst upwards and flooded the valley with light.

15

THE CARIBOU WATCHED THE LANDSCAPE WHITEN AND shape itself under the sculpture of the moon. It was a spectacle of incomparable beauty, the slopes bathed in lustre, the silver-edged darkness of the woods, the spectral purple of the hills against the sky, and it seemed as though all the beauty of the night had been poured out on the snow-dusted peaks.

A cathedral hush overlay all the land, and a sense of benediction brooded low—a divine kindliness manifesting itself in peace, in absolute repose. It was a time for visions. Peak beyond peak of rock and snow, bluish, transcendent in heaven. The moon rising higher, brighter, shining down over the gigantic outline of the mountain range. Clouds drifting for miles. There was a little sign of wind from the north. And down in the center of the ravine, the faintest wind from the westward. It was almost motionless, for all nature reposed under the eye of the quiet moon.

But on that particular winter's night this emphasized silence was gradually disturbed by a sound not easily to be verbally rendered. A wail? A cry? Its tone rising over the lower tone of the wind. Caribou could be expected to have the power of smelling and fled into the darkness before this event. A baby rabbit, terror ridden, squirmed through a hole. Everywhere the vastness and terror seemed to spread over the hillside and the valley; birds flew after the caribou. Now, in rapid succession, a moose, a pair of red foxes, red deer, roe deer, and elk continued after the birds. But why would they—anybody—stampede?

What actually happened was this: The moon had risen. Its great shield of gold stood over the east, and by its light a wild howling began, which seemed to come from all over the country,

as far as the imagination could grasp it. The howling had a cold
and beggarly sound, sometimes intolerably like an outraged voice.
The wolves were coming together.

The first howls were taken up and echoed through the forest. Their call started low, a singular uneasy moan that threaded
through the trees and gathered, as one by one the pack joined in,
their voices wild and raw, rising into a full-throated howl. In a few
minutes, however, low, shaggy clouds scudded over that part of the
horizon where the moon had just risen. The howling of the wolves
ceased altogether.

The moon had disappeared, leaving just enough of its faint
and fluctuating light to render objects visible, dimly revealing
their forms and proportions. So powerful was its radiance that the
clouds soaked up the light like a stain: some clouds to the west;
a swift cloud moving from left to right; vast clouds overhead,
writhing, curling, then uniting in one giant river. It was a murky
confusion—here and there blotted with a colour like the colour of
the smoke from damp fuel—of flying clouds, tossed up into most
remarkable heaps, suggesting greater heights in the clouds than
there were depths below them to the bottom of the deepest hollows
in the earth.

Now the moon-light shewed a bit brighter through the thickness of the gloom, faintly, as though the gale were a private mis-
fortune of her own, as if, in a dread disturbance of the laws of
nature, she had lost her way and were frightened. It became only
a matter of time until the overcast had thinned and split and
was beginning to curl up and pull apart into dark clots; the full
white circle of the moon came out now and then between them. It
seemed to rise out of a clear window in the sky, looking down from
far above like a captive. Then the clouds cut off the moon again,
and the moon feinted this way and that, trying for a shot past the
clouds. The clouds swept across it swifter than the flight of the
vulture. When the moonlight went, there was nothing to be seen.

Suddenly the moon came out and shone like a flashlight right
into the frozen forest. A beam of light threaded down through

the trees and found a shrew ripping to pieces a frog twice its size, spot-lighting them as though they were the main attraction of the evening. The spotlight punched out of the night sky was alien and unnerving. It was not the same.

As far as the eye could see, this light excited and upset. Moon was sending its faint light to cast strange, grotesque shadows among the forest, and by its light, an old wolf, gaunt and battle-scarred, came forward into a clearing.

The old wolf sat down, pointed nose at the moon, and broke out the long wolf howl. The others sat down and howled, a ring of wolves, with white teeth and lolling red tongues, with long, sinewy limbs and shaggy hair. They began to howl as though the moon-light had had some peculiar effect on them.

Viewed in this light the wolves became real, not an amusing reference in a casual conversation. There were seven of them. The presence of their knowing was electric in the air. They bunched and nuzzled and licked one another. Then they stopped. They stood with their ears cocked. Some with one forefoot raised to their chest. There were more wolves a-coming. Here and there dots moving singly and in twos and threes and larger numbers.

Just then a heavy cloud passed across the face of the moon, and the wolves disappeared. Nothing below the horizon was visible, but the living ring of terror encompassed the sides of the clearing and gave animation to the scene; a bright afterimage remained in the gloom. The world was then only that old sound of the wind, and the bitter cold.

When the moon came back as white as cocaine, the wolves were howling and moving north. They loped paler yet and grouped and skittered and lifted their lean snouts on the air, loping and twisting. Dancing. Tunneling their noses. Loping and running and rising by twos in a standing dance and running on again.

The wolves ran like streaks of shadow; they looked no bigger than dogs, but there were hundreds of them. The dry powder blew about them in the cold moonlight and their breath smoked palely in the cold, as if they burned with some inner fire, and the wolves twisted and turned and leapt in a silence such that they seemed of another world entire. They moved down the valley and turned and moved far out on the plain until they were the smallest of figures in that dim whiteness, and then they disappeared.

16

AS THE NIGHT ADVANCED, THE MEMORY OF THOSE WOLVES faded into a sweeping darkness of clouds. The membranes of foggy mist went over the moon and remained near an hour, blocking out nearly all the light. Then a new danger came on in stealthy and measured glides, like the moves of a chess-player.

Slowly at first, from far off over the mountains, the clouds were stacking up—new forms much different from their predecessors. Low clouds and ghosts of an upper-world made strange shadows on the ground, and a monstrous cloud forty thousand feet high blew over. It was not snowing, though the sky was heavy with it, an even pewter weighing on the airy white hills that rolled up to meet it, so that the world seemed reversed here: dark water above circling clouds.

Once the sky had clouded over, the temperature had dropped a degree or two. Wind gusted, stirring the snow-laden branches of the pine trees. It was freezing. Along the mountain's-side, wind whipped the snow that had settled in its rocky creases. Then the wind began running a long hand down a slope to where the land divided, and there the wind seemed to hit hardest, blowing the snow up off the ground in fiercer and more bitter sweeps.

It was some five minutes later when the wind changed once more, magnifying as it rose, till it whistled tidings of death and annihilation. It was about nine degrees, but the wind brought it down well below zero—so cold the air cracked like ice. Another five minutes, and the snow began to fall again, cutting off the peaks of mountains. Soon when the wind blew, big white flakes were whirling over everything. The scene was enveloped in snow.

Yes, a wild northwester was blowing, one of those storms that had followed the birds from the polar basin as a white pillar of a cloud, and individual flakes could not be seen. The blast smelt of icebergs, arctic seas, whales, and white bears. It was the breath of ice, almost unbreathable. The clumps of trees in the snow seemed to draw together in ruffled lumps, like birds with their heads under their wings.

The sky was invisible now. The snow was now falling more heavily, and swirled about fiercely, for the arctic wind was beginning to blow a capricious gale—now from the west, now backing around to the north, sending clouds of powdery snow madly in all directions. The air, afflicted to pallor with the hoary multitudes that infested it, twisted and spun them eccentrically, suggesting an achromatic chaos of things.

Visibility was poor. Everything was muffled, blurred, indistinct, out of sight. Gone! But there were times when there were pauses between the snow flurries and it was possible to see a great distance. Through the churning white of the blizzard, through flying spray, the presence of a shape approaching the indestructible wind might well appear but as a few atoms. Something which had seemed like a bird might actually be dead—a rock or something. At one moment, an unearthly, formless, chance-like apparition of life appeared. It was hard to see at first, but there it was, about two hundred feet from the upslope of the hill, looking as ghostly as the white waste of snow: a dead horse; that is to say, a poor horse which the wolves had killed, and at least a dozen of them at work, not eating him, but picking his bones rather, for they had eaten up all the flesh before.

After looking intently, a snow fall made sight impossible. The wind rose in a gust, driving snow against huge and ill-defined shapes. The darkness was shot with swirling whiteness. A coughing, whooping sound and bending, tortured shadows resolved themselves into fir trees being pushed by a screaming gale. Snow swirled and danced. Snow everywhere.

The crazily dancing snowflakes represented the whole of life, a dance of death spun on the edge of nothing. In the delirium of the dance, the wind whooped louder, came now in fierce bursts, and the snow was driven with fury as it swept in circling eddies. Would now the wind but had a body, it would have gone romping on top of that stupid hill, destroying everything one way or the other. Wobble, boom, the end. The empty end. Nothing seemed certain. Angles, colors, the riot of snowflakes, the din of the hollow sounding wind grew stronger and harsher. The twisted evergreens hissed. The deciduous trees were groaning and creaking, their dead white branches angling to the threatening clouds. The whooping and impersonal voice of the wind, so huge and hollowly sincere, came now with fiercer and more bitter sweeps, and more steadily from the north, and it was still coming down like a madman. Some of the drifts were over five feet deep. The wind was constantly changing them, sculpting them into sinuous, dunelike shapes as nightmarish as a moving gargoyle in the distance.

And soon the snow had begun to spit down from the sky like lead. In the hills, the snow was falling faster and more furiously on a dim world without feature. The animals were failing. Gray squirrels streaked down mottled trunks where shelter had once been. The caribou themselves, a group of five *dashing through the snow . . .* , descended through the impenetrable clouds of white mist into a bottomless chasm of vague greenish-gray pines, far away and far below.

The biting chill wrapped the scene! The air stung like acid. The murderous wind filled the night with spectral chaos, and the snow hurled up white hills that fumed like volcanoes. All nature seemed to tremble, everything in panicky motion. The steady knife edge of the wind cut back and forth, the low whistle of the wind cranking up to a womanish shriek. The caribou came down with occasional periods of quick descent, tearing down the snowy hill, the snow driving thick like white sheets flapping in your eyes. Through this white madness, the snow came harder, curtaining them off from the world, two or three caribou half-skidding back down to the more or less level surface of the snow, leaving the wind to build to the low-pitched scream that would go on all night, a sound they would get to know well.

17

ON THE MORROW THE SNOW LAY YARDS DEEP. THE DAWN took on ghastly substance, becoming solid except for the trees and mountains ripped like jagged black holes to space. Wild rams ghosted away up those rocky draws, and the wind swirled down cold and gray from the snowy reeks above them, a smoking region of wild vapors blowing down through the gap as if the world up there were all afire.

That day there was no sun, only a paleness in the haze, and the country was all grey, all grey! The world looked worn out. It wasn't snowing anymore, but every once in a while vapory drifts blew across the open slope, and it was cold. It was indeed cold, bruisingly, frighteningly, unnaturally cold. Colder than the nipple on a witch's tit!

Colder than a bucket of penguin shit!

Colder than the hairs of a polar bear's ass!

Colder than the frost on a champagne glass!

The cold air gave fictive power, an air of severity, to the scene. The blast wafted by. The wind, low and hollow, sighed mournfully in the gigantic pine trees and whispered in low hissings among the withered shrubs which grew on the rocky prominences. The black wraith of a deciduous creeper flapped, seemed to shiver with every puff.

All morning long, that blasted rogue wind blew. It seared the face of the slope, blowing snow sideways, veering, tossing, distorting, and splitting into different shapes, moaning steadily through the trees like lost spirits. About a mile farther, more wind came pouring into the trees, writhing over a hillside. Sometimes the wind came fiercely down the slopes, blowing sharp pellets into a dark spot on the snow. The spot was, indeed, a near relation of night. The spot was memorable also because it was here, or close to it, that the animal staggered out of hibernation too early, climbed onto the hill for a while. But there wasn't much to watch: A bear. A hollow way adjoining to a thick wood. Empty canals of snow into trees.

Passing the few unhealthy fir-trees, the bear stopped, lurched, and then leapt over a snowbank and skidded gently to a stop. The big brown bear was cold, hungry, and tired. All night he had been wandering in the falling snow looking for food. The falling snow had obscured the ice that hid the frozen fish.* Falling snow had obscured the world. The bear was defeated.

As the bear looked around and rubbed both front paws over his nose, a cold wind blew down from the mountains. The bear's teeth started moving up and down. Soon these teeth were chattering so loud and fast, the bear got scared he was a chattering skull. All of his warm fur would fall off, his skin and his veins. The teeth kept chattering and biting. He got real pissed and his claws came out, but he couldn't figure out who to claw, so the animal pawed the snow and swung his head restlessly from side to side. Why wouldn't his teeth stop? Why was he shaking like this? The bear had a fever. He wanted to run away, but he knew if he left this bondage, there'd be nothing else left in the world.

He stood still, very still. He did not know what to do. A sharp wind continued to beat about the winter branches. Winds gave the

---

* What are these fish doing in a pond at the time of year when the winter's tempests would be sure to fell them? Nothing. The fish don't go no place. They stay right where they are, the fish. Right in the goddam pond. Where would they go? You don't think them fish just die when it gets to be winter, do ya? It's tougher for the fish, the winter and all, than it is for other creatures—or this silly ass of a world—but they stay right where they are, for Chrissake. They live right in the goddam ice. It's their nature, for Chrissake. They get frozen right in one position for the whole winter. What do they eat, then? Their bodies, for Chrissake—what'sa matter with ya? Their bodies take in nutrition and all, right through the goddam seaweed and crap that's in the ice. They got their pores open the whole time. That's their nature, for Chrissake.

old brittle limbs such a shaking that the clashing trees resembled frozen soldiers in all the postures of saber-rattling.

The bear went down on all fours. He grunted, moving his head in that snake fashion that seemed natural to him. As soon as the bear got out to another sidelong sweep of snow, the wind was picking up, blowing sideways. The bear was walking on, at leaning angles into the snowdrifts, going deeper into winter stillness, a landscape of silence and ice.

18

AS THE HOURS PASSED, THE DAY TURNED EVEN COLDER, the wind more forceful. And by noon the sky had already begun to spit snow.* The clouds had upreared and stretched in two great arms, reaching overhead.

The snow did not fall this time, it simply spilled out of heaven, like thousands of featherbeds being emptied. Snow fell. And fell. Sky and hills mingled in one bitter whirl of wind and suffocating snow, and before long a no-man's-land of snow, wind, steeps looked like an arctic tundra.

Around, on every side, far as the eye could penetrate, it was a white world on which dark trees and tree masses struggled against the surf of wind. Here the snow had been swept into huge drifts

---

* It is always beginning to snow. All it does here is fucking *snow,* eternal snow and immortal peaks of snow and rock. The mountain top is covered in mist. The central body of it is hidden in white lines, a white spittle draining from the sky. So white that it's not there. And it is the whiteness that above all things is a very sulky looking fellow. Though in many natural objects, whiteness refiningly enhances beauty, as if imparting some special virtue of its own, as in marbles and pearls, there yet lurks an elusive something in the innermost idea of this hue, which strikes more of panic to the soul than that redness which affrights in blood. This elusive quality it is, which causes the thought of whiteness, when divorced from more kindly associations and coupled with any object terrible in itself, to heighten that terror to the furthest bounds. Witness the white bear of the poles, and the white shark of the tropics; what but their smooth, flaky whiteness makes them the transcendent horrors they are? That ghastly whiteness it is which imparts such an abhorrent mildness, even more loathsome than terrific, to the dumb gloating of their aspect. So that not the fierce-fanged tiger in his heraldic coat can so stagger courage as the white-shrouded bear or shark. In essence whiteness is not so much a colour as the visible absence of colour and at the same time the concrete of all colours; is it for these reasons that there is such a dumb blankness, full of meaning, in a wide landscape of snows—a colourless all-colour of atheism.

or long ridges and blew directly against the shapes of the high blue trees. Once, when the wind increased slightly, a tree shuddered a shelf of snow from its branches on to the ground. There a rabbit bobbed out and floundered in much consternation; little birds rose in a dusty whirr, much terrified at the universal treachery of the earth. Every once in a while you could hear a keening fox some-where, faint but clear. It seemed oddly muffled and small in the great expanse of snow.

Through the wild white scene the storm went on. The snows thickened and the cold increased in a degree almost too severe to support. The trees kept up a perpetual moan which one could hardly believe to be caused by the air.

Then, toward sunset, the snow had stopped. The clouds parted, revealing the higher regions of the air, where immense glaciers exhibited their frozen horrors, and eternal snow whitened the summits of the mountains. Over these crags rose others of stupen-dous height and fantastic shape, some shooting into cones, others impending far over their base: huge masses of granite, along whose broken ridges was often lodged a weight of snow that, trembling even to the vibration of a sound, threatened to bear destruction in its course to the vale.

Soon the sun burst in between low, lumbering clouds, which cast dark shadows over the mountains. It was bright in places. It was mixed. Yonder was the snowy summit of a mountain, so much higher than any around it that it reflected the sun's rays—that res-ervoir of frost and snow, where the accumulation of centuries of winters, glazed in heights above heights, concentre the multiplied rigours of extreme cold—while those below lay in deep shade.

In another place, another season, the sun would be warm enough to send a feeling of life through the mountains and onto the flat lands. Then there would be a slow suffusion of inutile love-liness across the landscape. Ditto the weather. But the sun did not sing that evening; shadows were gathering over the land, and the wind was mourning. When the heavy gusts of wind came unim-peded through the notches in the hills, the black trees shivered, and the adventitious wind rushed out and away into the fields beyond. In a short time suddenly it dropped, and the air was dead; not a breath stirred, and the cold grew by the minute.

By now the land was dim, the light dying from off it. Shadows were strong, and the pale, cold light of the winter sunset did not beautify—it was like the light of truth itself. In a few minutes, when the temperature dropped, when the smoky clouds hung low in the west and the red sun went down behind them, leaving a pink flush on the snowy blue drifts, then the wind sprang up afresh with a kind of bitter song, as if it said: "This is reality, whether you like it or not. All those frivolities of summer, the light and shadow, the living mask of green that trembled over everything, they were lies, and this is what was underneath. This is the truth."

It was as if the eye of awakening were being punished for loving the loveliness of summer. As if the air became an explosion of blinding cold fire, sudden and soundless. The appalling truth descended upon those forlorn regions of dreary space. A sign came down from the world of darkness.

It was true. Winter's arduous and multi-pronged advance across mountains and plains had triumphed. The drifts were one luminous gray. The trees were dark. The big motions of nature halted, seemed to hesitate, and then, like some cowardly thing, collapsed. Deepest silence fell with the light, and all the reality of the unreality seemed to settle into a mental picture of the place, a picture of the end of the world, a wild place that seemed poised on the lip of the abyss: endless snow and winter.

As early as a hundred million years ago, the earth had locked into the rise and fall of seasons. Winter and then spring and then summer. The same time every year. All winter long, every winter, every year, the temperature is near to freezing and the snow is heavy upon the ground; at a certain time the cold diminishes, the days grow longer, grass and flowers grow, the birds start their treestirm shindy; everything is miniature, neat, gently pastoral, locked into the rise and fall of seasons; the seasons make sense. But that night, as the flood of cold light sank behind the hill and the pine-boles turned from red to grey, somehow everything changed. The seasons and nature and creation appeared more like a scene of airy enchantment than reality.

The truth of the matter was that the sun had dropped and all color had faded from the sky, but something was wrong. Had always been wrong. The wind blew from the worst possible direction. The clouds were close, and the cold air scalded. The sullenness of the place seemed to say that the world was an experiment that had failed; the sun would set for ever, never to return more; every thing would soften and blur into anonymity, and nothing would transpire.

Such a thing would batter the whole universe in deep shadow, the wind eternally blowing, and every day and night without light. Each rolling mountain would never appear again. Surface animals would never reappear. Even the wheel of the moon wouldn't be visible. Dry years would come, and sometimes there would be no snow, no faint, weird like ghostly disorder; just wind coming out of whatever godless quadrant, cold and sterile and bearing news of nothing at all. In the winter of wet years, snow would appear as a density of dark and blustery nothingness, and yet not nothing; an ice-cold air-stream would go on and on, eventually transforming it into icy giant battalions marching in relentless order across the world, crushing, obliterating, destroying everything in their path.

And so everything eventually marvelous would disappear from the whole earth in time, perhaps. Light would have negative magnitude, and the timeless, frozen centre of the All would be changed. There would be nothing. Nothing . . . blank . . . nothing . . . blank . . . space without stars in it. No, nothing . . . nothing . . . One long, drawn-out eternity of the huge alien night, the snow, the destroying cold, the menacing unknown future. For ever! For all eternity! Not for a year or for an age but for ever.

Under the most adverse conditions, all would change. Weather would thrash along, stimulating extremes of climate. Soil absolutely bare of vegetation. The sky above absolutely colourless without the Sun. How long would it take for a new ice age to freeze out all life? Weeks? Months? Years? How many forlorn hours in thousands of degrees below freezing point or the absolute zero of Fahrenheit, Centigrade, or Reaumur?

Life would be quite impossible on a world of ice—only ice, snow, stillness, death; nothing but frozen silence. Air would disappear like a pull of smoke. Nothing would transpire. Nothing would be left. It would all never have been, like the sound a tree doesn't make when it falls in the forest and no one is there to hear it.

19

THESE PLAINS, THESE MOUNTAINS, HAD NEVER SEEN A sunset like that. It was as if the world had shrunk to its core, or the small circle of light had been overtaken by darkness, and a bright fierce truth descended upon the solemnity of the scene. The imagination seemed to spring to full life in inaccessible polar regions, in scenes of cataclysmal horror of a magnitude such as no being had ever conceived, in curdling temperatures that no fish, no birds, no animals could endure. Vague visions half blinded by the whirl of colossal storms and terraqueous distortions had filled the empty landscape.

And yet somehow that night, as time went on and the darkness sorted into near and far, those visions were replaced by creaking and sighing sounds which suggested the most imminent danger: another storm. Before long, the wind had really picked up and the cedar limbs were thrashing. Bare willows clicked like skeleton fingers. Snowflakes whirled madly in all directions. It was happening again: the end of the world.

The next day, it was the same, with every tree eternally blowing and every animal trapped within the crust of snow and ice. The same day returned once again, the same waste of snow and rock, very lonely and austere. The view had changed, appearing a shade lighter, but the country was of a deadly and a deceitful sameness.

So it went. It snowed every day now, sometimes only brief flurries that powdered the snow crust, sometimes for real. On the coldest days, the snowdrifts were deep and the pine needles in the glades were ossified with ice. On the days when the sun shone, it was only an instant. A bright speck. Then it was gone.

One could not imagine that matters could get worse, but they did. In a matter of weeks, in a blizzard, how it snowed so hard. Raged for forty-eight hours. Animals that occupied the land felt the wind of the blizzard increase, and overhead the sky grew dark with snow. The cold increased until it was thirty below zero. The very next morning, when the snow finally ceased falling, quickly the passion went out of the sky. All the world was dark grey. Although the breeze had now utterly ceased, the temperature had dropped ten degrees and made it memorable. On the north wall of the valley a mile away, seven deer had frozen on a rock.*

A long time passed in such weather. Cold and intangible were all things in earth and heaven. Colder and intangible but more disquieting. One cold winter morning, however, the patterns of cloud cover began to change slightly for the better. The wind was still blowing overhead. The snow was falling over the ice and hiding the ice. The snow was falling over the ice and turning to ice. The winter bareness spread drearily over the broken ground, suffused with sloth and sullen expectation.

Just before noon the light changed. The snow had stopped after dumping a fresh eight inches on the old crust. The wind had dropped and it was less cold when, when, all of a sudden, thank the good God, some strange light flared up—died away.

There came a pause, a hiatus to the cold sky. There was the smell of wood even if just for a few minutes. A change of air. Of course, every tree within the valley was destroyed, but their scent, one that mingled sweetness and decay, at once filled the still air so completely that its very memory lingered for hours afterward.

When the light began to come back to life at once, it was the

---

* How many more nights and weird mornings can this terrible shit go on? How could there be a winter gray enough to age the land itself? Perhaps one day the sky and snow-sepulchre will open, spring's softness will return, the sun and south-wind will reach; the budding of hedges, and carolling of birds, and singing of liberated streams, will call to kindly resurrection. *Perhaps* this may be the case, perhaps not: the frost may never thaw—the snow-world, the terrible, static, ice-built mountain tops may remain undisturbed but by the wind. Weather conditions were quite impossible.

clump of clouds and vapours that flared in the sky. The sun was an angry little pinhead in the gloom. Though in a matter of minutes the nameless clouds opened and, lo!—all of a sudden, for the change was quick as lightning, the wonderful comparative smallness of the sun shot a broken and discoloured light that partially hung upon the shattered boughs and cast vast clouds and snow and ice and rocks into such vivid relief that for the first few moments the sense of distance and proportion was almost annulled.

The sun stood high in the sky, staring down through the hole in a perforated cloud, waiting for animals and for the wind. For a moment, a few of those sudden shocks of joy that are so physical, so precisely marked, set out across the valley. The eye had an almost boundless range of craggy steeps, grey rock, bright ice, and, looking up, the sunlight was a veritable flood, crystal, limpid, sparkling, setting a feeling of gayety in the air, stirring up a faint effervescence that was exhilarating.

The sun, on account of the mist, had a curious, sentient, personal look, demanding the masculine pronoun for its adequate expression. His present aspect explained the old-time heliolatries in a moment. One could feel that a saner religion had never prevailed under the sky. The luminary was a golden-haired, beaming, mild-eyed, God-like creature, gazing down in the vigour and intentness of youth upon an earth that was brimming with interest for him.

Eyes opened wide upon the glorious golden shaft of sunlight shining through the great clouds that sailed in masses. Light slanted, falling obliquely. Here, it caught on the edge of a cloud and burnt it into a slice of light, a blazing island on which no foot could rest. Then another cloud was caught in the light and another and another, so that the sweep of flat land below the abrupt thrust of the mountains was burnished gold, arrow-struck with fiery feathered darts that shot erratically across the quivering tangle of reflections.

This light excited and upset. The valley was now much more pleasant than it had been before. But why? What was all this commotion? With just one glance, the sun had stirred up the clouds that had loitered in the heavens. For weeks—ay, months—winter had piled high drifts in every direction and as far as the horizon. Imagination completed what mere sight could not achieve. But now, with the sun overhead, it was like a pleasant sensation indefinitely prolonged. It was much more like a sensation than like an idea or an act of remembering.

The sensation of sunlight overwhelmed, was undisturbed but by the wind, which broke at intervals in low and hollow murmurs from among the mountains. It was a strange sensation, and it grew, and grew. Till soon the clouds broke and drifted apart, shining white in a clear blue sky. The valley seemed an enchanted circle of glorious veils of gold and wraiths of white and silver haze and dim, blue, moving shade—beautiful and wild and unreal as a dream.

20

NEVER HAD THERE BEEN SUCH WEATHER. EVERY MOMENT
of the afternoon was full of new things, and every hour the sunshine grew more golden on the ground. And it was still very cold—
below freezing—but there was one nice thing. Something special
in the wind. The storm was a thing of the past.

As the light grew, sounds joined the parade of perception—
sparrows haggling among themselves, a blue jay's squawk of excitement, the sharp whistle of a cock quail, and the answering whisper
of the hen quail somewhere near. All these animals, and others,
had felt so doomed up here in the eternal snow, as if there were no
beyond. Now suddenly, as by a miracle, they had returned to avail
themselves of the height of the ground, in order to examine the
glorious, the truly glorious, weather.

Other animals had gathered in the northeast corner of the valley and shone warmly in the light or gave off a dull, dry shine:
martens, minks, ferrets, otters, weasels, badgers, ermines, foxes,
and the small, gray-and-black tabby-striped wildcats. All these animals, and others, had fallen prey to the winter landscape. When
they got out for a breath of country air, and Sunshine raced across
the slope, it was something shocking.

An animal with four legs—a beast—came trotting up the hill.
Into the sun. Unlike the animals who knew only the present, this
animal, overseeing its offspring proudly and tenderly, could look
up into depths of pearly blue and see the golden world for what it
was: nightmare. Nothing but nightmare had seemed real all winter
long. Curds of bruised clouds hung motionless in the sky, memories of the bitter winter, but memories that the murmur of the
mourning wind carried across the treetops to distant east and west.

It was hard to tell if this turn in the weather, these blessed calms, would last.

On the other side of the valley, another animal that had lost everything that winter* came sludging through the snow. It was the sow bear, the mother, a huge, powerful, heavy thing breathing a stale breath of decayed old deer-hides and skunk cabbages and dead mushrooms.

The bear stopped, heard something. The sound repeated itself. It came from near at hand, from the thick shadow between the tree trunks on the hill. Then the bear went down on all fours, made for the nearest tree. And waited, because even the bear, all hot cold dark in her fevered confusion, needed to think what was best to be done. The bear made a gurgling sound deep in her throat and bared her long, curved, yellowish teeth, so good at ripping and tearing. Suddenly, crash! Two bear cubs burst from the bush and rushed pell-mell, tumbling head over heels straight for her. One flew flat on its face, bumping its nose and squealing. The other twisted in midair and landed in a heap on the ground, shaking its head in confusion. The bear boys looked at her, jumped forward.

The little cubs piled against their mother, clung to her. The mother of the little bears was overwhelmed by sunlight and the arrival of her cubs. For a long time the giant bear sat calmly with them in her arms and looked at the sky. There was a light wind. The sun moved on in its course until the bears were at peace with the world. Then, in no hurry, they rose in one piece of dark fur. They moved as if across a swale of moon dust, bulky and wobbling, trapped in the idea of the nature of time.

* The wolves were bad that winter, and everyone knew it.

21

WITH THE CHANGE IN THE WEATHER, A CHANGE HAD COME in the mood of the landscape and the appearances of the sky. The next day was very fine. It wasn't as cold as it was the day before, and the sun filled earth and sky. The heavens were idle and quiet, in keeping with the lonely, beautiful valley. The valley was full of a lustrous haze. Everything was perfect, a view so various and sublime that it gave little sensation of cold.

The effect produced was rather of a complete absence of atmosphere, as though nothing less tenuous than ether intervened between the white earth and sky—a sense of purity renewed, a sense of events in trembling balance flooded in from every corner of the world. Everything, everything seemed encrusted with portent. The soft colours of the clouds, the beauty of light on the glittering white stretches of land to the south and west. And when these sensations came, they started an ever so slight stirring of thought. A litter of broken sentences. Each thought became eternal thanks to the Sun.

With such a slow motion, thoughts, affected by the surrounding objects, gradually sunk into a pleasing and complacent rhythm around the snow-laden trees, a rhythm that began to vary only as the sun rose higher. Hour after hour, sunlight reflected off the snowy fields and forests, and through these great stretches, the light, like a thing alive, leapt and scattered, and the sensation of sunlight overwhelmed. The feeling of the wind—the real feeling of wind blowing in the country, in country living—and snow and other ways of feeling the world ran through the trees and the valley bottoms, and it seemed that the world was waking. The valley was a little different. Every valley was somehow new.

By noon the floods of light fell more nearly to the perpendicular. The stark colors of the morning were smoothed in pearl and opalescence. The wind, which had hitherto carried along with amazing rapidity, sank upon such a scene—the air so dry and pure, prolonged, stupefying, suggestive of an infinite quiet, of a calm, complacent life, centuries old.

This continued for many hours, and by sundown the temperature had risen to higher than usual. Soon cool draughts of air began to reach hard, firm, certain land, air that had been brushed through forests, through a stone gap in the mountains, through the cold shadow-radiance of the afternoon, through bush and solid rock, through the sunken fields, an air of enchantment from the south and south-east.

And so the days passed on, the weeks passed on. Now that the sun had been a regular occurrence, it was, somehow, an honest country, and there was a new song in that blue air which had never been sung in the world before. As the long winter ended, there was still a little chill in the wind, but it smelled of spring. The cold was less sharp, lapsing gradually to its end under the gorgeous loneliness of a cloudless, pale blue sky and the steady fire of an interminable sun. Between sunrise and sunset, meltings of snow and ice were visible in shining sight. Wet snow plashed into gleams. Everywhere there was a musical trickle and drip as the noon sun thawed icicles and snow crusts. The river ice buckled under the wet snow, the ponds split apart and the bigger lakes groaned and sang and cracked.

From every hill slope came the trickle of running water, the music of unseen fountains. Bearing down the snows of winter, a creek of considerable depth and plenty of water ran dappled from the mountains, catching the fragrant blizzard blown from the blackberry vines. The creek was swollen from the thaws and there were places where the water sprayed like a geyser in the hollows between the rocks.

All things were thawing, bending, snapping. The bare branches of the trees flung themselves up, yawning, taut with energy; the twigs radiated off into the clear light. The catkins on the hazel loosened their winter rigidity and swung soft tassels. The snow-dunes glowed scarlet, shrinking slightly from the touch of the wind, little streams of dark water gurgling cheerfully into woods, over the snow. And everywhere drip drip drip.

One day in the very last of the winter, in all this, a light appeared at a distance: atop a hill, near the edge of a cliff, which of course received the sun. Up there the snow had blown away in places, leaving bare spots. But in this clear climate of fantasy and perspiration, where every idea, sensible and insensible, gets vent, in this land was a Flower of the mountain yes a flower so new, so tender, so made perfect by inner light.*

In a few days the sun melted the thin snow at the foot of the hill, and soon there appeared in view more flowers, a few primroses and the first violets. Daffodils were craning forward from among their sheaves of grey-green blades. The cheeks of the flowers were greenish with cold. But still some had burst, and their gold ruffled and glowed. And then the light rain began, for on some days clouds would rest over the snowclad mountains and all and every the lands, meadows, marshes, woods, underwoods in the distance. And soon the snow was pockmarked from warm rain, and melting in patches to expose the yellowed grass beneath it. Sometimes on a sunny day a greenness grew over those brown beds, which, freshening daily, suggested the thought that Hope traversed them

---

* Flowers are fucked into being between the sun and the earth. It's a delicate thing, and takes patience and the long pause: A bird staggered in from some land far to the southwest, brought the seed in its bowels. As if in gratitude, it emptied its bowels on the waiting earth and evacuated a tiny seed which it had eaten on some remote island. The seed germinated. The sun shone, snow fell, winds blew for a long, silent time. Then the frosts of winter had ceased; its snows were melted, its cutting winds ameliorated. The little seed long germinating in the deep, dark furrows of the soil, straining, swelling, suddenly in one night had burst upward to the light, miracle of miracles!—this utterly silent, frozen world of the mountain-tops was not universal! After all this silence, life would develop. What was it like? A world, a glimmer or a flower? A flower. A yellow flower with flattened petals. A flower. A fresh, luminous flower. A flower of the mountain yes so mountain flower.

at night, and left each morning brighter traces of her steps. Flowers peeped out amongst the leaves; snow-drops, crocuses, purple auriculas, and golden-eyed pansies.

This flowering period represented the second division in the cycle of those superficial changes which alone were possible here; it followed the marks of the rabbits and birds in the white snow, the wind, the clouds, the rain, everything whirling along full lustre; and now the ghostly winter silence had given way to the great spring murmur of awakening life. This murmur arose from all the land, fraught with the joy of living. The birds fluttered and dashed. All through the day sounded long, sweet whistlings from the brushes. The vast blue sky resounded to the quacks of wild ducks and the honk-honk-honking of wild geese. The long, black-dotted lines of them were all flying north. All around there sounded voices of hundreds of white-throated sparrows. In the mild air they were singing cheerfully, sweetly; then later, loud, laughing shouts of bird triumph on every hand.

Even at a glance, it was obvious that Spring had come once more. Soon as the name was heard, the Woods shook off their snows. The melting floods broke their cold chains, and Winter fled away. There were still traces of grainy old snowbanks in the shadiest spots, but in places the sun was actually hot.

The days were unnaturally lengthy and spacious. Each day, as soon as the dawn was just breaking, the darkness lifted, and, flushed with faint fires, the sky hollowed into a perfect pearl. The sun rose on the other mountains and touched them with such light as made it seem as if the world were just being born. All day the curlews and killdeers and sandpipers chirped and sang in the creek bottoms. The crows cawed above the trees along the creek. The winds whispered in the new grass, bringing scents of earth and growing things. Often in the early evening thin flights of waterfowl were moving north before the sunset in the deep red galleries under the cloudbanks like schoolfish in a burning sea.

The nights passed. The spring grew warmer. In the daytime intermittent rains freshened all the earth, and each storm waited courteously until its predecessor sank beneath the ground. Then warmth flooded the valley and the earth burst into bloom—yellow and blue and gold. The flowers grew rapidly. Bud after bud burst forth, while those already opened expanded to full maturity. The colours of the flowers deepened, and as their odours penetrated deeper and more distinctly, the oak-buds were opening soft and brown. Everything came tenderly out of the old hardness. The curled heads of ferns. Buds, roots, fresh new leaves. Even the snaggy craggy oak-trees put out the softest young leaves, spreading thin, brown little wings like young bat-wings in the light.

The Source of Life was also the Saviour of spirits. As the sun became warmer and the light of day longer, the snow vanished, and one morning the whole land was green. Not one tree or bush decaying under the vines. To see a green spring beginning, it was a pleasant thing like it is to some to hear a cuckoo sounding and to be slowly convinced that it is not a clock but a live bird calling. It is a pleasant thing to come somewhere and be having such a thing happen a very pleasant thing.

Spring advanced rapidly. Days of blue sky, placid sunshine, and soft western or southern gales filled up its duration. The absence of snow was sensational, allowing fresh water to dissolve over and through the soaking earth. Now vegetation matured with vigour. The tree tops were all bright with reds and yellows, with brilliant gleaming whites and gorgeous greens. All the lower air was full of the damp haze rising from heavy soaking water on the earth, mingled with a warm and pleasant smell from all the open fields. And above all this was the clear, upper air, and the songs of birds and the joy of sunshine and of lengthening days. The languor and the stir, the warmth and weight and the strong feel of life from the deep centres of the earth that comes always with the early, soaking spring.

22

THE WORLD WAS NEW AGAIN. AFTER A WINTER'S GESTATION in its eggshell of ice, the valley had beaked its way out into the open, moist and yellow, and the plant kingdom of the ditches and the successional meadows and the stonier-sloped woods was fantastically green.

Obscene amounts of pollen were in the air, the trees burdened with the bright dust of their own fertility, the swollenness of their leaves. But in a short time—within a week—all the exciting, growth-heavy spring wind had blown away in places the mingled scent of wet soil and golden pollen. All that remained of sky and air was the wind, the breeze that blew carelessly through the clear air. The chestnut trees budded approval one at a time. The leaves winked.

Throughout the springtime, the wind did not blow very hard, but in warm, sweet gusts. The fields shimmered, multiplying the feel of the wind by two, and in the forest, mild Zephyrs breathed through blooming bowers like faraway rain—fainter, more wistful, gone. Down here there was a softer note in the sound of the wind. Now, if the wind blew a branch, a flower, it was solely for their good, that they might increase in strength and happiness. And what with the whistling and the chuckling of the wind coming over a hill, whenever the sound came again, stronger, it blew from a place that was old and whispered of youth. It blew down the grooves of time. It sang clearly the song of love. It breathed low of pure blue sky and the joy of freedom regained after winter.

The radiant promise it offered during the day was pleasant but less exciting than the wind at night. The whole long day was a blaze of sunshine and gentle breeze. Hundreds of purple and white morning-glories laughed in the meadows and the birds sang. A buzzing came faintly from all the trees in the creek bottoms. But all these sounds made a great, warm, happy silence at night. The whole long night was as clear as crystal, and very still. Could hear a distant coughing of a sheep. The sound of the night wind in the mountains was like one long indrawn breath.

In a quiet place, where any sound at night means something, such a wind could rise and meet the evening gloom in pure sympathy or in earnest, whatever be the mood it be in. The singing of the wind in the cliffs—it was only a gale, but as sweet a singer as any to be found on earth. It was generally better at night.

One day, or rather (because it's important to be precise), one night, just as the moon rose, the wind rushed against the trees, and the music of the wind, which rose in pitch, was comforting and reminded of the cow jumping over the moon. Many sounds came from the grasses, from the earth, from the broad tree trunk at the edge of the wood, where pink campions glowed. The air was drowsy. It smelled of damp roots and mud, and it was full of the sound of rustling leaves and of water running.

At such an hour, on such a night as this when the sweet wind did gently kiss the trees, the bees were asleep. In the grasses, in the trees, deep in the calix of punka flower and magnolia bloom, the gnats, the caterpillars, the beetles, all the microscopic, multitudinous life of the daytime drowsed and dozed. Larger animal species—the meadowlarks, the rabbits and the deer, the Disney book of wildlife—slept in the wide green meadows. Not even the minute scuffling of a lizard disturbed the infinite repose, the profound stillness.

But the wind was blowing down from the distant mountains. Grasses, more or less coating the hill, were touched in breezes of differing powers, and almost of differing natures—one rubbing the blades heavily, another brushing them like a soft broom. The trees on the right and the trees on the left chaunted to each other in the regular antiphonies of a cathedral choir; other shapes to leeward then caught the note, lowering it, happy that the world is such an excellent listener. Above the sky were ears. In all their different shapes they coiled, blurred ears, listening. And looking down, the wind was pitting the grasses and leaves, making little whirlpools, kitten-shaped ears, listening, listening.

For two or three hours the moon poured its light through the air. During these hours, the wind was still blowing, but now there were intervals of utter quiet. The only movement was caused by the movement of trees and branches which stirred slightly, and then the shadows that lay across the spaces of the land moved too. In this profound silence, one sound only was audible, the sound of a slight but continuous breathing which never ceased, although it never rose and never fell. It seemed to come from the earth, as a breath long-held and released. It continued after the birds had begun to flutter from branch to branch, and could be heard behind the first thin notes of their voices. It continued all through the hours when the east whitened, and grew red, and a faint blue tinged the sky, but when the sun rose it ceased and gave place to other sounds: the birds piping one against the other, and water mysteriously plashing, issuing southward, from a river in the meads. A little wind was running in from across the eastern plain, and in the new sun an old hen clucked her brood together. A bird twittered; two birds, three.

Cuckoo
Cuckoo
Cuckoo.

A duodene of birdnotes chirruped bright treble answer. Brightly the keys, all twinkling, linked, all harpsichording, called to a voice to sing the strain of dewy morn, of youth, of love's leave-taking, life's, love's morn.

As the sun rose higher, there was a certain thrill and quickening everywhere. The wind was cold, but not so tiresome, and the sunshine was like life itself, warm and full. Cocks were still crowing. Some young birds came along, flying a yard or two at a time and lighting. What birds were they?* They flew round and round. The air made clear their flight, their dark quivering bodies flying clearly against the sky as against a limp-hung cloth of smoky tenuous blue. Bird after bird: a dark flash, a swerve, a flutter of wings. All their darting quivering bodies passed: six, ten, eleven: were they odd or even in number. Twelve, thirteen: for two came wheeling down from the upper sky. They were flying high and low but ever round and round in straight and curving lines and ever flying from left to right, circling about a temple of air.

Birds were swinging and singing in tiny voices, but what did these sounds mean, and where, in this wilderness, could they be going? Up hill? Under the shadows of the pear trees? The Answer grew nearer and nearer: Birds were compelled to teach their nestlings how to fly. For the most part, they stayed up in the sun above the flowers and did not come down into the shadow of the trees. From time to time, they came to rest and then flew on. The cries: like the squeak of mice behind the wainscot: a shrill twofold note. But the notes were long and shrill and whirring, unlike the cry of vermin, falling a third or a fourth and trilled as the flying beaks clove the air. Their cry was shrill and clear and fine and falling like threads of silken light unwound from whirring spools.

By now the land was burnished gold like a dream of the world, and the great dome of air was warmed through and glittering with thin gold threads of sunlight. There was a rousedness and a glancing everywhere. A sallow tree in a favoured spot looked like a pale gold cloud; nearer, it had poised a golden fairy busby on every

---

* The wagrant wind's awalt'zaround and on every blasted knollyrock there's that gnarlybird ygathering, a runalittle, doalittle, preealittle, pouralittle, wipealittle, kicksalittle, severalittle, eatalittle, whinealittle, kenalittle, helfalittle, pelfalittle gnarlybird. Our pigeons pair are flewn for northcliffs. The three of crows have flapped it southenly, kraaking of de baccle to the kvarters of that sky with its high and light clouds, which are sure to melt away as the day waxes warm. This placid and balmly atmosphere is dearer, maybe closer to Heaven . . . O Paradise . . . for the birds, especially the small delicate dark terns that always live before the wind.

twig, and was voiced with a hum of bees, like any sacred golden bush, uttering its gladness in the thrilling murmur of bees and in warm scent. At the edge of the woods, the trees, with lifted fingers, shook out their hair to the sun, decking themselves with buds as white and cool as a water-nymph's breasts. At the foot of each sloping tree stood a family of flowers, some bursten with golden fulness, some lifting their heads slightly, to show a modest, sweet countenance, others still hiding their faces, leaning forward pensively from the jaunty grey-green spears. There the daffodils were lifting their heads and throwing back their yellow curls. The colts-foot discs glowed and laughed in a merry company right into the field.

Here in the middle of a sloping green field was a pleasant place bosomed in hill and wood. The air was warm with sunlight, and the daffodils continued their golden laughter and nodded to one another in gossip, never for a moment pausing. A furry bee came and buzzed round, sounded like a wind getting up, a sound caught by a spell just under crescendo and sustained. Then it began to scramble all over the tiny blossoms, a bee gravid with being, bending a flower to the earth. After a time, the bee flew away across the meadow, creeping into the stained trumpet of a Tyrian convolvulus. The flower seemed to quiver, and then swayed gently to and fro.*

Throughout the field, everything was serene, brown chickens running lustily near the woods, brown rabbits hopping everywhere, and bright white clouds flitting rapidly above. And all around was the country, woods and sounding water, the pear tree soaking in the alto chant of the visiting bees, the gold of the sun and the panting breath of the breeze. It was this new morning that

* So this was a marriage! A revelation. The motion was strangely gracious: There's the hum of the bee drone, a dust-bearing bee in the sanctum of a bloom; the thousand sister-calyxes arch to meet the love embrace and the ecstatic shiver creaming in every blossom and frothing with delight. So much for the forest murmurs . . .

broadcast a blue sky to every soul in the forest: Toads, frogs, spiders, birds, beasts, a woodpecker, somewhere a thrush. And like-
wise the flowers and shrubs—white-leafed thistle with round, pale
yellow flowers and yellow spikes; large, brilliant yellow ground-
sels; grape hyacinths, so blue they were almost black. Everywhere
the bud-knots and the leap of life! Grass undulating in waves, the
breeze rocking in a rustling green tree and woods and sounding
water, and the whole world awake and wild with joy. It was as
if the sun wanted all to lie in an ecstasy of peace, wanted all to
sparkle and dance in a glorious jubilee.

23

ALL MORNING LONG, THE SUN FELL WARM UPON THE LAND. This warm, scented light was streaming from the sun's chest, gushing out, cascading, splashing off trees, flopping to the ground. It was spilling everywhere, overflowing, just too much, too much to absorb. Treetops full of birds chirped and shrieked in ecstasy— the jays there in the trees, cawing, and the larks singing high up overhead. And not only larks, but throstles, and blackbirds, and linnets, and cuckoos pouring out music on every side.

It was a magnificent morning. It was a valley, full of birds, and flowers, and the low moo of cows calling across the meadows at the same time in every direction, as though it was the Valley of the World. It was pleasant under the trees, in the gold-flecked shade, with the whistle of quail and twittering of birds everywhere. It was pleasant and sunny out in the open, on rock, under a sky softly curdling with cloud. It was so beautiful, so perfect, and so unsullied. It was healthy. If you looked directly up at the sun, it was possible to see a feathery skyline of trees budding into bloom. Then, too, if you looked up higher and higher at the sky, it was pure, rooks dropping cool cries from the high blue. It was beautiful weather; it was a day of amber sunlight. It was a partially cloudy day with winds diminishing toward sunset.

As the hours passed, high towered the glorious Sun, and poured the blaze of day. Unhurried but steady, the clouds rose up like towers, and something had touched them into beauty, and poised them up among the winds, the luminous blue sky. With changing clouds, it seemed just a fantasy, like a piece of painted scenery. All that nature—the woods, the fields, the trees—was sucked in and out by the breeze; all was blowing, all was growing.

By the time the sun was overhead, the gusting winds had fallen to a soft breeze which gently stirred the blossom in the lime and carried its fragrance to merge with the sweet breath of the valley. Birds had congregated in the morning, but before it was even afternoon, everything had settled into place; birds would soar through into the upper radiance or alight on a branch pecking at the cherries, but there were so many hillocks and banks where birds and animals came to nest at this hour of the afternoon, and for some few fleeting moments, when the wind dropped and no birds sang, there was silence.

It was in this silence that the stream could be heard chattering over gravel. The stream sang on the opposite side of the field. There was a deep little dell, sharp sloping like a cup, and violets ran down in rivulets and cataracts, irrigating the hillside with blue, collecting into pools in the hollows, covering the grass with spots of azure foam. Below, in the first shadows under the willow trees, there was a clear stream where dace were swimming in pools. A little water ran trickling between grass and stones. A few forget-me-nots flowered by the water.

Along the course of the bright little stream, the earth was red and warm, pricked with the dark, succulent green of bluebell sheaths, and embroidered with grey-green clusters of spears and many white flowerets. The cliff of red earth sloped swiftly down, through trees and bushes, to the river that glimmered and was dark between the foliage.

The stream murmured down the descent by a channel which its course had long worn, and so wandered through to lose itself in the neighbouring wood. Going downhill awkward, and sometimes in flight, the clear, mountain, shrub-lined stream fell over little cascades in its haste, never looking once at the primroses that were glimmering all along its banks. Coming down fast, it broadened out just before it joined the river and the quiet, cool-looking slope beyond.

There came a quick gurgle from the river below. There was a wind running across, and on the eager water a flower, a fresh, luminous flower, floated like a little water lily, staring with its open face up to the sky. It turned slowly round, in a slow, slow little dance, as it veered away. Down river to the west, there were fish. Sometimes little fish vanished before they had become real, like hallucinations, sometimes wagtails ran by the water's brink, sometimes other little birds came to drink.

The winding river turned and turned down the hill, through the woods like an aluminum rainbow, like a vast smile of water, foam clinging to the lips. Its path through the chasms of the higher and the glens of the lower hills was shadowy and almost cold after the blaze of the fields. It flowed under the southern cliff and past the mounds of stone. Then the river softened up a way off, and, where it made a bend, washing around a boulder, the river— with fish in it, with the sky and trees in it—bubbled over stones.

Here the stream widened. Giant willowtrees trailed long green hair in the water, made an inviting grotto of cool green shade. Motionless grey shadows, herons, stood here and there in the shallows. A kingfisher waited ceremoniously on the branches. These fowls all lived among these low trees, and bred there. It was a private, peaceful, idyllic scene; violence was worlds away.

The kingfisher was the key to the magic world: He was witness of the border of enchantment. He saw birds come and dip their heads to drink and then flick their wings and fly away. He watched while two white swans sailed across the reflected trees with perfect blithe grace. They lifted their glistening feathers till they looked like grand double water-lilies, laying back their orange beaks among the petals.

The swans had gone out on to the opposite bank when the kingfisher suddenly heard something. It came from near at hand, from the thick shadow of the trees that bordered the stream. Along the shore the wild birds rose, peewits mewing fiercely, while from the wood's edge a twitter of lively birds exclaimed. Partridges and woodpeckers were booming and knocking when the kingfisher looked to where the sound came from, but nothing appeared there save the verge of the hillock and the forest.

The sound came nearer and nearer. The kingfisher was flapping and hopping. Finches went leaping past in bright flashes, and a robin sat and asked rudely: "Hello! Who are you?" He stood erect, looking round.

The woods were thick; the sound was muted and sporadic. Some creature stirred under the tree tops. Very little light penetrated inside, but something moved, flashed, turned a huge flank, exhaling. Breath snorted out. A pointed snout parted the leaves and looked out into the clearing. Nothing moved but a pair of gaudy butterflies that danced round each other in the dim light.

24

SOON THERE APPEARED IN VIEW AN AUBURN PONY. THE
horse shook its head, stepped out into the day. The sun lit the grass,
and the horse stood on the brow of a slope, watching the scene
below: a kingfisher tracing jeweled parabolas, ducks like white
cloudlets under the trees. The tall, lank pony seemed used to such
doings and ambled along unconcerned. Thus she passed under the
level boughs, stepped very carefully into the water, and drank.

And now more sound, more horses emerged black and shining.
The horses stepped archly among the shadows, the choppy blue
water gleaming. They scrambled down the bank to the edge of the
steady flow, sniffed at the water and began to drink, sucking up
long draughts of it.

The horses drank. The horses' silence lasted for minutes,
maybe centuries, and the river continually flowed away over the
sand, rocks, and stones. The birds sat still save that they flicked
their heads sharply from side to side. Now they paused in their
song as if glutted with sound. The dragon-fly poised motionless
over a reed, then shot its blue stitch further through the air. And
all the time the animals drank.

After a while, they lifted their heads and looked out downriver. They listened to the wood-pigeons call among the trees, and
the brown thrush singing. They saw the little minnows swimming
all together in the shallow places. They watched long-legged water-
bugs skate over the glassy-still pools when the green-coated frogs
with their white vests plopped into the water. They watched as this
stubborn little creature, a kingfisher, flew up the river and veered
and chattered and then swung back above the river again and continued upstream along the wooded shore to a distant sea of trees.

Eventually a few horses began to step sideways, sidling away. Three horses came up out of the river one by one and began to graze in the good grass along the bank. Occasionally one of the horses would tear off with his teeth a plant full of blossoms, and walk along munching it, the flowers nodding in time to his bites as he ate down toward them. Only one horse was seen descending the hill—the handsomest horse on the place. It had a substantial body, large, soft, gentle eyes, and a good mane. A way a lone a last a loved a long the riverrun, the horse ambled along for a considerable distance, chomping away, turning to scratch his behind against a tree with a big erotic motion.

The big red beast seemed to dance romantically through that dimness of green hazel drift, away there where the air was shadowy, as if it were in the past, among the fading bluebells. And as the animal breathed, while its tail moved slowly in sinuous and graceful undulations, the river went down as before yet more dark and darkening.

The horse trotted down the twisting river for a while. Then, coming over a little rise in the ground, he saw something at a great distance like a bright cloud in the air. The horse stopped, breathed heavily, shifting round its red flanks, and looking suspiciously with its wonderful big eyes upwards from under its lowered head and falling mane. Whether it was wind or water, mountain or cloud, he did not know. So brief had been that movement, that light, the brain had not been quick enough to interpret the cipher message of the eye. He did not know what to do.

The horse turned and looked again toward the light. Through a U-shaped notch in the treetops, which looked like an inverted tunnel, a fine view was to be obtained of the plain. It would seem that the whole earth lay before, an immense space—the wide plain with distinct hills arising on the left into bold romantic mountains, and on the right exhibiting a soft and glowing landscape whose tranquil beauty formed a striking contrast to the wild sublimity of the opposite craggy heights, high as heaven. Directly ahead, the carpet of the land unrolled itself to infinity. A river ran across the plain, as flat as the land, and appearing quite as stationary. The river glistened in a hieroglyph across the country, the flat fields stretching right away, broken now and then by taller plants.

The effect of the earth with its minute objects and colours and different forms of life was overwhelming. The whole view was exquisitely light and airy; the blues and greens of sky and tree were intense. Great beautiful clouds floated overhead, valley clouds that made you feel the vastness of an unbroken sweep of land. It was incredibly beautiful, so far as eye-sight has any virtue—and yet nothing could have been more beautiful than the deep light in the distance.

Now that the sun was on the wane, its light cast reflections from the river surface on the plain beneath. Reflections of the afternoon sun went farther and farther onto the plain to the very edge of the world. And there a light appeared at a distance that illumined the rocks and the horizon to a great extent. It was something of a miracle—as beautiful as the spring, the diffusion of daybreak, the apparition of a new solar disk. The horizon line streamed across the ground. The landscape seemed lying in a swoon: the blue and distant ocean terminated the view.

II. THE DEEP BLUE SEA

I

THE RIVER DESCENDED INTO A VERY LARGE VALLEY SUR-
rounded with hills, and those hills covered with the treeshade of
sunnywinking leaves.* Green sloping banks and bushes intercepted
the light of the full blaze of the sun, and sometimes the branches
of trees would catch the sunlight and spin in the wind like black
shadow, then a glisten of green, and all the time the bright river
swirling in a silent dance to the sea.

Then the river softened up away off, and emerged into the
romantic, free, beloved radiance of a great field. The sun shone
brightly on little showers of buttercup down the bank. In the fields
the fool's-parsley was foamy, held very high and proud above a
number of flowers that flitted in the greenish twilight of the grass
below. This was where the rest of the animals lived—a peacock,
guinea hens, sheep grazing, horses galloping away and tossing their
silvery manes among the tall flowers. It was a beautiful place, wild,
untouched, above all untouched, with an alien, disturbing, secret
loveliness. And it kept its secret.

The river and the meadows continued into the distance. They
came down into a level country where there were cattails five feet
high and great stretches of silent woods and long green stretches of

---

* In reality, the river falls five hundred feet . . . and look: opens out upon the
fields. Metallic at first, seen down through the trees. Closer still, it flattens, flat
as a street, cement-gray with a texture of rain. Flat as a rain-textured street even
during flood season because of a channel so deep and a bed so smooth. Today
there is nothing to indicate movement except the swirling clots of yellow foam
skimming seaward with the wind. A river, smooth and seeming calm, hiding
the cruel file-edge of its current beneath a smooth and calm-seeming surface. A
river going on and on and on.

pasture-land and many streams. And through these great stretches, this life of flowers, this world of colour, this chaos of perfume, down here, below the hills, there was no place that was not alive with something. The trees, the fields, the sky, the birds, the sunlight, the movement on the river, and the moving river itself. The tiniest breezes blew across the land and among innumerable scattered trees. Some purple violets were growing all over the grass, and wild jonquil. Everything was lovely. Along the edges of the river, some of the flowers, the young pale wind-flowers, had begun to shed their petals. They lay there dumbly as daisy petals in a summer meadow. Or they would simply fall into the water, carried away in the current, the blossom-covered surface of the river smooth, stretched taut from bank to bank like a polka-dotted fabric.

The river went on, the brilliant little discs of the daisies veering slowly in travel on the dark, lustrous water, a company of white specks in the distance. Occasionally the gurgle of the river was swift but not deep, for the river was still too wide; sometimes the river narrowed a little and sped towards the horizon. Its waters, in creeping down these miles of meadowland, frequently divided, serpentining in purposeless curves, looping themselves around little islands that had no name, returning and re-embodying themselves as a broad main stream further on.

If it had not been for the main stream of water, it would have been different. The land would lie exposed; the trees, coarse grass, and rank weeds would lie submerged in the bleak stillness of the marshes, the water a steely glitter. Instead, the wind and the water brought movement and turning and racing in places, top speed . . . then, and perhaps best, the wind and the water brought Joy, such as strikes deep to the heart on the river's bank when the kingfisher suddenly flares across the water or a torrent of wind starts again, brushing over, the air warm-cool and fluid. The "Highway of Water," as the river is referred to frequently, was as full of motion and change as the highway of the clouds above. It fell in an arrowy rush right down the hillside and across the north pasture, toward the sea.

Farther downstream the wind increased, steady, unbroken by gusts. The wind was warm. The land was greener here. And now you could just catch a glimpse of the bay in the distance when the river curved. Hills and trees permitted more of a view of the sea's hypnotic blue—where blue was visible. It was only a bright speck. Then it was gone. The river would wash it away as it disappeared around a bend.

Suddenly the river went down between the bare, reddish-yellow walls of earth, all ridged and wrinkled by forgotten rains. The view opened. The land fell and reached away. In the distance, at last, was a clear view to the sea, sparkling and shimmering like some kind of promise of salvation. Sea, shoreline, sand, stones. Tall grass, dunes. The sea and perfect peace. That was what the view was forming at last. The view inland was spectacular all right— flatland behind the dunes, trees past the flatland, a line of woods, all the way back round to these hills—but the sea shone summer blue and yellow far as the eye could see. The sun was dropping towards the west. The light was golden and mellow and carried the gaze out as far as the blue sky and white clouds.

The bold concave of the heavens, uniting with the vast expanse of the ocean, formed, a coup d'œil, striking and sublime magnificence of the scenery. The quality of the air, the exuberance of the flowers along the line of rocks overlooking the sea, the blue intensity of sea and sky, produced the effect of a closing tableau, when all the lights are turned on at once.

2

RIVER FELL. THE LAND DECLINED. ALL THE SOUNDS OF THE river were now a crescendo, and every phrase of this well-worn, familiar music was an unprecedented revelation of beauty that went pouring downwards over the landscape in its intense brightness.

Then the big humpbacked river with its mainstream leaping came coiling down to the sea. Ahead was the mouth of the river that flowed into the ocean. There to the left, the beginnings of the hills. To the right and toward the sea appeared a spectacular beach. From swerve of shore to bend of bay, it was a flat beach of two miles of yellow sand. The first dunes were a relatively short distance from the water's edge. The dunes far away were accessible enough. They were laced in undulating shades of orange and purple, and the white tips of the waves beyond sparkled with surprising brilliance.

Some miles north, the sea filled in all the angles of the coast smoothly, breaking in a white frill, and here and there across the bright sand, indeed, the shore was covered with innumerable turtles. Here was also an infinite number of fowls of many kinds and the green hills across the bay and, at the far point, beautiful especially to see up ahead north, a vast expanse of curving seacoast.

Looking out upon the west, the sun was so full of promise, and the sea was whipped white with a merry wind. Near to the shore the sea briefly imitated every land feature—every hill, every valley, every plain. Accelerated geotectonics. Around the world in eighty swells. Far out to sea, these sea-pastures, wide-rolling watery prairies and mild blue hill-sides, were calm as though they had earned the rest.

How big the sea was! From here there was no land to be seen anywhere—just a vast expanse of blue water rippling in the evening sun. The sea . . . so peaceful to-day—sometimes so cruel . . . The sea moved in solid brightness, coming towards the shore. And above it the brilliant, poised cloud masses swung their slow flight. There was a dreaminess in the view, too, which made it still more perfect and luxurious. The sun was dropping towards the west. The light was golden and mellow. It enveloped the great long misty sea-line in a golden glow, and suspended gulls flashed by like an improbable postcard.

Now more than ever, the fresh breeze blew steadily across the water, bringing with it, over the salt surface, the salty air. Yes, the breeze was freshening as if it blew from a far-away meadow and merged into the churning mist of sea and sky. From time to time, spray was blown off the crest of a wave and the sea was joyful and the taste of the salt water was the taste of hope and joy.

As the winds blew fresh at west, the waves kept tumbling the pebbles* and small rocks. The monotonous fall of the waves on the beach, which for the most part beat a measured and soothing tattoo to the act of thinking deep thoughts, seemed consolingly to repeat over and over again, curling, unfurling many crests; every ninth, breaking, plashing, from far, from farther out, waves and waves. One after another they massed themselves and fell; the spray tossed itself back with the energy of their fall. The waves were steeped deep-blue save for a pattern of diamond-pointed light on their backs which rippled as the backs of great horses ripple with muscles as they move.

And all along as the waves tossed and waved and colored beautifully from light to dark, clouds scudded across the sky and the

---

* The stones, so close-textured, so variously decorated, so individual. Some of them were beautiful with a simple wit beyond that of any artist: light grey with thin pink traceries, black with elaborate white crosses, brown with purple ellipses, spotted and blotched and striped, and their exquisitely smooth forms lightly dinted and creased by the millennial work of the sea.

sun had now sunk lower. Down the beach, birds flashed through the air. A gull. Gulls. Far calls. Coming, far! Till a crowd of a thousand seagulls came to dodge and whish. The shadows moved across the uneven ground below, swinging smoothly in wide, easy circles. They swung above the ocean to make new exploratory journeys like those long, strung-out flocks of long-necks that like to play that they are part of the sea and fly always a foot above the water, matching every swell, every trough, before finally settling to roost on the water like a speckled blanket.

But way off alone, out by himself hundreds of feet above the sea, a gull cried. A lone gull. It was strange. Yes, a hundred feet in the sky a large, fierce gull swooped down. He lowered his webbed feet, lifted his beak, and strained to hold a painful hard twisting curve through his wings.

The curve meant that he would fly slowly, and now he slowed until the wind was a whisper in his face, until the ocean stood still beneath him. He narrowed his eyes in fierce concentration, held his breath, forced one . . . single . . . more . . . inch . . . of . . . curve . . . Then his feathers ruffled; he stalled and fell.

3

SEAGULLS, AS YOU KNOW, NEVER FALTER, NEVER STALL. TO stall in the air is for them disgrace and it is dishonor. But this gull, unashamed, stretching his wings again in that trembling hard curve—slowing, slowing, and stalling once more—was no ordinary bird. Most gulls don't bother to learn more than the simplest facts of flight. They live in colonies where they forage and feed all day long. Solitude and reticence are unnatural to them. For most gulls, it is not flying that matters, but eating. For this gull, though, it was not eating that mattered, but flight. More than anything else.

The bird was fearless, off by himself again, far out at sea, hungry, happy, learning: Climb to a thousand feet. Full power straight ahead first, then push over, flapping, to a vertical dive. Then, every time his left wing stalled on an upstroke, he'd roll violently left, stall, his right wing recovering, and flick like fire into a wild tumbling spin to the right, crashing down into the water.

Time after time it happened. Time after time the gull rose higher in the air and circled again. The two-foot span arched and dipped in the wind. Then he dove suddenly and, careful as he was, he lost control at high speed and finally burst into a churning mass of feathers.

The key, he thought at last, dripping wet, must be to hold the wings still at high speeds—to flap up to fifty and then hold the wings still.

From two thousand feet he tried again, flapping his wings as hard as he could. For a few moments he hovered, his body rising and falling between his wings. Then he pushed over into a blazing steep dive toward the waves. In just six seconds he was moving seventy miles per hour, the speed at which one's wing goes unstable on the upstroke. Beak straight down, wings full out and stable from the moment he passed eighty miles—all pure, all noble—per hour, it took tremendous strength, but it worked. In ten seconds he had blurred through ninety miles per hour. A world speed record for seagulls!

But victory was short-lived. The instant he began his pullout, the instant he changed the angle of his wings, his body took on the appearance of a stumpy cylinder. He snapped into terrible uncontrolled disaster, and at ninety miles per hour it hit him like dynamite. The Gull of Fortune exploded in midair and smashed down into a brickhard sea.

4

WHEN HE CAME TO, IT WAS WELL AFTER DARK, AND HE floated in moonlight on the surface of the ocean. His wings were ragged bars of lead, but the weight of failure was even heavier on his back. He wished, feebly, that the weight could be just enough to drag him gently down to the bottom, and end it all.

As he sank low in the water, a strange hollow voice sounded within him like a bludgeon. There's no way around it. I am a seagull. I am limited by my nature. If I were meant to learn so much about flying, I'd have charts for brains. If I were meant to fly at speed, I'd have a falcon's short wings, and live on mice instead of fish. My father was right. I must forget this foolishness. I must fly home to the Flock and be content as I am, as a poor limited seagull.

The voice faded, and the bird now sunk a little more. But a new voice was heard in the lower part of his soul. Nevermore! he thought. Nevermore! the gull repeated. I am done with the way I was, I am done with everything I learned. I am a seagull like every other seagull, and I will fly like one. Without a moment for thought of failure and death, he opened his wings and rose, rather heavily, into the air. He pushed wearily away from the dark water and flew off in quite the opposite direction, away from shoreline and out of sight, cloud-bound, among irrelevances and repetitions, the stars and the moon twinkling on the water, throwing out little beacon-trails through the night. All so peaceful and still . . .

That night was brighter than usual. The moon was full, hanging quaintly above the scene, shining, dimming the stars and pouring metallic brilliance onto the sea and animating the water which undulated, shining like black silk. Even the wind, which

had been blowing strongly, seemed to be refreshed by the brightness of the light, for it picked up another knot or two, deepening
the swells. All was movement, all was change, and somehow this
was visible and yet unimaginable, a dancing play of black and silver that extended without limits all about.*

How vast and dark. How deep, how beautiful was the water
stretching so far away. Those clouds of dark vapor, waves of
shadow. The volume of things was confounding—the volume
of air above, the volume of water around and beneath, and the
plains of the sea that encircled the earth. From the sea, the sky
rose steep and enormous, and in between the two, in between the
sky and the sea, were all the winds, and the air washed profoundly
between. And in all this great space it was curious to think how
only the waters spoke. In the infinite series of the sea, with nothing ruffled but the waves, there was not even the whine of insects,
not even a bird. Just under the surface not a single groan or cry of
any sort, nay, not so much as a ripple or a bubble came up from its
depth. The world silenced. Only the sea's low-pitched hum.

How restful this moment was when compared to the roarings
of the giant ocean in the late afternoon, when marine life appeared
in great abundance, and in the early morning, with the light toes
of hundreds of gay fowl softly feathering the sea. In the daylight
sky such birds that fly, dipping and hunting, with their small sad
voices, can be seen in any large accumulation of water. Just the
same, strange forms in the water darted hither and thither: click-
ing dolphins, barracuda like swimming stilettos, silver blizzards
of sprats. One day a twenty-foot oarfish was seen, but at intervals, as the passing clouds yielded to the power of the full blaze of
the sun. And yet tonight, in the quiet of the night and the balmy

---

* With the light and the waves coming from the same direction, the constant
motion of the sea, though gentle, slid by in a body, utterly silent and swift,
intertwining among itself like some subtle, complex creature. The sea's black
hide heaved in the cobbled starlight, and the voice of the sea was absolutely
seductive, never ceasing, whispering, clamoring, murmuring, inviting the soul
to wander in abysses of solitude.

breeze and the maiden lustre of the moon, all matter of sea life was nowhere in sight. The sky and sea were beautiful, and the climate was congenial, but if the concept of paradise includes also life, then the scene was one that wandered about in Purgatory. The sense of loneliness was far more intense than it had been on land. This far out, water went whispering about, and high above, the clouds passed, in the vast, dim blur of the darkness, and that was all. Nothing else to be seen but the limitless sea. Although in little more than a minute and a half or so, something in the view had changed.

It was while gliding through these waters that one serene and moonlit night, when all the waves rolled by like scrolls of silver; and, by their soft, suffusing seethings, made what seemed a silvery silence; on such a silent night, at such a moment, a silvery jet was seen. Lit up by the moon, it looked celestial, seemed some plumed and glittering god uprising from the sea. That silvery, moon-lit jet arose and spread fan-wise into the air. A moment later it subsided and sank. Then once more arose and silently gleamed. Was it a whale? It was very big, had come out of the depth of the water, suddenly. It seemed not a whale, and yet if there's nothing else except the wind blowing, but what else is there? What else could make rays of light dance out of it? From here a fine view was to be obtained of its back, while the tip of its tail, a form of most exact and superior symmetry, shone with a long slant down into the silver light. It was only a bright speck. Then it was gone. And again the sky was alone with elemental things—night, silence, wind, and water.

Imagining, now, that nothing else would be stirring—or so it would seem—it was easy to be lost. "Down in the bottom," as they say. Now and then clouds would rest over the moon or the stars. Then the wind would sweep the face of the ocean, the waves would ripple and flash (buffet of wind made it seem alive). That was it. Was there nothing else? There was nothing, just the soft peace of silent spaces of sky above the waters, of oceanic silence. The mysterious sea, luminous, waited, alive yet empty.

But the sea was patient: it could wait. One day? One night? It was a complete mystery how long the waiting sea might last. In this case it lasted for hours. For now, little stars shone high up; little stars spread far away in the waters; the moon's reflection bored into the flat water like a hole into the sea. There was nothing else to be seen but the limitless sea, with some gusts of wind between bouts of extreme silence.

5

SOON THE STILLEST HOUR OF THE NIGHT HAD COME, THE hour before dawn, when the world seems to hold its breath. The wind dropped. The moon hung low, and had turned from silver to copper in the sleeping sky. Gradually the almost infinite size of this water and then the world began to change. The sky began to lighten. The illusion defined itself by imperceptible degrees: A corner of the sky changed colours. The air began filling with light. The calm sea opened up like a great book.

Still it felt like night—the prolongation of early coolness, the subdued, lingering half-light, the faint ghost of the night, the fragrance of its dewy, dark soul captured for a moment longer between the great glow of the sky and the intense blaze of the uncovered sea. It was natural that as the eastern sky was beginning to glow rosy-pink the hopeful birds were appearing on the sea and fluffy, radiantly white clouds were beginning to light up in a vast fathomless dome. Just then a sort of brightness, a point of gold, appeared above the sea and at once all the sky lightened. The sun, looking like an electrically lit orange, broke across the horizon.

With the very first rays of light it came alive: The delicate pink sky turned primrose, then blue. The water was the same colour as the sky, shifting with a quick small dancing movement, and scattered by the sun with little explosions of metallic pale-gold light. It had the look of a happy sea, and the sea, the air, the sun all spoke differently, now they spoke one language of unity. It was a cheery sun, which was aware of air, which was mindful of sea, which shared things with sun. Every element lived in harmonious relation with its neighbour, and all was kith and kin.

As the sun rose higher, the wind was blowing more strongly,

but not too violently. The tide was right. The strong, gentle lifting motion of the quiet waves reminded of the blooms of spring. And high above, the vast blue sky was scattered once more with the incredible small, tight clouds. The sunlight came and went, seeming blown quickly by a wind at its work. It was almost like the hither and thither of a leaf that comes unexpected; the sun kept going off and on, dodging behind first one cloud and then the other.

This kept happening, off and on. It'd be bright for a little bit, everything shining like chrome, waxy-looking, polished, then go dark as muddy water. Then bright again. At one point, as soon as the sun went behind the great rock (the exact description of the form of a cloud), a fine shadow was flung over the sea, the waves no longer blue. This shadow was dim and unsubstantial for a few minutes. It wasn't so bad. Then wind blew again and the color of a future light could be seen in the distance. The light wind strewed it with beautiful shadows and amoeba-shaped blotches of blue until the clouds opened, and a bright sun shone above bright as hell, like it was lit with more than light, like a movie-show screen when the film breaks and you got nothing to look at up there but the bright white light. Everything else is gone.

At that precise instant there was a vibration in the air and a splash—a dolphin leaping, true gold in the sun. It jumped again and again as a school of dolphin sailed in, curious and playful, chattering in funny click-tongue. Dolphins that leaped in pairs. They were very gay. Their plunging and turning and racing just beneath seemed to have no purpose other than sporting fun. Beyond, in the sun, hither and thither, on high, glided the snow-white wings of small, unspeckled birds. A flock of something—gulls? swallows? From time to time, animals higher up occasionally relieved themselves on the sea below—birds called grey albatrosses. Each flew by high in the air without taking any notice of anything. And the sun illuminated them as they went by, written on the walls of the sky. They were something supernatural and incomprehensible, sir. At one time, a short-tailed shearwater circled above, eventually dropping down. It kicked out its legs, turned its wings and alighted in the water, floating as lightly as a cork. Other birds arrived, and all the time numberless fowls were diving and ducking. Looking up at the sky and over the sea, you might, in a simpler world, have said it was magic: Birds would soar through into the upper radiance and hang on the wing sunning themselves, or alight on the waves, afloat all day upon smooth, slow heaving swells. Sun and wind would act upon them and, shooting from among the clouds, form a vast, sublime picture in the background of the scene.

Now these fancy things—these animals, sun and wind—were beautiful, that is true, but the most singular and beautiful object in all this scene was the sea. Its blue seemed vouchsafed by nature. It was a lovely place, the creamy blue surface of the sea only a small part of it; the real lure of the sea was beyond, down into its eternal blue noon, beyond into the deep water past where the ocean floor dropped to nothingness . . .

Looking down into the sea, you might chance on jelly-fish and dolphins, flying-fish, and other vivacious denizens of more stirring waters. But to and fro in the deeps, far down in the bottomless blue, rushed mighty leviathans,* sword-fish, and sharks. Through the 19,000 feet of ocean so many fishes. And in all this great space it was curious to think how the sea is a city, maybe even cities. Below were highways, boulevards, streets and roundabouts bustling with submarine traffic. In water that was dense, glassy, and flecked by millions of lit-up specks of plankton, fish like

---

* Among these, the great whales of the sea: I., The Sperm Whale; II., the Right Whale; III., the Fin Back Whale; IV., the Hump-Backed Whale; V., the Razor Back Whale; VI., the Sulphur Bottom Whale. Whales of middling magnitude: I., the Grampus; II., the Black Fish; III., the Narwhale; IV., the Thrasher; V., the Killer. The smaller whales: I., the Huzza Porpoise. II., the Mealy-mouthed Porpoise. Any of the following whales: the Bottle-Nose Whale; the Junk Whale; the Pudding-Headed Whale; the Leading Whale; the Cannon Whale; the Scragg Whale; the Coppered Whale; the Elephant Whale; the Iceberg Whale; the Quog Whale; the Blue Whale; etc.

trucks and buses and cars and bicycles were madly racing about, no doubt honking and hollering at each other. The predominant colour was green. At multiple depths, speeding fish came from all directions and disappeared in all directions. They were like those time-exposure photographs you see of cities at night, with the long red streaks made by the tail lights of cars. Except that here the cars were driving above and under each other as if they were on inter- changes that were stacked ten storeys high. And here the cars were of the craziest colours. The dorados—there must have been over fifty patrolling beneath—showed off their bright gold, blue, and green as they whisked by. Other fish were yellow, brown, silver, blue, red, pink, green, white, in all kinds of combinations, solid, streaked, and speckled. Only the sharks stubbornly refused to be colourful. But whatever the size or colour of a vehicle, one thing was constant: the furious driving. There were many collisions— all involving fatalities—and a number of cars spun wildly out of control and collided against barriers, bursting above the surface of the water and splashing down in showers of luminescence. It was a spectacle wondrous and awe-inspiring: silly silent cities in the sea, slickered o'er with scum of histories.

Much farther down, marine animals were the same color as the sea. Whales were seen especially when they paused and were sta- tionary for a while; their vast black forms looked more like lifeless masses of rock than anything else. Even deeper down into the dark water, shapes of innumerable obscure creatures could be indis- tinctly seen, giving no distantly discernible token of movement. Fathoms deep, there was of course nothing to see. No light. When up looks up, up is down . . . But there is no up. No down. No in. No out. No forward or backward. Just this cold, this unnameable continuum of merging and dissolving. Groundless.

6

AT A GREAT DISTANCE BELOW THE SURFACE, THERE WAS NO real sense of motion. Five hundred feet. Eight hundred feet. Nine hundred fifty feet. You'd never notice. The water had an inky quality that swallowed light.

Moving down, temperature differences in the water were spaced out at safe intervals, the first major one appearing about three hundred feet (water temperature had dropped ten degrees). A mile and a half under the ocean—the unrelenting pressure of water all around—water temperature, ah, thirty-six degrees Fahrenheit. Almost freezing, yes, sir.

It was a long way down, and the water was dark. Deep enfolding darkness. Amniotic darkness. From time to time throughout this story, the pressure, coupled with a swift acceleration of speed, amounted to hundreds of tons to the square inch. To a fish that was common enough; much more unusual were the smallest of white flecks that would appear and disappear into a perfect dark distance.

The sea's darkness swept down around the white flecks and down there through the water without wavering, all the way down to a dark underwater kingdom in which there live and swim the many-sensed creatures of the lightless ocean deeps, a cloud of good or bad angels, the invisible yet active forms. It was so utterly dark, and yet pale phosphorescent shapes ranged beyond the limits of sight: a species of fish with faint flashes; and another with an extraordinary brilliance; and sometimes some eerie bioluminescent fish could be found, a fish with incredibly exaggerated jaws, wide at the mouth.

Now suddenly, as by a miracle, such an animal flickered into

visibility as a line of lights flashed out along its body. It appeared
to be quite large, but it was hard to judge. Hanging from a point
just below its gills was a long tendril, ending in an unidentifiable,
bell-shaped organ. Its light dimmed and glowed again with intense
green. Then a chorus of screams broke out, a pandemonium.* It
was a steady background, into which all individual sounds had
been blended. Not one thread in the tapestry of sound could be
disentangled and identified. It was so alien, so remote. At the
sound, Nature seemed to tremble; the great luminous fish—
the little, eerie bioluminescent fish mentioned earlier—suddenly
flashed on all its lights in a frantic signal of alarm and departed
like a meteor into the darkness of the abyss.

The fish swam steadily through the night water, propelled by
short sweeps of its tail. There was little other motion: an occasional
correction of course by the slight raising or lowering of a pecto-
ral fin—as a bird changes direction by dipping one wing and lifting the other. It was after another twenty minutes of descent that
the bioluminescence lit the ocean floor, mistifying the gardens of
the deep.

Beneath, a range of low hills was passing, their outlines curiously soft and rounded. Whatever irregularities they might once
have possessed had long ago been obliterated by the ceaseless rain
from the watery heights above. Even here, far from the great estuaries that slowly swept the continents out to sea, that rain never
ceased. It came from the storm-scarred flanks of unnamed mountains, from the bodies of a billion living creatures, from the dust of
meteors that had wandered through space for ages and had come
at last to rest here in the eternal night.

---

* A school of whales, about ten kilo-metres away. What are they doing? They're
mating. And what a wondrous thing. Flukes grinding back and forth somewhere in the depths, their song became a symphony vibrating across the ocean,
and maybe continents vibrated.

7

AY. WHAT A NIGHT IT WAS. GOOD LORD. AN ANCIENT SEABED, fathoms deep. The sea-weeds and the pallid monsters of the very bottom. A submerged mountain jutting up from the hidden plain. They all had a story. A sea story. Such ceaseless strife; such dark, unlit depths.

These "moonbeam-bodied creatures" lived their lives between the echoing cliffs and a flat, dead, dull-brown plain stretching away. They lived so deep—and only a few years before a predatory fish would come streaming through.

Down where life was rhythmed by reflex, such things do happen, and here is an example: Once, a venomous-looking creature with gaping jaws swam slowly across a half-concealed cleft. The fish swam by cautiously, as if testing the water after a long sleep, when some great dread came in the shape of oncoming sound and movement. The fish turned. So swiftly that the eye could not follow the movement, a long tentacle flashed out and dragged the struggling fish down to its doom. And that was all. In the depths of a restless sea, life was certainly very interesting . . . and short. Over and done with in an instant. A fish that was strong and driving wildly always knew this as it rode the earth of deeps and wildernesses.

Yes, the battle for life was taking place there, but the event—a tiny dead fish—was actually of no lasting significance, for in the long history of the ocean many such events occurred. About two billion years of history had taken place. So many animals, and the sounds of animals, had gathered and dispersed in the deep sea, and very ancient mountains had deposited sediments that had accumulated to a remarkable depth. For millions of years, an extent of time so vast that it is meaningless, the closest of these mountains, hidden away in this inaccessible corner of the world, had grown so patiently in the deeps. Only the ocean knew that with the passage of time and in the presence of great pressure, small amounts of liquid rock seeped out on the floor of the sea, each forcing its way up through what had escaped before, each contributing some small portion to the accumulation that was building.

This mountain and its ravines could not have been any more than forty million years old, but throughout its brief life it had always been a lively infant when compared to the roarings of the giant ocean. It's true. Millions upon millions of years ago, back to ancient times before the mountains were born, there existed, then as now, one aspect of the world that dwarfed all others: water. Secretly, far beneath the visible surface, it moved slowly, coming and going at different depths. There was something ominous about it, and yet it was wonderful, an intoxication: its taste: its universality: its democratic equality and constancy to its nature in seeking its own level: its vastness: the restlessness of its waves and surface particles visiting in turn all points of its seaboard: the independence of its units: the variability of states: its hydrostatic quiescence in calm: its subsidence after devastation: its sterility in the circumpolar icecaps, arctic and antarctic: its preponderance of 3 to 1 over the dry land of the globe: the multisecular stability of its primeval basin: its luteofulvous bed: its slow erosions of peninsulas and islands, its persistent formation of homothetic islands, peninsulas and downwardtending promontories: its alluvial deposits: its weight and volume and density: its gradation of colours in the torrid and temperate and frigid zones: its violence in seaquakes, torrents, eddies, whirlpools, maelstroms: its vast circumterrestrial ahorizontal curve: the simplicity of its composition, two constituent parts of hydrogen with one constituent part of oxygen: its infallibility as paradigm and paragon: its variety of forms in loughs and bays and gulfs and bights and guts and lagoons and atolls and archipelagos and sounds and fjords and minches and tidal estuaries: its solidity in glaciers, icebergs, icefloes: its submarine fauna and flora (anacoustic, photophobe), numerically, if not literally, the inhabitants of the globe.

Water was life. The alchemy of the open water had the capacity to produce enormously, to encourage natural life to develop freely and radically up to its own best potential—more than the glorious sunlight or the land. In fact, the origin and evolution and fate of all life began in earnest at the bottom of the deep ocean along a line running two thousand miles from northwest to southeast. One day, a rupture appeared in the basalt rock that formed the ocean's bed. By some chemical process, or from some genetic chemical jumble, incalculable trillions of billions of millions of imperceptible molecules united to one another. Different compound substances formed, and one was part of a separate system: one closed seed of life falling through dark, fathomless space and time itself. In this case, the molecules separated from one another and, over millions of years, spread themselves broadcast over the face of the earth. The world began.

Consider all this: for millions of years, tens of millions, hundreds of millions—no one knows how many millions—the central areas of this tremendous ocean were empty. No life. This eternal sea existed, larger than any other of the earth's features, vaster than the sister oceans combined, wild, terrifying in its immensity and imperative in its universal role. How utterly vast it was! How its surges modified the very balance of the earth! How completely lonely it was, hidden in the darkness of night or burning in the dazzling power of a younger sun than ours.

Across a million years, agitated by a moon stronger then than now, immense tides ripped across this tremendous ocean, keeping it in a state of torment on the surface. At some point during this time, far away down at the bottom, atoms of matter were being formed; the birth of life-building slime. The ocean continued its swift gleam of bubbling white water, and in its dark bosom, strange life was beginning to form, minute at first, then gradually of a structure now lost even to memory. Microbes, germs, bacteria,

bacilli, billions of cells building microscopic civilizations, civilizations that would perish and be built again in time and perish. Life
was of a curious microscopic sort. A million years passed, and then
a million more, and the first sentient animals were of course fish.
They permeated the ocean, coming and going as they wished. But
they could not be said to be a part of the subtleness of the sea;
down into the blue, its most dreaded creatures grappled, unappar-
ent for the most part and treacherously hidden beneath the loveliest tints of azure, carrying on eternal war since the world began.

These battles were fought in the endless night of the ocean
depths, where the sperm whales hunted for their food and sometimes schools of squid. When a predator (i.e., a spouting fish—a
full-grown Platonian Leviathan) met its prey (a giant squid at least
fifty feet from head to tips), it was food that objected strongly to
being eaten alive. A terrific, most pitiable, and maddening sight:
The whale wrapped in the tentacles of a giant squid. The long, saw-
toothed lower jaw of the whale gaping wide, preparing to fasten
upon its prey. The creature's head almost concealed beneath the
writhing network of white, pulpy arms.*

This was the restless surge of the universe, the violence of
birth, the cold tearing away of death. The universal cannibalism
of the sea writhing and wrenching in agony! And yet the years
passed, the empty, endless, significant years. The sea fluctuated
between life and death like a thing struck by evil. Sometimes mol-
ten lava would rise through the internal channels and erupt from a
vent in the ocean floor. A thousand years, or ten thousand, would
silently pass before any new eruption of material would take place.
At other times the climate was changing—the heat would be too

---

* With one tentacle already a truncated stump, there could be no doubt as to the
ultimate outcome of the battle. When the two greatest beasts on earth engaged
in combat, the whale was always the winner. For all the vast strength of its forest of tentacles, the squid's only hope lay in escaping before that patiently grinding jaw had sawn it to pieces. Its great expressionless eyes, half a metre across,
stared at its destroyer—though, in all probability, neither creature could see the
other in the darkness of the abyss.

hard on certain creatures. Species would bloom and disappear the next day. All life would be choked off, noiselessly. Noiselessly floating corpses amid the mingling glooms.

And still, at wide intervals, the years passed. The sun swept through its cycles. The moon waxed and waned, and tides rushed back and forth across the surface of the world. Through hard times, the alchemist sea changed. Over its brooding surface immense winds swept back and forth, whipping the waters into towering waves that crashed down upon the world's seacoasts, tearing away rocks and eroding the land. Bit by bit, over a hundred thousand years, the sun shone, rain fell, winds blew, currents flowed. The sea built up hills, the sea dug up valleys. The land and all its dreariness lost. The ocean won. Every time.

Timelessly, relentlessly, by day, by night, in storm and sunshine, the waves came on and on. New-forming land would rise from the sea to be weathered by storm and wind, the headlands and backbone diminishing regularly. Far out to sea, where there was no land, it was curious to think that the sky was the same. The same wind and waves with the same violence. The dern storms would learn to get here at any time of the day or night. When they would creep in like sea-wraiths, waves would be generated which would circle and crash upon themselves. A burst of rain would come in a great glistening mesh. The lightning would play round it and jab into it and into the sea. And the thunder would go rumbling and grumbling—chain-explosions which would go on and on hour after hour.*

Storms like that were frequently seen rolling across the sea for days at a time. Night after night, summer and winter, the torment of storms, the gigantic chaos streaked with lightning, could

---

* During a storm, nature can put on a thrilling show. The stage is vast, the lighting is dramatic, the extras are innumerable, and the budget for special effects is absolutely unlimited. The ocean is inviolate. Nature primeval, a spectacle of wind and water, an earthquake of the senses, that even Hollywood couldn't orchestrate.

be heard booming, tumbling and tossing, as the winds and waves disported themselves like the amorphous bulks of leviathans whose brows are pierced by no light of reason, and mounted one on top of another, and lunged and plunged in the darkness or the daylight, in idiot games, until it seemed as if the universe were battling and tumbling in brute confusion and wanton lust, aimlessly by itself. And yet in those moments the sea was gentle compared with a century storm.

A century storm. You might call it some act of God, a typhoon perhaps, or the storm that comes along once every hundred years . . . in that kind of sky . . . that kind of wave . . . It produced a huge shift in nature—the colour of the sea, everything else. There was too much wind, too much tidal effect. The sky's attack and the sea's treachery, combined with the wind pressing itself against the water, so odd in its shape, formed one of the world's major structural forms: chaos. Science's finest hour produced a wild effect. The whole setting was wild: the monstrous waves coming down, the high-pitched shriek of the wind, and showered salt rain. The heaviest rain.

Luckily, Nature had provided the perfect deterrent: clouds and monstrous storms like that came only when accompanied by hurricanes. A herring or a cod might live a century and never see such a storm. Years would come and all the time there was bright sunshine, the night was dark, cool, and quiet, the heavens were starry bright. In the years ahead, endless expenditure of beauty and capacity, tireless ebb and flow and rising and subsidence of the ocean. No storm. No clouds. And then, one day, somehow everything changed.

8

THAT MORNING, AS ON ALL THE OTHERS OF THE FULL TALE
of mornings since, the sun had already risen, and the ocean was
a smooth skin reflecting the light with a million mirrors. The sky
was dappled with small, white, fleecy clouds. The wind was fair
but fitful.

By eleven o'clock the wind had somewhat abated but was still
blowing. The sun was already high and the sea was a glittering
azure, shifting and flashing as if large plates of white were floating
on the surface. By midday, a stillness almost preternatural spread
over the sea, however unattended with any stagnant calm. The sea
had become glass. There was not a fleck of white visible on the surface. There was no freshness in the air. It was sultry and oppressive,
reminding of the old term "earthquake weather." The silent sea and
the sky appeared formidably insecure in their immobility.

For a long time nothing happened. Not a whisper of wind was
stirring; the sea was like polished glass. It seemed like hours, the sun
and the birds lost in melancholy musings. The fish had disappeared,
and in this foreshadowing interval, too, all humor, forced or natural,
vanished over waves monotonously mild. Then the sweet voice of a
bird burst forth amidst the universal stillness. And then, just then,
the faintest possible whisper of air passed by. It was from the east,
and like a whisper it came and went. The wind blew again, and in
this profound hush of the visible sphere, a strange spectre was seen.
This time there existed, on the distant sea and beyond the bulge
of the earth, an iron-dark line on the horizon, wiggling or just lolling
about between the sea and sky. A heavy mass of horizon cloud.

The clouds were building up now for the trade wind, and, with
that heaven-rolling mountain range of clouds moving slowly over

the sea, the whispers of wind became puffs, muttering and puffing stronger and stronger. The stagnant air of the day changed into a fitful breeze, with the promise of more wind behind it.

In another hour, the wind had much increased, and the sky was more overcast, and blew hard. Slowly the whole eastern sky filled with clouds that over-towered like some black sierra of the infernal regions. There were high cumulus clouds and enough cirrus above them that so clearly could one see canyon, gorge, and precipice, and the shadows that lie therein, with the land no more than a cloudy dream within a dream . . . For a moment one looked unconsciously for the white surf-line and bellowing caverns where the sea charges on the land. The illusions merged and flew about, joined into long illuminations in the eerie, storm-coming light.*

According to the caprice of the wind, the clouds passed above. The wind had been momentarily increasing, and the sun, after a few angry gleams, had disappeared, leaving behind nothing but the naked, desolate sea. And then, where a vagrant shaft of sunlight struck the ocean and turned its surface to wrathful silver, louder sea-shine lightened, for the waves were full of god-head and the light that saves . . . until the sun slowly disappeared again.

Then there were silent flashes, extraordinary lightings up of the whole horizon, like vast distant fireworks or some weird atomic experiment. Not a sound of thunder, just these huge displays of quick silent yellowish-white light. Then one faint noise as of thunder, of thunder infinitely remote, less than a sound, hardly more than a vibration, passed slowly, as if the thunder had growled deep down in the water. Its quivering stopped, and the faint noise of thunder ceased all at once.

The western half of the sky had by now grown murky. The light

* Don't you think that a very remarkable sky? Cast an indifferent glance at the ill-omened chaos of the sky. Watch light climb into the rounded summits of high-altitude clouds. Clorets, Velamints, Freedent. As a sunbeam from between watery clouds comes swiftly moving over the sea, the sea is agitated, a very dark blue with white crests. Other clouds cast broad shadows upon the deep troughs of the waves. Eventually there are only a few lozenges of light in a greasy sky.

had almost gone and faded out of sight. It was two in the afternoon, and a ghostly twilight, shot through by wandering purplish
lights, had descended. In this purplish light the wind was rising.
The sea was in a restless fussy mood, dark blue in color, that grim
cold northern blue which even in summertime can convey a wintry menace. The sky too had its northern look. There was something ominous about it, and in intangible ways one was made to
feel that the worst was about to come.

Slowly the afternoon advanced with renewed grumblings of
distant thunder. The wind blew continually, and the sea was like
liquid jelly, rising and falling with a thick, smooth, dense movement. Then some time very presently now when yon clouds grew
darker, the smooth swell became more powerful, the waves higher
and stronger. The sea had turned a dull leaden grey and grown
rougher, and was now tossing foaming whitecaps to the sky. The
wind-pressures changed, rising then, with an extraordinary great
sound.

Now the temperature dropped, and the wind was straight
out of the northeast. A terrible wind out of the catalog of winds.
A wind related to the Blue Norther, the frigid Blaast, and the
Landlash. A cousin to the Bull's-eye squall that started in a small
cloud with a ruddy center, mother-in-law to the Vinds-gnyr, the
three-day Nor'easters. Earlier when the sky had clouded over, the
temperature had dropped a degree or two. This nameless wind
brought it down some thirty degrees, began to make a singular,
animal-like sound against the foaming sea.

As the weather grew worse, a cloud of doom settled over everything. The wind howled, and the shadowy waves rose higher, and
a few drops of rain began to fall. They dropped on the mighty
waves. They fell on birds, on fish, atoms sustained in the vast
expanse of air. The sound of the rain was like the swelling sound
of the sea, which hissed and coiled and twitched like a vast cloth
spread over snakes.

Steadily the rain increased. Heavy drops of fresh water plopped
loudly and wastefully into the sea. As for the sea, it looked rough.

Waves were reaching up, and their white foam, caught by the wind, was being whipped into a frenzy. Yet even these waves were low, compared with the measureless crush and crash in the distance. Waves bursting on the horizon, caught at intervals above the rolling abyss, were like glimpses of a far shore with towers and buildings. When at last they arrived at this place, the seas previously encountered were as ripples compared with these, which ran a half-mile from crest to crest and which upreared almost directly above.

The rain did not stop. The ill-omened chaos of the sky hung unbroken, darkening the twilight. The heavy clouds that loaded the atmosphere, and the thunder which murmured afar, appeared to be steering west-south-west or something south, as though for some distant island. Everything in a blur. As for hearing, the sound was instantly sucked away by the wind. But as the lightning came closer, thunder came with it. In the immediate foreground now the sky suddenly cracked as if from an ax. Right after, a white splinter came crashing down from the sky, puncturing the water. It was some distance, but the effect was perfectly visible. The water was shot through with what looked like white roots; briefly, a great celestial tree stood in the ocean.

The clap of thunder was tremendous. The flash of light was incredibly vivid, pulling the ocean into a state of exalted wonder. A group of birds fled with a clatter of wings. Suddenly a bolt struck much closer. There was an explosion of water. For two, perhaps three, seconds, a gigantic, blinding white shard of glass from a broken cosmic window danced in the sky, insubstantial yet overwhelmingly powerful. Ten thousand trumpets and twenty thousand drums could not have made as much noise as that bolt of lightning; it was positively deafening. The sea turned white, and as quickly as it had appeared, the bolt vanished—the spray of hot water had not finished landing, and already it was gone.

Between thunderclaps the punished swell returned to black and rolled on indifferently. But the sea—having upon it the additional agitation of the whole storm—was most appalling. In the difficulty of hearing anything but wind and waves, the wind tore up whirlwinds of water and gave you an idea of what the water-spout must be;* the rhythm of the waves, the volume of sound, was startling. Everything was screaming: the sea, the screeching bitter winds, fifty-foot waves thrashing around, thousands of sea-birds and fish. It was like the bottom of the ocean was going to come up.

Then it descended, pandemonium broke loose. The heaviest rain. A fresh burst of Thunder. A deafening noise on every side. Suddenly everything happened at once: rain was lashing down from the sky in knotted sheets; a wave of lightning surged across the sky, widening as it travelled westwards, flooding the water below with a rolling tide of radiance, a twist of lightning that admits the eye for an instant into the secret convolutions of a cloud. As the lightning was retreating across the sky, some great wave's deafening sound was transformed into an immense, crush-ing weight. The wave was too close, a huge, inverted pendulum, the arc of which, between the greater rolls, must have been seventy feet or more. Once the terror of this giddy sweep overpowered, starting from a windward roll, the wave over-topped—the over-curl lit by slow lightning; the translucent, rushing green backed by a milky smother of foam—and tons of water crashed down at the marred sea. Annihilation—hey!

* To those who have not chanced specially to study the subject, it may possibly seem strange that in seaquakes/waterspouts, fishes not commonly exceeding four or five feet should be trying in vain to escape approaching doom. That night the waves of the sea sped in disorderly flight; the sea birds, the dolphins and flying fish, hurtled frenziedly through the air. The sea absolutely went mad.

9

THANKS TO THE THUNDER, THE LASH OF RAIN, THE FULL force of the wind, it was going to be pretty ugly—it was easy to see that—for some time. Atwixt the first fury of the tempest and now, the clouds had moved on to their vast destination, followed by steady jets from the new, enormous structures of storm cloud behind them. To the east there was always a shadow somewhere. A different sea. Colder.

That night there was no question of moon. What little light was left in the sky came from the serried stormclouds, heavy with preponderant excess of moisture. When the lightning glared out, angry waves were seen by reflection. In the foreground, and beyond, much rain also could be seen snaking about, the nearest drops making glistening darts as they descended across the throng of invisible ones behind. The waves massed themselves, curved their backs, and crashed. The rain came down, straight and silvery, like a punishment of steel rods.

The night went on and on. Shifts in the wind changed the direction of the rain, but thunder still rolled and echoed, and it was still raining. Beating rain. Pounding rain. Sweeping gusts of rain came up like showers of steel. The sea came in with black waves as high as church towers and mountains. It was a night of listening, a night given to the continuous splash of falling water, the constant grumble of the skies, and the howl of the wind. And it was a wild night, a rain determined to go on for a long time. Extraordinary.

But all of this merde began to change its mood, trembling ever so slightly, as the morning came. The mystery of the AW SEA began to coalesce and there began to appear inklings of light, although

there was no sun, only a paleness in the haze. The rain was exhibited in the light as if it were an illuminated grille, and as if each
raindrop were separately visible, faintly vibrating in the brilliant
grey air.

Viewed in this light, the wonderful comparative smallness of
the rain, or the busy whisper of the rain—a steady, keen noise—
combined with the scenery produced a striking and sublime effect.
The sky was many clouds at many levels, some thick and opaque,
others looking like smoke. The sea, it looked rough, but the sea
is always impressive and forbidding, beautiful and dangerous.
Waves were reaching up, and their white foam, caught by the wind,
was being whipped against . . . more waves coming.

Throughout the day the scene was enveloped in an impenetrable cloud cover. The wind was blowing strong and hard, and the
waves and clouds seemed to be racing each other across a single,
vast firmament. In a while the rain slowed and then stopped,
though a huge sea was still running and a stiff wind blowing. At
evening it returned, not coming so close this time. The sky was a
distant black curtain of falling rain.

For the next few days the weather remained the same. In the
twilight of the morning, everything fish-grey. The sky a dense
blanket of grey clouds that looked like bunched-up, dirty cotton sheets. The ocean, bruise grey under the strained wet light.
In the afternoons came the rumble of thunder, like great sheets of
rippling tin. The nights were very dark and cold, gunmetal grey.

Day after day the rain fell. The thunder would go rumbling
and grumbling away, and the wind would blow the rain in gusts.
Every day the awful featureless scene did not change: the same
derelict sea and salt air, the same faint lustre of grey sky and black
water, was visible. And yet some variations occurred. There were
many skies: The sky was a heavy, suffocating blanket of grey
cloud. The sky was black and spitting rain. The sky was a featureless milky haze. The sky was a density of dark and blustery rain
clouds. The sky was nothing but falling water, a ceaseless deluge
that wrinkled the sea. There, too, were many seas: The sea roared

like a tiger. The sea whispered in your ear. The sea thundered like avalanches. The sea was dead silent. The sea hissed like sandpaper working on wood. The sea clinked like small change in a pocket. At its worst, the sea sounded like ghosts vomiting. And in between the two, in between the sky and the sea, were all the winds. And there were all the animiles, sir.

All the animals in the sea, at the distance of a league, and above it experienced wild fluctuations. Because of the erratic whisper of old storms, or the approach of a new storm, animals were tiring, and some were dead. Some animals were drowned in vast weights of unexpected water—gulls and other surface water birds.* Nature seemed indifferent to life itself. Early one morning, a bird with a broken wing was beating the air above, reeling, fluttering, circling disabled down, down to the water. Later in the day, tarble storm. Tarble wind. Little chance the bird lived and breathed as it had lived before.

---

* The storms held no terror for creatures of the deep—halo-like, these "moonbeam-bodied creatures" lived so deep, so far below the level of the ocean that no odor of fear came to them. Thoughts of elemental things—night, silence, wind, and the terrible hail—were only part of the domain of the surface.

IO

THE WIND, THE ROLLING WAVES, AND DAYS WENT BY. THE vicious rains fell in sheets and in columns. And every day and hour was shrouded in clouds. It seemed that the end of everything had come until finally, early in the fourth day of greyness and wild rain (or third, sixth, tenth?), the wind changed and blew directly at west, w.s.w., or s.w. by w., and never further from the west. When the wind changed once more, it's true there was rain, but it wasn't so very hard. It certainly wasn't a driving rain, like you see during the monsoons. There was wind—some of the gusts would have upset umbrellas—but it was different. It was beginning to look like a different ocean.

Soon the weather was changing rapidly. The sea, so immense, so breathtakingly immense, was settling into a smooth and steady motion; the wind was softening to a tuneful breeze. Within a few hours, the rain slowed to a drizzle. The sky was lightening here on the east side, a paler gray-white, and miraculously, as if the mist and wind and rain and the cold had been a test, the sky began to clear.

The clouds thinned, were perfused by a faint light of humour. The first light had been deep and vague in the mist, and then the sun flashed and a great yellow glare fell under the clouded sky, calm, mysterious, still. For a time the sun was whole beneath the cloud, then it rose into eclipse, and a dark and certain shadow came upon the waiting sea.

When the sun returned, his light found the world transformed. The wind had fallen to a soft breeze which gently stirred upon the surface of the waves. The slow-moving clouds above were interspersed now with great holes of deep blue sky. It was the dawn of a beautiful day.

With the rains over, the sunlight turned crisp and golden. Some distance off, the patterns of cloud cover already moved on to the south, and the waves seemed to flee with the clouds. The wind blew with a faint, warm breeze and the sea moved about kindly, the water peaking and troughing like groups of dancers in a circle who come together and move apart and come together again, over and over.

In just a few hours this change had taken place in the weather. The change was as quick and radical as stepping back a season. The sun was shining, the breeze was steady, and seagulls shrieked in the air above. It was as if the sun were shining through a mist, but a mist made out of the blue globules of the sky itself. The cloud cover had vanished. But for a few wisps on the horizon, a few wispy pink clouds above, the sky was clear, a vast fathomless dome of delicate pale blue.

It was a perfect morning. Warm. No fog. No storm. Balmy breezes. A creamy, moving cloud. Two clouds. And the fish! Ah, god. A fish jumping out of the water was most agreeable: A fish jumps. An idea of a fish jumps. A fish jumps, hangs in the air suspended, flesh turned to icon. Then it drops and softens, the circles widen, it becomes an ordinary fish again, an animal returning to the noise of the waves—all this was real.

Yes, a mighty change had come over the fish. All alive. All color. All sounds gathered intensity from the swelling colors of the morning, punctured now and then by the voices of the birds, the trembling sound as flying fish left the water and the hissing that their stiff set wings made as they soared away, the exhilaration of a whale breaching after a long submarine chase.

The sea, the sea, yes, the sea was alive. All sorts of whales began to swim in thickening clusters. Yes, visible that day across the water, humpback whales spouted mists as they breathed, playfully breaching in the water. Sometimes, against all probability, a sperm whale had suddenly—not by the peaceable gush of that mystic fountain in his head, but by the far more wondrous phenomenon of breaching—appeared in the distance, tossed himself salmon-like to Heaven.

That white whale seemed incapable of surge or anger. It was not so much his uncommon bulk that so much distinguished him from other sperm whales, but a peculiar snow-white wrinkled forehead, and a high, pyramidical white hump. These prominent features revealed his identity, at a long distance, to those who knew him, but disappeared into the waves after a pause in the air.

Eventually the whale broke water within two ship's lengths. A vast form shot lengthwise, but obliquely from the sea. Shrouded in a thin, drooping veil of mist, it hovered for a moment in the rainbowed air, and then fell swamping back into the deep. Crushed thirty feet upwards, the waters flashed for an instant like heaps of fountains, then brokenly sank in a shower of flakes, leaving the circling surface creamed like new milk. Hoveringly halting, and dipping on the wing, the white sea-fowls longingly lingered over the agitated pool that he left.

It was some five minutes later when the Sperm whale returned to the surface. The whale came breeching up towards the warm and pleasant sun, and all the delights of air and earth. For an instant his whole marbleized body formed a high arch, and then sank out of sight like a tower swallowed up.

At noon that day, this breaching was regular. Whales, with dromedary humps, zoomed up from the deep, topping the waves like a building, falling back with a crash. Beneath this atmospheric waving and curling, and partially beneath a thin layer of water, also, the whales were swimming: successive pods of whales, eight and ten in each, going round and round like multiplied spans of horses in a ring; and so closely shoulder to shoulder that a Titanic circus rider might easily have overarched the middle ones, and so have gone round on their backs. The innermost heart of the shoal presented that smooth, satin-like surface, called a sleek, produced by the subtle moisture thrown off by the whale in his more quiet moods.

In that enchanted calm floated the nursing mothers of the whales and those that by their enormous girth seemed shortly to become mothers. Floating on their sides, the mothers seemed quietly eyeing the gulls that flew over a school of turlehide whales, faint and high in the distance. A little farther away two sea birds (gannets?) flying low in the middle distance produced a hazy, distorted reflection as upon a convex metal surface. The glow from them was gentle and friendly. But most lovely of all was the skill with which they flew, their wingtips moving a precise and constant inch from each other. They flew toward a glowing arch of sky overhead, white as the clouds beneath the blaze of noon.

II

AS THE BIRDS FLEW, THE CROWD OF REPOSING WHALES—
beaked whales, pike-headed whales, bunched whales, under-jawed
whales, the submarine bridal chambers and nurseries—slowly
vanished. The birds went still further and further from the circumference of commotion and far off, beyond the outermost
whales. It was a flight of great beauty, gannets with creamy heads
and black-and-white wings. With the waves at heel, they flew over
the sea. There was a light breeze now, and all the watery region
round about there was flattened and wrinkled by the wind. The sea
glowed, transparent with light, ornamented with gulls. Thousands
of seabirds circled and swooped into the clear cold water.

Through this vast region, past flocks of buffleheads and pin-
tails, gulls and terns, and in between, the two shadows fled. Two
birds, large gannets, flying low, their wings skimming the tops of
the ripples. They flew round the sparkling sea shoots, over waves
monotonously mild, past herds of seals that began to dot the sea.

Out across the ocean, the view was not robbed of sharpness by
mirage. Everything was bright and sweet. Big white shining clouds
floated high up in clear space. Their shadows floated over the sea,
beyond which was faintly seen, skirting the horizon, a dark form.
A small black speck.

It was hard to see it at first, but there it was—a pixelation, a
form, a figure? Hard to say. Under iridescent cauliflower clouds,
such weather, it was clear there was no harm in it; birds flyin across
the sea seemed luminous and magnificently indifferent. Obviously
it would be something very simple—the simplest impossibility in
the world, as, for instance, the shadow of a passing cloud or aura
resembling steam in the daylight. Could it be sight of land? The

question then was whether the water was shallow again. The birds signalled affirmation when the speck showed dead ahead. The waves nodded, too, their indolent crests, and across the wide trance of the sea, east nodded to west, and the sun over all.

As the birds flew farther, the speck grew by steady degrees to a spot. It grew larger, and so swiftly. Its dimensions were deepened. It appeared to be a firm substance, the bottom flat, smooth, and shining very bright, from the reflection of the sea below. The gannets saw plainly the tops of some hills at a very great distance. The tiny point of black projected itself from these hills. It was land. Land! Land!

12

IT WAS NO FALSE ALARM. THIS WAS AN ISLAND CLAMBERING among pink rocks, with the sea on either side, and the crystal heights of air. Just as the birds know where to go when it rains, they knew the wave which cannot halt, but flows unceasingly in the direction of the nearest hill.

The clouds that had blazed so brilliantly above the sea were now coming and going in numbers over the island. The waves were big, breaking on the beach. The birds came flying over and found the island to be all rocky, only a little intermingled with tufts of grass and sweet-smelling herbs. These nameless birds came quite near to three things: a honeycomb of caves awash in a rush of foam, a rock in the shape of a great dog, a small neck of land jutting out into the sea. They flew round and round the central ridge of the island and came to rest beneath the palms, high up on the rocky spine.

Up there, the same two birds were still. There was a cool breeze from the sea, the lemon-blossom smelled wonderful, the view was glorious. One could see the waves breaking in white splinters like smashed glass upon the rocks. One could see lines and creases in the rocks—a series of large boulders that punctuated the waters. One could see a coral reef, and beyond that, the open sea was dark blue. Within the irregular arc of coral, to the north, and not far away, a group of naked rocks thrust above the sea. Between the steep rocks one could see the distant headlands of yet another example of how the earth's material was used: another island; a rock, almost detached, standing like a fort, facing this island of solitude.

On that island, nothing could be relied upon to sustain life

adequately. There were a few pandanus trees. There were a few
tree ferns. But there was nothing else. The shore drifted in a long,
slow curve, outward to a point, beyond which three steep islands
of diminishing size continued the sweep of the land toward the
depths, tentatively, like an ellipsis. Looking out over the water,
beyond these, was the glitter of the sea and more land. There were
many small islands, some of which floated up and became clouds.
A distant gently-peaked archipelago.

For miles, as far as the eye could see, were the violet, round
archipelagoes of romantic isles, islands clearly cut against the alter-
nating depressions of the watery horizon.* From island to island
large gannets and smaller terns skimmed across the waters, while
frigate birds drew sharp and sure navigation lines from the ocean
right to the heart of the islands, where they nested. Those rocky
islands—especially the small delicate islands stretching away to the
southeast—were also the resort of great numbers of seals, some
young seals seen peeringly uprising from the water like commas
and semicolons.

There was something magical about an island—the mere word
suggested fantasy. You lost touch with the world—an island was a
world of its own. A world, perhaps, from which you might never

---

* Each seems isolated, yet in reality all are linked by the bedrock from which
they spring. If the oceans were to vanish, that would be the end of the islands.
They would all be part of one continent, but their individuality would have
gone. Some of the other islands:
  - A small, bright verdant island of almost impenetrable rain forests. Lush
    plunging waterfalls, barking deer, and goat.
  - A narrow little island arid and treeless, uninhabited save by birds and turtles.
  - An island conveniently situated between two tremendous rocks. It is an
    unforgettable island with picturesque clusters of trees, and animals graz-
    ing far in the distance: antelopes, alligators, ants and attractive anthills
    anywhere about, again and again. Always as an afternoon abates an ant
    advances, also antelopes, alligators. Better beaches and air. Ahhh, as birds
    chirp; biu, biu, biu, ahhh . . . Contentment.
  - A desert island. Surrounded by seaweed. This island was at a greater dis-
    tance, had a nickname, too, a shadow name that was rarely spoken: the
    Island of the Dead.

return. And so in these beautiful islands, waiting in the sun, in the archipelago of islands, tips of sunken hills, here, in the sunny day, in this place, life formed a parenthesis of beauty unmatched across the entire ocean continent. There was no other adjective; it was not just pretty, picturesque, charming—it was simply and effortlessly beautiful. Its beauty was rare even in the blessed sunlight and beautiful sea and blue sky. If paradise consists solely of beauty, then these islands were widely hailed as paradises. The same gay place from island to island.

And yet somehow that theory departed when one looked round the whole ocean. Each island, at any given moment of time, was a chimera, a play of the mind. By the same token they were beautiful, that is true; their cliffs, where the restless ocean had eroded away the edges, dropped clear into the sea, and birds nested on the vertical stones; the shores were white and waves that washed them were crystal-smooth and blue. But the infinite number of islands which lie in these seas were not really paradises. Twenty-four hundred miles almost due south there did exist an island which merited that description. A sunny island where peace dwelt, sanity reigned, and the sun forever shone, the blessed island lay golden in all the watery region round about there. The capital island of the seas, there was not tree or a blade of green upon it, not a handful of soil, that was not the special treasure of this particular island. Something of a miracle.

13

THE ISLAND STOOD ON THE HIGH SEAS, SHAPED SOMETHING like a leaf stood on end. An island environed every way with the sea: no land to be seen except some rocks, which lay a great way off, and two small islands, less than this, which lay about three leagues to the west. Nine-tenths of the island was covered with layers of greenery. From its backside, which faced south, a vast, sheer cliffside of almost six thousand feet, rising assertively from the waters beneath it, which collected at its base in a thick, beery foam. Eastward into the sun, the island sloped steeply downward and began to appear as a massive wedge of cake that had been tipped to its side.

A coral reef enclosed more than one side of the island, lying perhaps a mile out and parallel to the shore. The coral was scribbled into the sea as though a giant had bent down to reproduce the shape of the island in a flowing chalk line but tired before he had finished. Inside was peacock water, rocks and weed showing as in an aquarium; outside was the dark blue of the sea.

The surrounding shores were beautiful, with semitropical verdure—trees tiered upon layers of grasses, and mosses, and snaky snarls of succulents, all of them colored those improbable parroty shades of green you encounter only in jungles. The bark of the trunks was green and the cheeks of the flowers were green. In fact, it was chlorophyll heaven. A green to outshine food colouring and flashing neon lights. A green to get drunk on.

Out to the east the plant life grew wilder and denser, so that the forest pushed all the way to the very edge of its earth, and the water surrounding it was covered with a busily kaleidoscopic skin of its leavings—wind-tattered hibiscus flowers and sunburned mango leaves, hard little nuts of unripe guavas and scraps of ferns. The leaves shifted in a million spangles along the shore, or bobbed in the sea. It was beautiful all around here, although there was no beach; that lay on the side of the shore yonder, behind that forest to the east where the mountain dropped down into the wash of the sea. There, the physical dimensions of the land and water met on equal level, making a bay. It lay like that on the sea, did it, with a dent in the middle—a wonderful beach—and two sharp crags at the ends.

The sun was bright on the beach and the water a lovely swimming-pool green. Tiny seagulls, like specks of spray, wheeled above the line of surf and down the beach. Below them in a thin, hot line, the sand was pearl white, smoothed and shining. Some eighth of a mile further down, the sand showed whiter beneath the very beautiful line of cliffs stretching out from the beach, and the big round boulders of the bay leapt out from the water and sloped steeply up to a ridge perhaps sixty or seventy feet above the sea-level and irregularly set with trees and undergrowth, chiefly a kind of palm that stood or leaned or reclined against the light.

Watching the panorama of sandy beach and palm trees, there seemed to be no need to comment upon the beauty of things. It was quite enough that the caressing air beat upon the long leaves of the palms in playful gusts, that kestrels glided over the bluff and out to sea, their wings motionless, their bodies seeming to drift backward when the wind was strong. With the birds, with the wind warm and the sky far above, it was easy to settle these plain things, give up, relax, and live in the perfect present, a pure sense of place. And yet a strange and brilliant light lay upon the world, and all the objects in the landscape were washed clean, and a word extending itself ever outward, a word that carries the sunlit ardor of an object deep in drenching noon, seemed to leap forward in the brilliance: beauty. Pure beauty. More beautiful than anywhere else on earth. It ran lightly on the surface of everything in view, tinting the edges of the palms in the background, and the waves and the sand. Beauty was born on this beach, that child of Shower and

Gleam, of sun and loveliness. The water shone pacifically. The sand gleamed above the shallow tide. The whole landscape—beach and headland and sea and rock—quavered like a stage backcloth.* And the sun was everywhere. The sun touched the tops of the hills in the distance, teeming jungle, and far above, polished mosaics of cliffs, familiar, safe, benign. The sun was hot and bright, and its light cast shadows and reflections. It was supremely beautiful through the clouds and as it fell through the air. When it touched the ground, it instantly made the land, and particularly animals, come to life. It was most agreeable; the animals seemed to enjoy the sunshine so much. Gold-eyed birds darting in between the leaves and back out to sea, turtles basking on logs in the golden sunlight. Viewed in this light, everything seemed like a vision of heaven or, if you prefer, an authentic natural paradise where each growing thing had its opportunity to develop in its own unique way, according to the dictates and limitations of the island's famed beauty.

It must always have been God's day on that island. Nothing was there but things of high import. Calm as summer, with singing of birds. The hum and heat. The landscape as romantic as a cardboard background on the stage, and the mountainous island but a wooden screen against a sheet painted blue and white. Up from the beach, the hills showed green and new washed. The country rose from the ocean in hill and tableland, almost uniformly clothed by primeval forest. Thousands of trees, hundreds of thousands of trees. Branches ad infinitum, leaves in perpetuity.

From time to time a flock of birds would explode shrieking from the tangled greenery, but the jungle looked so impenetrable; the trees seemed to obstruct any movement. How could one bird

---

* The whole time on the island, the heat was intense. Even the air that pushed in from the sea was hot and heavy with humidity. But the wet, heavy, bird-interpolated silence was a mystical experience. The purity of the heat seemed to cover the miles as if by magic. There was a haze over the bay. The big round boulders looked hot, as if the stored-up heat which they were exuding were shimmering visibly. They had a solemn, almost religious look. The dark yellow seaweed stains upon them looked like hieroglyphs.

ever make its way back to the nest? By the shore edge, a large dark bird nested easily. The rocks themselves were where all the birds of the sea—seahawk, seagull, curlew and plover, kestrel and capercallzie—found high cradles. In the forest, there was confusion. There the wild herbs and the wild fruits and the forest fungi were twisted in odd ways; all upland birds—ebony toucans with their bright orange beaks, red-headed blackbirds, paradise tanagers in clear primary colors, scarlet ibises, spike-billed jacamars clothed in metallic green, miniature darting hummingbirds—struggled through brush and vines. The jungle was not short on trees, natural obstacles, and diverse other plants. At the edge of the forest, they touched and twisted around each other so that it was hard to imagine how birds were able to fly into it.

Then one of the sea birds, beautifully darting, whirled around and flew with unimaginable velocity into the canopy of the woods. Another and another followed in quick succession. But how could this be? One aspect of the question was beautiful and mysterious, gold-shot with looming wonder. It was like an open door that nobody could shut. Quite another aspect was troubled with sundry misgivings.

Where the birds had begun to flutter from the air into the forest, the land and the trees were no more than a glimmering outline—like a curtain. To know what had happened and what was going on behind it and the hills close about it, to know the virtue and goodness of any of the fruits or plants, to grasp the way of things among the branches of the towering trees, through the creepers, among the thorn, there was only one answer: here and now, it was time to know this island.

14

IN THE SHADE OF THE TREES AND PALMS, NATURE STEPPED quietly forward. Very close around, the wood flourished high and dense, more palmy than palms. The land seemed to glisten and drip with steam: colossal tropical trees with rank creepers twining endlessly about their trunks and a long thicket of these oaklike trees, the boughs curiously twisted, the foliage compact, like thatch. In some places the trees touched leaves and knit together a canopy, cutting the light into leaf-shaped shadows.

It was a wondrous sight. The wood was green as mosses; the trees stood high and haughty, feeling their living sap; the industrious earth beneath was as a weaver's loom, with a gorgeous carpet on it, whereof the ground-vine tendrils formed the warp and woof, and the living flowers the figures. All the trees, with all their laden branches; all the shrubs, and ferns, and grasses; the message-carrying air; all these unceasingly were active. Through the lacings of the leaves, the great sun seemed a flying shuttle weaving the unwearied verdure.*

Now, amid the green, life-restless loom of that jungly stuff, there was more light than one would have expected. Sometimes the branches of trees would open and splinter into an open space where bright flowers grew and butterflies danced round each other and the air, hot and still, became an integral part of the scene. In

---

* Oh, busy weaver! unseen weaver!—pause!—one word!—whither flows the fabric? what palace may it deck? wherefore all these ceaseless toilings? Speak, weaver!—stay thy hand!—but one single word with thee! Nay—the shuttle flies—the figures float from forth the loom; the freshet-rushing carpet for ever slides away.

one place it gleamed fiercely. The whole space was walled with dark aromatic bushes and was a bowl of heat and light. Since they had not so far to go for light, the creepers had woven a great mat that hung at the side of the open space. A great tree, fallen across one corner, leaned against the trees that still stood, and a rapid climber flaunted red and yellow sprays right to the top. A crochet of spider-webs stretched between two trees, glinting like a tangle of jeweled necklaces.

Deeper into the jungle, as the ever-woven verdant warp and woof intermixed and hummed around, some rare flies, of amazing forms and colours, buzzed in a great peace. Even deeper, flies droned, and the other sounds began to rise: the deep forested chirping, the caw that came from the tops of trees, the chattering of lower primates, the incessant sawing of insect life. It was not unlike the overture of the opera in which the well-trained listener could draw forth the piccolos, the soft French horn, a single meaningful viola.

The air was vivid with conversation—honks and clucks and shrieks and chirrups—and every bird and monkey, spot-billed toucanet and insect called insistently. But the most singular and beautiful sound came from an almost extinct race of large singing lemurs known as the Indris. The Indris, those happy creatures, symbols of life in peace, on a higher plane. The gentle affectionate ways and strange melodious voices of these near-legendary creatures had made a great impression on the jungle. Was it their nearness that abolished despair and dread? It seemed more their sweet, eerie singing. Their strange songs. With their enchanting other-world voices, their gay, affectionate, innocent ways, they had become symbols of life as it could be on earth, a message of hope from another world; a world without violence or cruelty, in which despair was unknown.

Further in, the lemurs were near, and the scratch-scratch of other animals merged with their song. Then, yet further in, a lot of very green trees opened into misty, new places abloom with torch ginger, orchid, heliconia, saplings, and bushes, and leaves the size of frying pans, with boulders here and there obscured by armies of trees. Sometimes a score of animals would reappear—the silhouettes of large birds, whose bodies are hooked; monkeys dancing; mongeese leaping; snakes swaying; every animal and insect to be found in almost every kingdom of animated nature. And always, almost visible, was the heat.

15

THE SAME BIT OF SCENERY RECYCLED INDEFINITELY. JUNGLE flowers, wild roaring beasts. Aisles of giant fern, eucalypti. Bush and more bush. The heady fragrance of jasmine, frangipani, narcotic sizzle of ginger. This rain forest, the trees, continued far into the island—the great factory of leaves pumping oxygen into the atmosphere, the tireless photosynthesis of plants turning sunlight into energy. And the green cloud of trees gave off the resin smell of the hot day and a greenish glow.* Then there was the matter of the jungle's profligacy, as if the jungle were constantly showing off to itself—every rock, every tree, every surface that would stay still was trimmed, bedecked, baroque with greenery: there were fistulas of bushes wrapped with creeping vines and spotted with moss and lichen and trees draped with great valances of hairy, hanging roots from some other unseen plant that lived high above the canopy.

On and on the jungle went, so unceasing in its excesses that it was hard to tell where one tree ended and the next began. The sky had been all but blotted out by the treetops, the blobby swatches of blue growing tinier and more infrequent. The trees' roots had braided themselves into a slippery latticework, and the creepers and bushes were so close. So thick was the vegetation that there was no breeze, which only made the trees and bushes seem more

---

* Across the jungle, the sky, the water, the bark of the trees, everything that wasn't green became green. Bright green—green as grasshoppers. A green so bright and emerald that, next to it, vegetation during the monsoons was drab olive. There were so many shades and tones of green—serpent, aphid, pear, emerald, sea, grass, jade, spinach, bile, pine, caterpillar, cucumber, steeped tea, raw tea: how inadequate is our vocabulary for color!

unreal, more statuary, although all around was their smell, a com-
plicated and insistent perfume of loam and rot and sugar.

The scent was very sweet and strong deeper and deeper into
the thraldom of that green world where the birds had voices like
creaking wood and all the snakes were blind. Here and there was
a smell of ferns and a smell of dead flowers mixed with the fresh,
living smell vanishing slowly into the odors of the jungle. In the
turbid, miasmic state of mind which the jungle induced, the
humidity, the bugs, the stenches of animal refuse—a sort of gassy
vinyl scent—seeped up from the ground.

A great way into the woods, high jungle closed in—so thick
was the foliage that the sun became unnuanced and unreliable. The
air here was dark, too, and the wild, overgrown land was like the
sea. Things flew up from the floor and trickled down from the tree-
tops. Here a patch of rock came close to the surface, and the creepers dropped their ropes like the rigging of foundered ships.

Here also were a billion billion billion little animals. Insects
were clustering round the soft soil, and the creepers and bushes
were full of the whisper and scurry of small lives. In the undergrowth, a rat snake rubbed itself against a stone. Hopeful yellow
bullfrogs cruised the scummy pond for mates, a winged visitor
buzzing in and out now and then. It felt like there were millipedes
crawling all over. Those were the same trees; this was the same hill;
but, the weather being hazy, the bugs had multiplied hideously in
the heat, the floor heaving with unseen layers of worms and beetles
like the wet innards of a large dozing beast.

Through the Kingdom of Bugs, independent worlds of ephem-
erons were passing their time in mad carousal, some in the air,
some on the hot ground and vegetation, some in the tepid and
stringy water of a pool, a vaporous mud amid which the mag-
goty shapes of innumerable obscure creatures could be indistinctly
seen, wallowing with enjoyment. Amidst all these deadening
influences, still strange insects appeared like ideas: Happy earthworms frolicked purple in the slush. Crimson dragonflies mated
in the air. Doubledeckered. Deft. A little way further on, there

was a caterpillar letting itself down on a thread, twirling slowly like a rope artist, spiralling. The caterpillar was squirming in a luscious, unreal green, like a gumdrop, and covered with tiny bright hairs. Just a few minutes ago it had been poking in and out of the branches. Now it was feeling around in the air with its blunt head, its huge opaque eyes like the front end of a riot-gear helmet. A furry bee came and buzzed round it for a moment. After a time the bee flew away. It seemed like anything could happen. Maybe an awkward beetle or a small coterie of flies, in great, lazy orbits except when they came close to each other, would come swirling around in sight above the caterpillar. Maybe a minute would pass before any new eruption of material would take place.

At other memorable spots throughout the jungle there seemed to be no usual busy life at all, no birds, no insects, just this dark place of unnatural quiet. The silence of the forest was more oppressive than the heat, and at one place where the trees were thick, the myriad noises of the jungle seemed far distant and hushed to a mere echo of blurred sounds, rising and falling like the surf upon a remote shore. There the wild animals were silent, furtive—enormous fleecy sloths the size of Labradors hanging from branches, and spiders, their backs daubed with glittery blue specks, picking their way across spun-glass webs—and the jungle was a bath of heat.

Across the haunted and fragile land, past ancient trees cloaked in vines, the sound here was of no sound, of a place holding its breath, overpowered by the cathedral-arching trees. Their canopies had become more massive and umbrellalike in their reach, making the air increasingly dark and humid, muted in light and muffled of sound. Behind leaves and stalks and branches, tall dark trees seemed to materialize from the bushes. Then more trees. Then ground creepers. Rocks. Black silhouettes of blade-leafed jungle plants. Huge ferns. A startling shoeflower.

The gloom and dead stillness of the forest went on for ever. The silence went on and on, and the heat was thick. Through the screen of leaves, the jungle closed behind like a tomb over and over again. The birds and the hum of nature, even the salamanders were gone. Even the trunks where fresh yellow butterflies had once rested to dry their wings now were gone—the matted undergrowth banked so closely between the huge trunks that the only opening was through the upper branches of the trees, where the wind did not blow.

This stillness of life did not in the least resemble a peace. It was the stillness of an implacable force brooding over an inscrutable intention. It looked at you with a vengeful aspect, an edgy, bitten-back quiet, as if it would at once explode.

16

IT WAS IN THIS SILENCE AND STILLNESS AND INACTION THAT the thing fell from the sky, something wet and heavy that landed with a juicy, suggestive thwack, like one slab of raw meat falling smack against another from a very great height.

It was disgustingly priapic, about eighteen inches long and fat as an eggplant, and that particular sugary newborn pink one finds only in tropical sunsets or dahlias. But what really distinguished it was the fact that it was moving—something was forcing its thin, unspeckled skin to swell into small bulges before smoothing flat again, the ripples undulating up and down its length like rolling waves.

The thing turned out to be a fruit. A manama fruit. They only grow at this elevation. Out of the fruit squirmed a large writhing mass of grubs the approximate size and color of baby mice, which fell from the fruit to the ground and began wriggling off. Against the moss of the floor, they looked like rivulets of suddenly animated ground beef, worming their way toward some sort of salvation.

Further into the dense uncertainty of the jungle, the manama fruit fell with muffled thuds, each time landing with the same unnerving violence. On the rising parts, other trees—like the kanava, which had heretofore been ubiquitous—began to be replaced by the manamas, until eventually everything, everything seemed to be surrounded exclusively by them and the air seemed to smell faintly of something unclean—new excitement.

Soon the sky seemed punctuated with floating tumors, attached to nothing but suspended overhead like strange pink moons. Below them on the ground, pigs lay, bloated bags of fat,

sensuously enjoying the shadows under the trees. A little apart
from the rest, sunk in deep maternal bliss, lay the largest sow of the
lot. She was black and pink; and the great bladder of her belly was
fringed with a row of piglets that slept or burrowed or squeaked.

The scenery, not to speak of the change of climate, was too
unexpected to be true. The manama fruit falling with greater fre-
quency beside them, on and on, now east, now west. The animals
panting from the heat. Pigs and fruits and concepts moving in
three dimensions. This continued till, fifteen yards from the drove,
suddenly burst into life the noises—squeakings—and the hard
strike of hooves.

Here and there among the creepers that festooned the dead or
dying trees, the squeaking increased till it became a frenzy. It was
seen at some distance between the trees: something a hawk had
dropped in fierce, ecstatic flight: a piglet caught in a curtain of
creepers, throwing itself at the elastic traces in all the madness of
extreme terror.

Its voice was thin, needle-sharp and insistent. Its cry was
echoed presently, and something squawked in the forest, a gaudy
bird from a primitive nest of sticks. The pig continued to scream
and the creepers to jerk, and the bird called and cried. This cry
was echoed by another. Another followed, and soon a great cloud
of birds hung screaming and circling in the air, echoes set ringing by a harsh cry that seemed to come out of the abyss of ages.
A wraithlike monkey shrieked from a tree. Unseen insects peeped
and scraped from the sky. EVERYTHING about the jungle growing
louder, more persistent, more powerful, an inexorable sound—the
rustling of millions of leaves—the buzz of insects—the voices of
birds and monkeys—amphibious croaks. The screams of sea-birds
deafening, their wraak, wraak, wraak. The monkeys screeching.
Insect chirpings and whirrings. Clouds of birds wheeling and crying over the woods. But in less than a minute the piglet tore loose
from the creepers and scurried into the undergrowth, the birds
were down again, and the pattering of pig's trotters died away in
the distance. All was once more silent. There was an echo, some

falling twigs. The rustling of leaves then quietly faded. In that total stillness, a bird gave a wild laugh, a monkey chuckled a malicious question, and, as fire fades in the hot sunshine, his words flickered and went out. There came a pause, a hiatus. Then the heavy well of silence.

17

IT WAS EASY TO SEE THAT THE JUNGLE WAS NOT PARADISE, but a life-and-death terrain. The silence and the emptiness flowed through everything. Every creature, everywhere in the island, knew its rules and regulations—it was an ominous part of the universal problem of all things. Silences were inevitably appended to all activities, however ecstatic the choir of birds or insects.

From the old wood came an ancient melancholy. There was silence and the unspeaking reticence of the old trees. They seemed a very power of silence, and yet a vital presence. They were waiting: obstinately, stoically waiting. Perhaps they were only waiting for the end, the end of the forest, for them, the end of all things. But perhaps their strong and aristocratic silence, the silence of strong trees, meant something else, because these things—these trees, the vines, all the wildflowers—grew far into the distance. And farther out, acres of forbidding trees, a criss-cross pattern of trunks, kept going north, reminding that the island was not an island in the conventional sense of the term—that is, a small landmass—but was rather of leviathan proportions and seemed as if it would go on for ever . . . serpenting in slow woodland pattern far into the sky.

And yet this world of trees and giant creepers began to change farther uphill. Suddenly the air was drier, the trees less assertive, the sun casting shifting, fuzzy-edged parallelograms of light across the elaborately ferned and twigged forest floor. On the lip of a circular hollow, just where the shadows ended and the sunny part began, came an opening where the country seemed to descend to the east, and looking over the gravelly edge of the sheer cliff that dropped into the valley and led to the sea, the country appeared so fresh, so green, so flourishing, everything being in a constant

verdure or flourish in the sun. But it was too hot. The wind had
fallen off, so that the broiling afternoon sun and a shimmering
heat distorted objects at a distance: rocks, cliffs, treetops, and
a steep slope enveloped in a fulgor of sunshine that killed all
thought, oppressed the heart, withered all impulses of strength and
energy. And under that sky the sea, blue and profound, remained
still, without a stir, without a ripple, without a wrinkle.

From the top of that cliff, the island was roughly boat-shaped,
humped near this end with the jumbled descent to the shore. Birds
wheeled in great arcs overhead, over the ocean and back. Gulls,
albatrosses, barnacle geese, one of those vexing toucanlike birds
whose aggressive, phosphorescent yellow feces streaked the tree
trunks like oil paint. Down towards the sea, the birds gathered
about a small natural amphitheater which the jungle had left free
from its entangling vines and creepers, a clear piece of land, near
three acres, so surrounded with woods that it was entirely land-
locked: on one side the wall of green, on the other the hills. It was
a large central space filled with plants. The upper part of the field
was hemmed in by huddled trees: coconut, cashew, mango, bil-
imbi. Two little rivers, or rather two swamps, emptied out into this
pond, as you might call it—a small lake with orange banks, the
thick, viscous water covered with a luminous film of green scum.

Beyond the swamp that smelled of still water, through tall
grass, the sun gazed down like an angry eye, and the foliage had a
kind of poisonous brightness. A peculiar stagnant smell hung over
the open space—a smell of sodden leaves and rotting tree trunks—
and the air was buzzing with bees, grasshoppers, and wasps. A
bit further away from the water, the tree of life grew there. But
it had gone wild.* The tree was not as large or as tall as the ones

---

* Perhaps this then was the tree of death. Or despair. Like the talking tree of
the fairy tale, legends and stories nestled like birds in its branches, its wildness.
It reminded of the Tree of Knowledge, which had become fruitless, splintered,
lopped, and distorted by the fierce weather. Or like the broken, leafless twigs on
the tree of evolution. Or maybe call it the Tree of Heaven—no matter where its
seed falls, it makes a tree which struggles to reach the sky. This tree was a mystery.

inland, and, more exposed to the elements, it was a little scraggly and not so uniformly developed as its mates. The trunk was about the width of a chest. The bark was greyish green in colour, thin and smooth. Swollen parasite vines veined its branches and trunk; wild pines sprouted like coarse hair from every crotch; and it was hung with lianas. The head of the tree had the full roundness of a mango tree, but it was not a mango. It wasn't a lote either. Nor a mangrove. Nor any other tree.

From the long sloping field, bright little birds hovered like insects over the tree. Then birds of prey, winging from the sea, rising from marshlands, swooped with a flurry of white wings, hovered over the wild plants of field and hill. Other aquatic birds had congregated downhill at the pond yonder—another pond just where you see the rise in the ground. These birds bent their beaks to the pond and began to drink greedily for only a moment, but in that brief instant they noticed things they had never consciously noticed before: The water was colder than anywhere else on the island. The water seemed to have icy light.

A bird, perched on an ash-coloured twig, sipped a beak full of cold water. Another bird arrived to drink of the water. Other birds arrived: the gannets and the migratories and all the birds of the rockbysuckerassousyoceanal sea, all sighing and drinking water. The pond was almost calm, like an oasis in a desert starved for color, for life. The new sense of coolness came into the field quite suddenly. The water had eaten the sun's rays but was nowhere near as hot as swamp water and cypress stumps . . . It was a delight.

Amid swarming gnats and flies, the animals drank the water with enthusiasm and flew up into the air, laughing, the air so drenched with moisture that the birds seemed to swim about in it. After making nearly a semicircle around the pond, they diverged from the water-course and flew around and settled again some-where to the left of where the old, velvety surface of the pond became a streambed full of juicy rocks. Some of these stones were a mossy and vegetable green, and some were as white as bits of tooth, and some of them were hazel, and some of them looked like rock candy. Between the rocks, they drank and drank from the water, which was cool and tasted faintly salty, oceanic, as if it had been mixed with fistfuls of ground-up seashells.

This stream bank, this junction, this spring up in the hills was profound. Small orange flowers trimmed its edge. The grass was wet and thick. Farther downstream the little bright brook that came from the weedy, bottom pond came over the grass and down toward the trees, setting cold waters free to join the edge of the brush and other ornaments of the arboreal world with which that region is thoroughly well supplied.

The edge of the forest was tight as twenty chain-link fences stacked together. This was the divider, the barrier. A natural barrier, a prison. But these trees were without a doubt the gates back into the forest, the arboreal city with more bustle in it than anything known on Earth. Even with the going downhill, the course of the stream winded through it easily. The rocks themselves were absolutely level and smooth, with hardly a stone larger than a bean—nothing to distract attention from the water that shot over them and washed past, swerved at the bottom of the hill and disappeared into the trees.

18

THE THIN THREAD OF A STREAM RAN THROUGH BRUSH AND vines of the dense forest. Past a deepblue beetle balanced on an unbending blade of grass. Past giant spider webs that spread like whispered gossip from tree to tree. The air was warm, thick, heavy, sluggish. There was no breeze other than what was stirred up by a hundred thousand wings of flying insects, but there was still bright green herbage here where the watercourse purled. There was a brightness, a beauty, a fragrance along the stream that seemed to enhance farther down for a distance of some two hundred yards.

Farther downstream was like traveling back to the earliest beginnings of the world, when vegetation rioted on the earth and the big trees were kings. The great trees which embowered the water seemed to have thickened, trees whose roots grabbed at you like snakes. It was perhaps fortunate that the stream disappeared in a split at the base of immense rocks for a moment. Then, past the rocks and roots and damp earth, the captured water returned to the over-shadowed distances. Downstream from this, the stream bed broadened soon into a shallow trough where the water tumbled from pool to pool among the bushy scrub. Three untidy banana trees grew in the ground, from which right-angled ribs of earth had risen and enclosed space. A little way further on, there were more banana trees, beyond which a river glimmered through the foliage.

Far below, the thin thread of the meandering stream went falling from ledge to ledge, and the ferns that drooped to the water were bathed in spleandor. After a broken cataract of about twenty feet, the stream was received in a general confluence, and the river was proportionately voluminous and deep. Away at the foot of the rock, the river was coming with the breeze and lots of driftwood going by. The river had stolen from the higher tracts and brought in particles to the vale—all this horizontal land—and now, exhausted, aged, and attenuated, lay serpentining along through the midst of its former spoils.

The descent down the mountain was timbered or rocky: tangled jungle undergrowth, jagged cliffs. The broadening waters flowed through a mob of breathing vegetation. It swept past enormous boulders and the coconut trees that bent into it and watched with coconut eyes. It was warm, the water. Graygreen. Like rippled silk. With fish in it. With the sky and trees in it. On silvery sandbanks alligators sunned themselves side by side. Under the mangosteen tree, the quiet deep-swimming fish and the gossamer wings of the dragonflies danced past.

Down river was wider, and the slender arches more open. Looking along the edges of the river, over the same slippery crosshatch of roots, and the endless march of green, the plants had changed: gone were the rapacious fly-eating orchids, the saucy, vulgar bromeliads, the squat cycads, and in their place were frilly wedges of sober-colored mushrooms and whorls of tightly closed ferns.

The rushing river led into more open forest. With openness came the sun and a little spot which seemed less thickly overgrown than any ground yet encountered. About a quarter of a mile downstream from this, the trees receded a little, a little more sky appeared, and instead of bald trunks supporting a dark roof there were light grey trunks and crowns of feathery palm. Beyond these, a glimpse of the spread sea, which glittered lazily, postcard-perfect, through the trees.

19

THOUGH YOU COULDN'T SEE IT FROM MANY DESERTED coves round the west side of the island, the swollen river forced its channel to the sea. It fell in cascades among a litter of boulders and broken rocks, a waterfall with the flattened ocean at its foot. The water fell in spouts and dashed from the high cliffs overhead. The cliffs were marvellous and the waterfall spoke of a power mighty as Omnipotence, and there appeared a faint line of luminosity, a rainbow, in its cooling vapours. In one place it gleamed fiercely out of the water and wavered in the air.

About a mile from the romantic waterfall, the coast ran on southwest in a series of low headlands and hidden coves, two or three different coves where light gusts were toying with the leaves and rocks glistened with inner light. On the firm sand of the smallest of the three coves, the waves broke soundlessly—wind blowing through—graceful curve of coconut trees—arc of golden sand—crystalline water—majestic rollers. The ground rose steeply into a little cliff, a crumbled and creviced reddish wall; as if it was some fortification.

The cove curved in a very flat concave arc not fifty yards across at its cliffed mouth. It was like a giant bowl cracked in half, the other half washed out to sea. On this side, the wall of the cove curved around and protected the beach from both the surf and the wind. And along this wall was a reef ledge that started at the edge of the beach and continued out past the cove, where the waters became rough. On the other side of the cove, the wall was more jagged, eaten away by the water. It was pitted with crevices, so when the waves crashed against the wall, the water spewed out of these holes like white gulleys. Past the entrance to the cove was yellow and wrinkled—some of the tallest cliffs on the island, a hundred feet or more high. Behind was the jungle, sodden and creeping and thick with secrets. Like something in a fairy tale.

All afternoon an eddying cloud of sea-fowl circled, and hovered, and swooped around the cove, and the waves kept tumbling against the earth with the methodic regularity of a clock ticking. Time passed, flowed with the gentlest undulation. The scene insensibly tranquilized the spirits. In the early evening, the light was still very bright but, in the mysterious way of southern light, was gathering itself together and would soon be gone.

As the sun got lower and lower, colour appeared among the trees, by bronze, by gold, in oceangreen of shadow. Birds began singing and calling, unseen, hidden in the branches and vines of the forest: raucous croaks and whistles, and four clear sounds in a row, like a bell. Towards the beach, birds were shying and crying all around. Birds swooped and circled high up in the air. Some fell like a net descending, landing with a snap roll just before touchdown. When they touched the ground, it was beautiful; the rocks were red and the sand of the cove was yellow and the water clean and now amber clear over the sand. It was all one.

By now the westering sun was just above the horizon in a valium sunset, smoky and golden. It was a placid explosion of orange and red, a great chromatic symphony, a colour canvas of supernatural proportions. In a matter of minutes, the sun was beginning to pull the curtains on the day. It was a relaxing moment. The breeze came in from the sea. The sun, touching the water, was like a disc of iron cooled to a dull red glow, ready to start rolling round the circular steel plate of the sea, which, under the darkening sky, looked more solid than the south-west part of the island.

Then the sun went fairly down, and with the last light shimmering on the sea, the hard stone of the day was cracked and darts of bright light poured through its splinters. Red and gold shot through the waves, in rapid running arrows. Meanwhile the shadows lengthened on the beach. The rocks lost their hardness. The sea, although it looked calm because it was so exceedingly glossy and smooth at the horizon, where the sun was setting, was, closer to shore, coming in in large sleek humpbacked waves which showed no trace of foam until they met the rocks in a creamy swirl.

Soon the sun was gone,* but he had left his footprints in the sky: the vault of the world was magnificently tinted. There were pinkish bars of high cloud in the still strong light. And the sea held light, as if light was warmth and did not fade as soon as the source was removed.

It was not long before the western horizon was the palest yellow, then a luminous pale-green, then a limpid stained-glass blue. The shades of evening were beginning to fall pretty freely, and the stars were eager to participate; hardly had the blanket of colour been pulled a little than they started to shine through the deep blue.

The sky darkened. The sea paled to a nacreous grey. Now there was only the liquid shadow of cloud as it waned into dusk. There were more stars now, and the water was a dark blue, so dark that it was almost purple, the sky beyond still not quite drained of afterglow. A big detached cloud floated dark and still, casting a slaty shadow on the water beneath. And then, almost as abruptly as if a curtain had dropped, night was on.

---

* It darkles, (tinct, tint) all this our funnaminal world. Yon verge is visited by the tide. Alvemmarea circumveiloped by obscuritads! Yonder, by ever-brimming goblet's rim, the warm waves blush like wine. The gold brow plumbs the blue. The diver sun—slow dived from noon—goes down. It's like the setting of a comedy. Act one, sunset; act two, dusk; act three, moonlight.

20

OVER THE NEXT COUPLE OF HOURS, THERE WERE MORE stars, the water churning beneath shifting winds. The sea whispered and hummed like a great shell held to the ear, and the dark air around was alive with its noise.

The clouds were always there, huge, sharply described. And clouds were blowing in from the west. Soon the darkness was full of clouds and stars dancing secretly in a round, twining and coming steadily together. How beautiful to watch the night sky build and thicken, full of solitude, thought, and anticipation.

Within an hour, on the east side of the island—where the bay was located, the white curve of sand from so early that day—the moon rose full and wide as a corner of the sky, her orb seeming to look up, hanging upon the horizon with a great red halo around it. No one had ever seen a moon so large or so strangely coloured: it was almost as if this were some other lunar body, seemingly reclining on the viewless air, a form of most exact and superior symmetry. As it rose, the moon became as bright as polished silver, and each star sparkled with scintillations of inexpressible whiteness. Pleasing images lit the lapping waves and the swells that were rolling from the horizon; millions of mixed shades and shadows, drowned dreams, somnambulisms, reveries dreaming, dreaming, tossing like slumberers in their beds; the ever-rolling waves but made so by their restlessness.

For a time, it was a nice moonlit night, and even this one small cove on the south shore of the island was affected: the light fell full a little way in the water, in contrast with the rocks. But by the time the white orb of the moon was high in the heavens, the light disappeared. The wind had changed direction, bringing with it a terrible noise, and within a few hours, the heavens were clothed in driving clouds, piled in vast masses one above the other. The stars were gone.

The scene without grew darker; mud-coloured clouds bellied downward from the sky like vast hammocks slung across it, and the texture of the air was especially rough. Birds raced in the furrows of the wind and turned and sliced through them as if they were one body cut into a thousand shreds. Birds came reeling past the water and dived straight into the jungle while other things darted up trees.

Then there was more wind in the sky than there had been, the sand whirling up from the shore, the waves breaking on a pair of needle-shaped rocks. The waves sounded hoarse on the stones beneath . . . in the rough sands of the sea . . . a cabletow's length from the shore . . . where tide ebbs . . . and flows . . . out to sea and around the mouth of the cove, and further beyond an immense phalanx of gray rocks.

The swell became more powerful, the waves higher and stronger, roaring into the cauldron of the cove, the bingbang cove with its seas booming inside caves and slapping out. At the one end of the beach, the water churned itself into a circling froth in its desperate haste to escape through the narrow outlet under the big elbows of Rock, and as it met head-on the whipping power of the sea wind, and the wind was blowing so hard, the cauldron became an equally furious sucking whirlpool.

Across the cove there was the same current, the same water plollocking all around, crashing out foams, the boom and pound on the sand, the sand dipping quick on the beach.* The waves of the ocean were breathing, sucking down, then boiling back. And

---

* One must remember that this beach cove was a terrible place, full of wet shadows that chilled and invisible specks that flew into eyes and made it hard to see the dangers. As the wind roared with laughter, that then was really the time to feel frightened, to feel the wind blow and roar, to hear waves crashing up on these crazy rocks. The waves slapped the rocks and wailed and sucked in and out of the crannies with a noise which was a burden to the spirit.

the waves going, "Raw roo roar"—"Crowsh"—the way waves
sound especially at night—the sea not speaking in sentences so
much as in short lines: "Which one? . . . the one ploshed? . . . the
same, ah Boom." The waves all up and down the sand in different
tones of voice "Ka bloom, kerplosh, ah ropey otter barnacled be
crowsh, are rope the angels in all the sea?" and such. The sea again,
louder, by caves in the crashing dark. The sea saying—*(with a voice
of waves)* "Aum! Hek! Wal! Ak! Lub! Mor! Ma!" The waves with
their blank mouths saying, "Yes that's so," and,
   Shoo—Shaw—Shirsh—
   Go on die salt light You billion yeared
   rock knocker—
   Gavroom
   Seabird
   Gabroobird awike in wave risurging into chrest
   Ker plotsch—
   Shore—shoe—
   god—brash—
   God rush—Shore—
   Shaw—Shoo—
   —Rest not
   —Plottit, bisp tesh, cashes,
   re tav, plo, aravow,
   shirsh—pish
   rip plosh—
   Ah cave, Ah crosh!
   —Creep
   Crash
   —Ah back—Ah forth—
   Ah shish—Boom, away,
   doom, a day—boom the
   earth—Arce—Shaw,
   Sho, Shoosh,
   flut, frup—
   —coof—patra—

coof, loof, roof—
ravad, tapavada pow—
Which one? the one? Which
one? The one ploshed—
The ploshed one? the same,
ah boom—
Glum sea, silent weed,
the chicken of the sea
go yak! they sleep—
Aroar, aroar, arah, aroo—
geroom—
gedowsh—gaka—gaya—
Gavril—
Gavro—
Shhish—listen: a fourworded wavespeech: seesoo, hrss, rsseeiss,
ooos. They were the big four, the four maaster waves. Vehement
breath of waters amid rocks. In cups of rocks it slops: flop, slop,
slap: bounded in barrels. The sea dont say muc'h actually . . .
Gosh, she,
huzzy, tow—Terplash, & what difference
make!
Go brash, Topahta
offat—Xcept when tumble
boom! O Boom de boom dey
the sea is the sea—hie bash
rock—ak—bedoom
Shurning—Shurning—plop
be dosh—
—Burning—Burning—
Churning, Churning,
Aye ee mo powsh—
Arree—Gerudge nada
Ssst—
Sea—Sssssss—see
Nada—Ah Mar—Gott

Thalatta—Merde—Marde
de mer—Mu mer—Mak a vash—Mar or murmury mermers,
to the mind's ear, unchartedrock, evasive weed
    Mai! mai! mai! ma! says the wind blowing sand—
Clock—Clack—Milk—
Go—Come Cark—
Care—Kee ter da vo
Kataketa pow! kek kek kek! Kwakiutl! Kik!
Kara VOOOM
the wave of roary and the wave of hooshed and the wave of
hawhawhawrd and the wave of sim—sin—Horny?
    Corny?
No, no, no, no, no, no—
Oh ya, ya, ya, yo, yair—Shhh—
here we go, ka va ra ta
plowsh, shhh, and more, again, ke vlook
ke bloom & here comes
big Mister Trosh
—more waves coming,
every syllable windy
Boom—call it
the Civil War of Rocks
—Rocks 'come air, rocks 'come walters of, hoompsydoompsy
walters of. High! Sink! High! Sink! Highohigh! Sinkasink! Waves
& rock rocks—
Kara tavira, mnash grand bash
—poosh l'abas—croosh
L'a haut—Plash au pied—
Peeeee—quite
appro priate ly—
Pss! pss! pss!
Ps! the boom,
Arra! Aroo!
Ah si—Ah so—
Seet! Seeeeeeeeeee

eeeeeee—kara—
curlurck—Kayash—Kee—
Pounders out yar—
shoot—shiver—mix—
Tatha—gata—mana—
ha roll—tara—ta ta—
Ah Ratatatatatat—
the machinegun sea, rhythmic
pouring in with smooth eglantinee
in yr pedigreed milkpup
tenor—
Tinder marsh aright arrooo—
—mnavash la vache
arrac'h—arrache—
Kamac'h—monarc'h—
Tamana—gavow—
Ger der va—
Va—Voovla—Via—
Ami go—da—che pop
sea
poo
Farewell, water meeting water—
O go back to otter—
Term—Term—Klerm
Kerm—Kurn—Cow—Kow—
Cash—Cac'h—Cluck—
Clock—the noise of the waves—all this was real. The sea roar
bashing and barking like a dog in the fog down there. Sea sea-
birding here below . . . These were the strong, troubled, murderous
thinkings of the masculine sea. The snotgreen sea. The scrotum-
tightening sea. A boiling fury of opposing waters and frenzied
creaming foam.

21

A LONG TIME PASSED, HOURS WATCHING THE WAVES COM-
ing flying through and killing themselves in fits of rage in the deep
enclosed rocky area. The sight of the rushing foaming water spilling back from folds and crevices. The weight of the surf falling on
the hard, wet sand. Boom, clap, the waves still talking. But now
the sea, having upon it the additional agitation of the whole night,
was infinitely more terrific. Every appearance it then presented
bore the expression of being swelled, and the height to which the
breakers rose, and, looking over one another, bore one another
down, and rolled in, in interminable hosts, was most appalling.

The wind grew stronger, whisked under stones, carried up the
hills. And not only that: the wind kicked up the crashing high
waves. Waves bursting against the headlands. Exploding water.
Huge black rocks rising like old ogresome castles dripping wet
slime, a billion years of woe right there, the moogrus big clunk of
it tangled in the ferns, and for a time the land looked more flight-
ful than the sea. But in a very little while, the tempest came on,
and the waves seemed mountainous.

Down the coast the tremendous sea was all on a sudden covered over with foam and froth; the shore was covered with the
breach of the water, a heavy, booming noise of a great body of
water falling solidly all the time. In the agitation of the blinding wind, the flying stones and sand and the awful noise in that
nether world was begun. The high watery walls came rolling in,
and, at their highest, tumbled into surf. As the receding wave
swept back with a hoarse roar, it seemed to scoop out deep caves in
the coast, as if its purpose were to undermine the earth.

The sea shook the earth. The angry tide raced in and out. The wind brought a noise between shrieking and singing, roaring and clattering, like the sound of the sea. Everything was drowned within it, drowned and lost. The wind blew keen frae west to east. It blew harder and harder, bearing down on the world.

Suddenly something fell from the Rock above, a dead limb that had blown from a wild tree. It was not a very large branch, now swinging through space at the end of the beach, but it was just the beginning; more branches would fall upon the little accumulation of rocks and sand and floundering fishes. Then there was a single, nuclear flash of lightning that was followed some milliseconds later by a clap of thunder that could have cracked the world in half, and then, because these things come in threes, there was rain. Heaven opened and the water hammered down. It clattered onto the rocks and pitted the sea. The thunder made some sounds like a grand piano falling downstairs. The flashes of lightning joined into long illumination which made the rocks a blazing ochre yellow. The broad expanse of vivid lightnings quivered upon the waters and, disclosing the horrible gaspings of the waves, served to render the succeeding darkness far more terrible.

And a terrible storm it was. The thunder, which burst in tremendous crashes above, and the loud roar of the waves below conspired to heighten the tremendous sublimity of the scene. It was a sight full of quick wonder and awe! The vast swells of the omnipotent sea; the surging, hollow roar they made; the knife-like edge of the sharper waves—all this was thrilling and terrible, like poetry within language.*

The noise of the storm was constant, as was the rain that fell,

---

* Enthron'd amid the wild rocks,
        Involved in clouds, and brooding woe,
The demon Superstition shocks,
        And waves her sceptre o'er below.

Around her throne, the mingling glooms,
        Wild—hideous forms are seen to glide,
She bids them shade earth's brightest blooms,
        And spread the Desolation wide.

the mud that forever seeped up from the ground and dashed from
the high cliffs overhead. Chunks of bark and debris were indeed
moving rapidly down toward the sea. And every second or two
there'd come a glare that lit up the waves for a half a mile around,
and you'd see the island through the rain, and the trees thrashing around in the wind, then a H-WHACK!—bum! bum! bumble-
umble-um-bum-bum-bum-bum—and the thunder would go
rumbling and grumbling away, and quit—and then RIP—another
flash and another sockdolager, startled gulls flapping airward in a
frightened flight.

The rain grew stronger and the sea rougher. As the wind
howled on, and the sea leaped, the lightning steadfastly shot
her red hell further and further into the blackness of the sea
and the night. Sometime after midnight, a terrific flash split the
air, luridly lit up a sudden flurry of movement—the falling tree
limbs, rogue waves. The thunder seemed to crash against one cliff,
then against the other, and to go shrieking off into the jungle in
search of higher ground. A sinister wind accompanied the terrible thunder. It seemed like the whole Ocean was blowing with
all its might right into the jungle, causing all trees to shudder
as the big groaning howl came newsing and noising. The thin
trunks of palm trees were bending but not breaking. The pointed
foliage flapped like the feathers of giant birds, like battered wind-
mills that churned the sky. (Imagination played a major role in
the jungle, especially during a storm.) A little inland, when it hit
the great wall of vegetation, the wind raced faster. The great trees
bent in unison as though pressed earthward by a mighty hand.
Farther and farther toward the ground they inclined, creaking,
groaning, crying for mercy, the contemptuous wind not caring for
these abject things. (Let them live.) Howling, shrieking, laughing, the wild blast blew the multitudinous leaves up and down
and then, suddenly, the jungle giants whipped back, lashing their
mighty tops in angry and deafening protest. A vivid and blinding
light flashed from the whirling, inky clouds above. The deep can-
nonade of roaring thunder belched forth its fearsome challenge.

The deluge glistened, and the water just poured out of it, and the wind came back, raised to a roar of noise, screaming and waving in all directions in such a confused mass that even the lower leaves and branches of the trees were whipping the moving air—all hell broke loose upon the jungle.

Now a great wind blew the rain sideways, cascading the water from the forest trees. The lightning, darting and flashing through the blackness, showed that blasted rogue wind topping down trees a mile away with an advancing roar. Trees were torn up by the roots, blown away with all those crazy scattering leaves. Water bounded from the mountain-top, tore leaves and branches from the trees, poured like a cold shower over the soulless stirring of the ooze and slime, on every old broken-down tree. You could see the undergrowth was shaken. Such stress of wind and water. It seemed as if the jungle, having tired of its playthings, were ejecting them unceremoniously from its territory, a rending and upheaval of all nature.

22

THIS HELD ABOUT THREE HOURS AND THEN BEGAN TO
abate. The wind shifted. The clap of empty thunder settled to a
softer continuous rumble, which was almost drowned by the
sound of the rain.

The wind might have by this time lulled a little, but the wet-
ness spread with perverse determination. Rainwater poured off
leaves all around. Branches dripping onto the long grass. The leaves
in the heights of the great nipa palms spread like immense green
cupped hands, swelling. The trees—so incessantly thirsty as stands
of throats, greedily swallowing every drop they could—sweated
water, which disappeared into the pelts of moss that clumped
around their bases. The ground grew squelchy and spongy, bare
soil crawling with pale pink scorpions and a seething mass of dun-
coloured earthworms. Oozing lumps of fleshy fungi lay scattered
about like the rotten liver and lungs of some colossal animal.

What an imperfect place this island was: here everything
sagged and burped water. The trees were swollen with it; the
ground was fecund with it. Streams of water sluiced between the
trees, past the roots of gum trees and broad fields, sudden mud-
slides tumbling down to jagged cliffs and finally coming upon
flooded stretches where the brown current ran swiftly out of the
heart of darkness, bearing down towards the sea with a large
admixture of interlacing branches, leaves overlapping leaves, rotting vegetables, animal droppings, and patches of slimy grass. And
all the time the rain fell.

In two hours more it was dark still, but there was light enough
to see by. The wind had freshened, and as the sky changed slightly,
the rain let up and leveled out. The flood had calmed down at

last into the circular stillness of water. Through a vastness of wet air and the tops of high trees, there was no noise save the drip and trickle of water that ran out of clefts and spilled down, leaf by leaf, to the brown earth of the island. On the shadowy land, things began to take life; plants with great leaves became distinct. The maze of the darkness sorted into near and far, and although the breeze had dropped away, trees leaned over, cracked against the earth.

Downhill toward the bay, the appearance of the island was altogether changed. Low vegetation, broken shadows of tall bamboos and tree ferns, and the soft green velvet of the moss. Out of the forest and into the open there were views of the bay and the two headlands, the restless ocean stretching out to infinity under the clouded sky.

Across the bay was like a scene viewed in a diorama. Gulls flew up from tidal pools. Sand fleas swarmed over drowned surf birds and a dead seal. There, down there by the sea, the long waste of foreshore lay moaning under the dawn, and the shore was littered with driftwood and jellyfishes—the monstrous red stinging kind that looked like wounds along the shoreline. Seaweed was strewn everywhere—rockweed with air bladders like textured orange grapes, lonely scraps of sea lettuce, tangled nests of rusty kelp caught in the waves, gloomy waves, breaking with the rhythm of fate, so monotonously that it seemed eternal.

Up and down the beach, the sea was teething. This endless breaking of slow, sullen waves of fate stretched far to the north, beyond the inner bay, as if the water was breeding corruption. The rain buzzed pensively against the sand and sea, adding drop after drop . . . a sleepy tune that seemed as if it would go on for ever . . . Rain, for ever raining.

And this continued for many hours. Or at least that's what it seemed like at the time: a mockery. It was absurd. It continued raining, though with no wind at all. The sky lower than it should be, the horizon unfixed.

Then the world began to change. Miraculously out of the

heavens, in four great waves, Nature spoke. First, the pulse of colour as the eastern sky was beginning to glow. Second, like the weirdest cloud of insects, those clouds of spiritual wonderment and pale dread were changing, wafting through, sailing over dense heads of trees, past the shore of a sombre and hopeless ocean, sometimes breaking into separated clouds. Third, in sweeping away with the dawn wind, the rain slowed to a drizzle and then stopped; the seaward sky was still grey and uninspiring, but there was a nice line of light where it met the water. Then, finally, after cold minutes or hours, by the increasing light, the darkness melted away from the sky. Over the gloomy sea the sky grew red. Quickly the fire spread among the clouds and scattered them. Crimson burned to orange, orange to dull gold, and in a golden glitter, a line of white heat, the limb of the sun rose eastward beyond the projection of the bay, splashing its radiance across the sky and turning the dark sea into a weltering tumult of dazzling light. Soon the sun leapt up over the rim of the world—nature smiled once more.

23

THE COAST REACHED OUT AND MELTED INTO THE MORNING. Out there island clouds emplaned upon a salmoncolored othersea. Seafowl in silhouette. Downshore the surf boomed. Mustard sunlight reflected like a digital display over splashing waves, and the waves came on and on, crests streaked tangerine, breaking, receding with the knock of rolling cobbles.

The sun rose higher, dribbling fierily over the waves. Bars of yellow and green fell on the shore, making the sea-holly and its mailed leaves gleam blue as steel. Down the beach, streaks of morning light were beginning to penetrate the palm trees, the dripping leaves and branches, and the moist petals of gorgeous flowers glistened in the splendor of the returning day. There was water everywhere, lapping on smooth stone, reflected in a dapple of light.

Up from the beach there was a brightness, a beauty making the forest glisten. And in the new sun, the peaks and the hills to the south and west. The view was superb. And then, in the blowing clouds, there appeared a strange optical effect: a band of faint iridescence colouring in faint colours a portion of the hill. The hovering colour like the outspread wings of a waterbird, a rainbow forming itself.

Steadily the colour gathered, mysteriously, from nowhere, it took presence upon itself. The arc bended and strengthened itself till it arched indomitable, making great architecture of light and colour and the space of heaven, its pedestals luminous, its arch the top of heaven. In one place it gleamed fiercely and curved down into the leaf-bright forest to shine and fade and leave lingeringly some faint essence of its rosy iris in the air.

Weather had put on another of its transformation scenes, glorified by a rainbow, as if Heaven itself had put its seal upon the day. All storms were past, the silence of Eden regained. A faint, vast rainbow joined land and sea, sea and land. The eternal struggle was gone. Instead there lay a beautiful promise in the sky.

Aside from the pure pleasure of the rainbow, there was even more enchantment—some act of God beneath the light of an eternal dawn, the music that never gains, never wanes, but ripples for ever like the tideless seas of fairyland. The birds sang their blank melody, the white-coated animals returned to the eye in rays almost dazzling.* A few stagey cloud puffs were travelling from right to left. And as the sun rose higher and the sky grew bright, clouds soaked up the light. The sunbeam gently kiss'd them with a flood of splendour, diffused gaiety and gladness, the bold concave forms perfectly distinct and as bright as the insufferable splendors of God's throne. Heaven was a partly cloudy place.

* The bright fantastic birds were flying overhead, gulls that were returning to the big opening in the clouds. The flock had elements of grace. Yet, one of the Flock flew off, sweeping majestically into the distance, now out to sea, out of sight, cloud-bound. All the other gulls fluttered northward, but the one bird, taking its way, flew with unimaginable velocity to the south. The two gulls that appeared at his wings were pure as the air, and the glow from them was gentle and friendly.

III. THE VOID

I

SO THIS IS HEAVEN, HE THOUGHT, AND HE HAD TO SMILE at himself. It was hardly respectful to analyze heaven in the very moment that one flies up to enter it.

As he came from Earth now, above the clouds and in close formation with the two brilliant gulls, he saw that his own body was growing as bright as theirs. True, the same young Seagull was there that had always lived behind his golden eyes, but the outer form had changed. He was flying over a sea, sailing through clouds and out again into the comparative clearness. All earth below for leagues and leagues.

It was strange to look down and see the earth, not flat or gently curved, but as a segment of a round ball, the sea light blue, the land yellowish-green, islands scattered over the sea. A very few seagulls were working the updrafts out of the clouds below him. Away off to the north, at the horizon itself, flew a few others.

To see these sights, and not only that, but to observe the ebbing and the flowing of the clouds, the beauty of light on the water, the quiver of wavelets like crumpled tinfoil, the distant shores patched with dark woods, silvery mirages, and streaks of light; it was all peace, elements and void, golden air and blue distances. These sublime and magnificent scenes touched him with new sights, new thoughts, new questions. Why so few gulls? Heaven should be flocked with gulls! And why was the wind singing across the empty miles of air? The wind's high song was a different song from the singing of the wind in the cliffs.

As he flew a loop, living in this ideal world became more delectable to our hero. The wind was a whisper in his face. Those clouds of spiritual wonderment were still all of a brilliant white.

He narrowed his eyes in concentration, held his breath. He held in thought an image of the great gull flocks of another time, and he knew with practiced ease that he was not bone and feather but a perfect idea of freedom and flight, limited by nothing at all. He swallowed, swooped with a flurry of white wings, and then flew higher, away from the other birds.

The bird was fearless, went higher in the air and circled, his wings motionless, a smooth, beautiful, aerodynamic airship. He took in new ideas like a streamlined feathered computer. He discovered the loop, the slow roll, the point roll, the inverted spin, the gull bunt, the pinwheel. Then he flew around a cloud and then another cloud.* As he flew out toward the far veil of high cloud, his escorts called, "Happy landings," and vanished into thin air.

By the time he arrived at the clouds, how far off had the animal been from the others, and how high above the water and land—the eternal possibilities—had he risen? Very high, and very far away. The light air about him as he flew at altitudes—at high, cold altitudes like the topmost geographical feature on the planet— felt crisp and cold. He didn't appear to notice, but the winds kept blowing through.

Further up, so powerful was the wind that it was difficult to breathe while facing it. The changing winds of various altitudes took the figure where they would, and it was clear he could go no further that way. Only the lightest atoms of matter, such as hydrogen gas, could move forward into the atmosphere, trading speed for distance through the wind, subject to a different sort of gravity, new rules. He had travelled a long way, had set a world record for seagulls, but the atmosphere was changing, and the wind was

---

* Jesus, look at that cloud! Look at that cloud face. The lips are opening—*God in the sky in the form of huge gold sunburning cloud seemed to point a finger and say, "Behold, the sun! Behold, the angels! Sorta." A dull, prolonged roar vibrated in the air. The sky was spread over with God's light. Whatever the light touched became dowered with a fanatical existence*—now the form is slipping away—it's gone.

rough. The bird tired, took fright and fled, now dropping and dipping into the clouds.

In the other direction, moving so smoothly, atomic and sub-
atomic particles drove before the wind on their way to their nests
in the stars. Directly overhead, far, far above the clouds, helium
atoms were going faster than heavier forms, fellow-electrons were
revolving at a steady pace, and behold, those electrons moving
around hydrogen atoms in the vast expanse of the air were carried away on this smaller mass at great speed: a party of electrons
zipped by.

These particles did exist. It was true that they were small and
round, around each atom an electron acting as a satellite, a particle
of negative electricity—a real existing thing—riding on the back
of a particle of gas. Urged forward, caught in the mad whirl of particles or atoms, it seemed those moving around hydrogen atoms
were having the time of their lives . . . at the smallest scales and
atomic increments.

Of course there were myriads of similar atoms all around,
being urged forward, with electrons capable of revolving at all the
different rates. Upward into the shoreless void, atoms added to the
pure, soft motion of the air: atoms united to one another; positive and negative particles in the air quickly recombined; fellow-
electrons were carried away on the incalculable trillions of billions
of millions of imperceptible molecules. Electrons were escaping,
surging to and fro from atom to atom. The attraction between
atoms, and again between molecules, was like something—like
sudden splashes in the æther ocean, larger congregations of electrons forming other little worlds of their own.

These atoms were, of course, dancing high in the sky, hurled
up from the earth, pure joy, pure death, burning in the upper layers of the atmosphere. In their endeavour to escape, they produced
a strain or stress in the surrounding æther, and this caused the
force of gravity of the earth to pull, strongly and slowly. The effect
on the orbit-distorted atoms was apparent, even atoms of oxygen
and nitrogen felt it was hostile. Of course the very atoms heavier

than the hydrogen atoms were the bricks of the universe; they fell from dizzying heights down to Earth. The conflicting forces of gravity, magnetism, and the spin of the earth trembled high up into the atmosphere, forced the unwanted atoms of matter in such a way that they spread themselves broadcast over the face of the earth. Hydrogen, being the lightest substance—this triumph over matter—sped onwards through the now almost unbreathable atmosphere.

Now gravity's pull to earth was a slightly menacing swell, but the difference in temperature kept every atom in constant danger. Climbing through the atmosphere, the temperature plunged, heated to hundreds of degrees, and then down. At one mile up, it was cold. At two miles, it was noticeably colder. At nearly three miles it was bitter. And seven miles up, it dropped to -50°. It continued this way to an altitude of about twelve miles, and then things went haywire, as if an entire new set of rules applied, for at sixteen miles, the temperature started to rise sharply until, at thirty miles, it was a comfortable +48°. But this soon changed, for at fifty miles, it dropped to a severe -100°, where it remained for some time. But at about fifty-five miles, it started a dramatic leaping; it reached more than +200°. And then at some point, an almost unbelievable phenomenon would occur: the temperature of the atmosphere would be -200°. It was a crazy ambience, this vertical pillar of atmosphere, but it was the portion of the universe through which an atom of matter must move if he wished ever to enter space.

2

BEYOND THE EARTH'S ATMOSPHERE, WIND AND SPACE WERE banished. Passing from cold to hot to burning hot and freezing cold, any atmospheric disturbances ceased. The planet's immense gravitational field was not dragging. Oxygen and pressure both could be said to have vanished. Only an increasing exhilaration and a delightful effervescence of thought remained.*

Above the earth, between it and the sun, through the absence of an obscuring air, the sky had taken on an unfamiliar aspect. It made things different. The Sun, ordinarily, was nothing to wonder at; the minor portion of its light that was scattered into blueness by the atmosphere was sufficient to blank out the other stars altogether. Here, so far out on the other side of the sky, into the unending sunlight, was the absence of atmosphere, the eternal night, yet there was no question of being able to see the stars, they were so overridden by the Sun.

In the opposite direction, its visible face illuminated, the Earth appeared now as a great bright orb hundreds of times larger than the full moon. In its center a dazzling patch of light was the sun's

---

* At the outer edge of Earthspace, basically there is no up or down, hot or cold, day or night. *What is there?* The absence of oxygen and atmospheric pressure. A universe teeming with radio emission. All these radio emissions are natural— caused by physical processes, electrons spiraling in the galactic magnetic field, or interstellar molecules colliding with one another, or the remote echoes of the Big Bang. *How cold is space?* It depends on how high you go. The higher you go, the colder it gets. In orbit around the Earth, it's only at 120 degrees absolute; 150 degrees below zero, if you prefer. The cold of interstellar space is thousands of degrees below freezing point or the absolute zero of Fahrenheit, Centigrade, or Reaumur. The whole point of space is to give molecules a chance to cool down after they come shooting off the surface of giant stars.

image reflected in the ocean. The planet's circumference was an indefinite breadth of luminous haze, fading into the surrounding blackness of space. The spectacle was strangely moving. It was a huge pearl set in ebony. It was nacreous, it was an opal. No, it was far more lovely than any jewel. Its patterned coloring was more subtle, more ethereal. It displayed the delicacy and brilliance, the intricacy and harmony, of a live thing. The blue represented all the water on the earth, and the bits of other colors the continents and islands, their vague browns and greens indenting the vague blues and grays. Much of the northern hemisphere was an expanse of cloud-tops. Toward the equator, where the air was clearer, the ocean was dark. A little whirl of brilliant cloud was perhaps the upper surface of a hurricane.

For a long time (a few hours following), the Earth revolved on its axis at a speed of more than a thousand miles an hour at the equator, turning from west to east as it has obediently done for nearly five billion years. Earth was marvellous, impossible blue, lit up like an indigo lantern with its own interior glow, its ancient airs, the tectonic murmur of its still-beating heart, a misty breadth of sunlight. And the Earth—the ceaseless turning of the Earth—was infinitely inviting with its swirls of white on blue and its peeping glimpse of tan.

Then, tantalizingly blurred by the distance, a glimpse of something very strange. Many miles away, the golden landscape reared toward the night side of the planet. Between the areas of night and day, a belt of shade now marked the area of deep dusk. Earth was waning.

Time passed with dream-like slowness. The earth turning, the sun moving. The probing beams of sunlight slowly swept westward along with the day till the sun hovered at the horizon and cast its light through that atmosphere, cleaving white billowing clouds and glittering salty seas. The straight lines of light shone kindly and steadily with the lovely, blue-green crescent of the waning Earth as a backdrop.

During the final minutes of the sun, obscurity unveiled a star.

One tremulous arrow of light, projected how many thousands of years ago, now stung with vision. A farther, dimmer star came into simultaneous being. And one star after another came out. At the edge of the world there appeared a faint line of luminosity as the last hues of sunlight faded.

It was rare that any geographical features could be identified in that ever-shrinking arc of light, but even the darkened portion of the disk was endlessly fascinating. It was strangely moving, for the sheer beauty of the planet surprised in its size and in its perfect serenity, majestic without severity, impressive without showiness, emphatic in its admonitions, grand in its simplicity. From this high look-out, no visiting angel, or explorer from another planet, could have guessed that this orb teemed with vermin and reptiles, fish and all, thousands of birds in the air.

Soon the sun was physically eclipsed by the Earth, and all colour disappeared. Everything vanished into blackness, although a grey, bright afterimage remained in the sky.

In another moment the pale stars alone were visible, only because they were so near. The earth below was like a huge circular table-top, a broad disc surrounded by darkness and faint stars. At about the same time some brilliant stars were seen away from Earth, slowly gleaming in the Void, and in a few minutes, as darkness settled, every star had seemingly flared up into higher magnitude. The heavens blazed. Silver and black. The major stars were like the headlights of a distant car. The Milky Way, no longer watered down with darkness, was an encircling, granular river of light.

3

HOW MAJESTIC IT WAS, HOW INVITING. THOSE WHO HAVE only seen the starry sky from the earth cannot imagine its appearance when the vague, half luminous veil of air has been withdrawn. The stars seen on earth are the mere scattered survivors that penetrate the dim and misty atmosphere. But now, up here, the brightness was intense; that airless, star-dusted sky could realise the meaning of the hosts of heaven!

Looking from star to star, the more obtrusive of the constellations asserted their individuality. Pisces, Aries, Taurus. The zigzag. All were duly patterned, posing on fields of ink. And though for the most part the great and familiar lights of the sky stood forth as near neighbors, dim lamps were visible at a great distance. Through gaps in the nearer parts appeared vista beyond vista of luminous mists.

Looking calmly and majestically over the shivering light-clouds, imagination was now stimulated to a new, strange mode of perception, moving into the steady night regions of eternity and deep perspectives of stellar populations. The parallax or parallactic drift of socalled fixed stars, in reality evermoving wanderers from immeasurably remote eons to infinitely remote futures, formed a grand and sublime picture in and from other constellations. The hologram sky glittered with new forms much different from their predecessors, fanciful constellations suggesting playing cards, the faces of dice, a top hat, a martini glass. Peering between the stars in the outer darkness, among many millions of other faint stars, there were stars of sweetness—an eighth-magnitude star, a nineteenth-magnitude star—and nascent new stars. There were other areas of this tremendous ocean of gold: stars of (presumably) similar origin which had (effectively or presumably) appeared in and disappeared from the constellation of the Corona Septentrionalis; a perceived vortex of star streams; also, as mere flecks and points of light, other such vortices, such galaxies, sparsely scattered in the void, depth beyond depth, so far afield that even the eye of imagination could find no limits to the cosmical, the all-embracing, galaxy of galaxies. The universe now appeared as a void wherein floated rare flakes of snow, each flake a universe.

Gazing at the faintest and remotest of all the swarm of universes was crazy and cockeyed and extremely strange: distant galaxies and objects smaller than galaxies, red dwarfs, asteroids and iceteroids, the fixed stars and variable suns, energy spontaneously given off by matter leaking from another Universe. All else was rayless obscurity, profound darkness and nothingness.

It was very big to think about everything and everywhere. Since the ultimate stuff of the physical universe was now said to be multitudinous and arbitrary "quanta" of the activity of "spirits," only God could do that. The scale of the scene was too immense to comprehend. The meaning of time, the nothingness of space eternal. What was all this about? What was after the universe? Was there anything round the universe to show where it stopped before the nothing place, or even another Universe, began? Asking such questions was difficult going. Such questions were incontrovertibly old and everlasting. There were many answers. It would be hard to say.

Yet in matters that really counted, simple thought was slowly filling the darkness with a dim gold of stars and no space and no light but stars. It was reassuring, on such a night, to see the stars looming against the nothingness of paratheory, to know all this was real, it was really happening, but with a quality of the unreal; it was reality happening in quite a different way than on the level land on Earth. Unlimited energy was everywhere, and distance was crowded with swarms and streams of stars. But in a strange vertigo, the majestic universe of stars and galaxies seemed to fall away into the profound darkness with the lambent edge of the galaxy shining behind them . . . the separateness of the Milky Way. Perhaps the Galaxy—the completed hoop of the Milky Way—was more important, more real than all the galaxies; the ringing reassurance of a full house of stars at just that distance made everything seem more physical than before, and pleasanter. But this galaxy was too big, perhaps the grandest sight to be seen, too perfectly detailed to really be described.

Could try. An asteroid, passing by at ordinary speeds, would see this scene time and again: the infinite lattiginous scintillating uncondensed milky way marked by an infinite number of stars and variable suns and telescopic planets, astronomical waifs and strays. Through the milky spread of stars, not only had every star been accorded due prominence, but there were also star-forming regions; wispish, gently glowing veils of condensing gas in which were embedded the hottening embers of embryo suns. There were newly formed stars surrounded by disks of protoplanetary material and planetary systems themselves, ticking round their central suns like microscopic orreries, at a vastly accelerated rate. There were also aged stars which had ejected shells of their own photospheres into space, enriching the tenuous interstellar medium: the basic protoplasmic reservoir from which future generations of stars and worlds would eventually be created. There were regular or irregular supernova remnants, cooling as they expanded and shed their energy to the interstellar medium. Sometimes, at the heart of one of these stellar death-events, a newly forged pulsar, emitting radio bursts with ever-slowing but stately precision, like the clocks in some forgotten imperial palace which had been wound one final time and would now tick until they died, the time between each tick lengthening towards some chill eternity. There were also black holes in the hearts of some of these remnants, and one massive (though now dormant) one at the heart of this galaxy, surrounded by an attendant shoal of doomed stars which would one day spiral into its event-horizon and fuel an apocalyptic burst of X-rays as they were ripped asunder. If such a thing had happened once, it must surely have happened many times, in this Galaxy of a hundred thousand million suns . . .*

Yes, the Galaxy was enormous. Stars might exist within hundreds of light-years or, for all anyone knew, billions of light-years in any one direction. From one star system to another, the stars would still seem quite the same: still the same tattered streamer of star-dust, the starry archipelagoes, the white breakers of the milky way.

Stars shone through all. It was as though all the stars smeared light across the elaborately crowded parts of the Galaxy and all the dim stars, not just the bright ones—it was utterly impossible for an object as massive as a dead sun to sneak up unobserved. In a way, it was a pity. An encounter with a dark star would have been quite exciting. While it lasted . . .

---

* As long as the bloody universe holds together. The universe is a goddam awful place. The Universe is a junkyard; with everything in it, there's nothing out there. Earth is stupid too. The Planet drifts to random insect doom . . . All the universe is straining toward the obscure significance of a Fisher Price toy whose spring has unwound to its very end. Earth has nothing to do with it, except that it gets wiped out, too.

4

ALL OVER THE GALAXY, THERE ARE PLANETS AND PLANETS. Virtually every star has some sort of planetary system or other, and planets are just stars that are too small to be stars, you see.

Of all the planets in all the star systems, the Galaxy will have two kinds of worlds: worlds completely empty, lifeless, and worlds with water and with air, whirling in sunlight and darkness. A world can be the right size and temperature and still be uninhabitable for any of a variety of reasons; suppose it has a poisonous atmosphere, or is incredibly volcanic, or has a high level of radioactivity, touched with grayed-out pink or purple trees and red moons and a green sun. Another world might be wandering through space between stars at this very moment; a world that has an atmosphere, plenty of oxygen, a world with a normal gravity, a breathable atmosphere, a pleasant temperature range. Far from the center of action where new stars are being born, far from those centers of the universe where new galaxies are being born, in that other world, the sea is seductive, never ceasing, whispering, clamoring, murmuring, inviting, an organic soup waiting to be shaken into life.

Such a world marched in a silent procession far out in the uncharted backwaters of the unfashionable end of the western spiral arm of the Galaxy, not far from a small unregarded yellow sun. Orbiting this sun at a distance of roughly ninety-two million miles, the world floated like an apple in a tub. To the east, although this term meant little, the Sun lost energy at a rate which must imperil it after another fifteen or twenty billion years, poor fated thing. To the west, or away from the Sun, shone the blinding splendour of the moon. Most impressive of all rode the planet Earth, its features ascertainable when in daylight, barely suggested when its spinning carried one half the surface into darkness. How big it seemed at times, how small now.

Past the Earth, now at a right angle with the meridian, the Moon lay beautiful in the cold light. Not far from full, it was black and white; a mild and delicate white. And the black was somehow softer, too. From a height of fifty thousand kilometers, the Moon's geography came into view: the great craters, the dark scar of a valley—its eastern limb wrinkled with easily visible mountains formed a dazzling background. Closer to land, the mottled silver disc of the Moon was different. Now the jagged peaks and the ground bore a gray dunce's cap of dust. The huge craters, which looked so impressive from Earth, turned out upon close inspection to be gently rolling hills, their relief grossly exaggerated by the shadows they cast at dawn and sunset. There was not a single lunar crater whose ramparts soared as abruptly as the precipices and slopes of Earth. The land lying below, the whole earthward-facing side of the Moon, proved unexpectedly simple.

In the other direction, far, far away, Earth hung in the sky—a half-Earth that lay towards the sun. How strange that the familiar blues and greens of Earth shone with such celestial glory when one looked at them from afar! That blue-green crescent, even in her last quarter, had the power of a dozen full moons. Of course, the Moon had a few specialities of its own. Like the two-hundred-below-zero nights, and the dust that shimmered on the rocks and crags. What else did the Moon have to offer? The Moon quietly and efficiently accompanied Earth on its path around the Sun, through hundreds of thousands of miles of vacant space. Day after day, month after month, the Earth was turning; the moon moved but did not grow distant. As it swept through space (a bubble lit by slow lightning), the moon went about its business, so delicately counterbalanced by the centrifugal force generated by the Earth's mass. It was a dance where the dancers spun on the edge of nothing, puissant and lonely.

But the earth and moon were not alone; the stars and the sun shone, and hundreds of other things might be in the vicinity. Here in the Solar System, there were many types of flying objects that had been seen over the centuries: asteroids by the tens of thousands and comets by the tens of billions; meteoric stones moving at a certain speed, their vast elliptical egressive and reentrant orbits from perihelion to aphelion.

Close to the earth, it was all so peaceful and wonderful. There were only two or three asteroids at the moment, and not too close to the planet's immense gravitational field. Somewhat beyond the orbit of Earth's moon, the Meteors and wandering, hirsute comets orbited in a circle. One of those meteors, a wailing black meteor, traveled through empty space as if shot from a gun, round and round. The meteor was familiar with the moon and the planet, for it was traveling back and forth between the Earth and the moon, but it's really weird. It's like . . . start at Earth, then it's at the moon seven days later, then it flings up way out of the Earth-moon plane and comes back to the moon: Moon → (deep space out of Earth-moon plane) → Moon → Earth → (deep space in Earth-moon plane) → Earth → Moon. And it repeats that over and over. As helpless and inert as any comet or asteroid, a powerless prisoner of gravitation, the meteor goes through a cycle with each step taking seven days. Somewhere in there, it just sits in an elliptical orbit around Earth for a couple of weeks . . . until the heat works its way through that rock in low-Earth orbit and makes that streak of light over the Earth.

IV. THE ENDLESS SUMMER

I

DESCENDING FROM A HIGHER ORBIT BROUGHT THE EARTH into spectacular view. There was considerable cloud cover, but blue-green lines of the continents and oceans could be seen in the distance. And ice caps . . . under a kiss of atmosphere, like morning dew, soon to be boiled off in the day's heat.

The glowing meteor detonated kilometres from the clouds, a great stone mammoth burning out to waste in the vacant regions of the atmosphere. So powerful was its radiance, that it thoroughly illuminated the dense medium of cloud below with a rolling tide of light and colour. It brought signs in heaven, or portents on the earth beneath, as if it were the light that is to reveal all secrets.

In all its undashed fearfulness, its groaning roughrock Creation throes, the phantasm advanced towards the blooming clouds in the form of small rocks and wailed, hurtling through like the sound of a bugle through a long weight of silence. The great vault brightened like the dome of an immense lamp, meteoric stones goin out through there and just a squallin.

Lord didnt they come. The hawk-flight of imagination followed them as they curved downward below the clouds. But you know what? A falling meteorite on a burning and unclouded course disappears so quickly. There wasn't much to watch at that precise instant. There was a vibration in the air—that previously solid rock now a succession of showers and gleams—followed by more pieces.

As the fragments fell under the controlling influence of gravity, new rules arose. The winds were pushing and piling against them for a good many hundred miles. Farther away, in a ten-thousand-mile arc, the micrometeorite damage would glide down into the atmosphere, swiftly moving over the sea, past strange formations and lonely stretches of land that's got nothing in it but furze, sandy flats, tufts of long grass, scrappy trees.

The rocks went suddenly past the meadows that sloped golden in the light of the already late afternoon, over more of the wide lands and mountains, obscured in darkness, yet still displaying their black outlines. As they passed into the unilluminated night side of the planet, they were so unpredictable and devoid of reason. The rocks kept breaking up, breaking, moving, following the scatter of swift-flying birds in the sky and the wind, which broke down more rocks. Their senselessness sped onward through the gloom . . . and shadow, miles and miles of it, far into the night.

From time to time promising features would appear on the distant horizon—ravines, mountains, maybe even hills again; up, down; and suddenly the vast expanse of vallies, luxuriant in shade, were frequently embellished by the windings of a lucid stream, and diversified by clusters of half-seen mulberry-trees. The great levels of sky and land stretched around further off, landscape beyond landscape, till meteoric stones—the charred fragments—were over the horizon in a magnificent burst of sound, and a burst of brilliant light. The light grew stronger, whiter. The horizon was lost in the radiance, sparkled an instant then went out, bereft of light. The illusions merged into the sky, and the ground disappeared into the darkness.

2

THERE SEEMED TO BE NOTHING TO SEE; NO CREEKS OR trees, no hills or fields. There was nothing but land, silent empty land. Nothing moved. Nothing stirred. The silence was profound.

No, there was nothing but land—slightly undulating. Up at the sky there was not a familiar mountain ridge against it; there were no hills. But this was the complete dome of heaven, all there was of it.

The sky was like a bowl of light overturned on the flat black land. A marvellous stillness pervaded the world, and the stars, together with the serenity of their rays, seemed to shed upon the earth the assurance of everlasting security. The sensation was new; it was inexplicably pleasing, as if the sky were not meant to darken, but, beginning again with each turn into night, and through night, to bless the zone of shadow under which the land lay, stretching away in every direction.

As soon as the eyes became accustomed to the dim light, it became clear that this land was not wholly dark. You could see little dark spots in the gloom. And there were more fireflies out there than, perhaps, since that land emerged from the waters of geologic ages. Thousands of them everywhere, just drifting up out of the grass, extinguishing themselves in midair. Not much to look at right here apart from the steady shimmering of their light.

After a while, when the moon came up, a sheet of thin, fleecy clouds skirted the horizon, leaving just enough of its faint and fluctuating light to render objects visible, dimly revealing their forms. There were plenty of grass and weeds around and low bushes. Even with hardly any moon, the stars were bright enough that every bush cast a shadow. The only landmarks were shadows, low shadows. Every time anything moved, the stars and moon-light illuminated the edges of things, made suggestions out of shadows—owls and buzzards, cottontails. These forms was inter-changeable. Except for some random dark patches far out over the land, these forms were the only things around.

All that land lay cold and blue and looked as if no eye had ever seen it before. Only the tall wild grass covered the endless empty land, and a great empty sky arched over it. And for miles and miles, the breath of the moon, mist and silver, lay on the fields. The land fell and reached away as far as the eye could see, the hills folding together and the gray grass rolling in the plain.

As the moon rose, new forms much different from their pre-decessors were beginning to appear: masses of trees less than three miles away, a thin silver ribbon to the north that could only be a river. Across it, for miles and miles in the soft clear moonlight, illimitable, covering the earth from horizon to horizon, lay the Wheat. The growth, now many days old, was already high from the ground. There it lay, a vast, silent ocean, shimmering a pallid green under the moon and under the stars.

What would you call this—this scene? The desert of wheat? The earthy-smelling plains? The land seemed to be full of a prairie-like placidity, born of royalty. And it was indeed the most splen-did thing. The elements couldn't be more simple, more mysterious. Still, when there was nothing to see around but a few horses suck-ing water, with thousands of miles of grass resting under the sky, one glance told the eyes that have looked on them what it might possibly mean: a prairie.

3

THE BALD-HEADED PRAIRIE STRETCHED AWAY IN ALL DIREC-
tions. The moon rose higher and grew yellow as a melon, casting a
strange gleam on the gray grasslands. Somewhere in the nameless
night, a nightingale began to sing. The cool wind moved over the
prairie and the song was round and clear above the grasses' whispering. The bird sang on and on. A pheasant sounded to the east.
Now and again their songs ran together like the interlacings of a
mountain stream whose waters foam and then mix.

Soon the unvarying emptiness of the country was full of
music, and part of it came from the great, bright stars swinging so
low above the prairie. The stars were singing. The whisper of the
sweeping wheat was swallowed up in their song, as if glutted with
sound. Other sounds began to rise from the prairie. Gradually
the skittering life of the ground, of holes and burrows, of the
brush, began again; gophers moved, and the rabbits crept to green
things, the mice scampered over clods, and the winged hunters
moved soundlessly overhead—wings that zigzag maddeningly,
flapping around.*

How alive everything was! Nearly all the time winds rushed
over the fields, faded to small breezes, subsided into stillness, gathered again. Trees dipped and curtsied, the thousands of acres of
wheat rippling like a skirt. Very low, very misty, very tender, the
stars shone—the moon rising higher, brighter—and over all flowered the smell of growing things, of fecund earth, overpowering.

---

* Ba. What is that flying about? Swallow? Bat probably. So blind. Have birds no
smell? Ba. There he goes. Funny little beggar. Wonder where he lives. Ba. Again.

It was a night of overwhelming beauty, magical and mysterious. It was a night of smells and the mist, a night of listening, a
night given to the faint soughing and sighing stirring, the shy sab-
bath of leaves and petals and the air that eddies there as it does not
in other places. But as the night advanced, the wind became softer
and softer. In the distance the sounds of life dropped off, and it was
pleasant. The prairie had a hushed look. From time to time the wind
came chill over the dark-green fields, but the dark plains were peaceful and quiet, and the stars flowed down in a slow cascade over the
western horizon. Sometime after midnight, the moon slid away.

On a hill during a clear night such as this, the roll of the world
eastward is almost a palpable movement. The sensation may be
caused by the panoramic glide of the stars past earthly objects,
which is perceptible in a few minutes of stillness, or by the better
outlook upon space that a hill affords, or by the wind; but whatever be its origin, the impression of riding along is vivid and abid-
ing. The poetry of motion is a phrase much in use, and to enjoy
the epic form of that gratification it is necessary to, on a hill at a
small hour of the night, long and quietly watch your stately progress through the stars.

On such a silent night, after such a nocturnal reconnoitre, it
is hard to get back to earth. The consciousness of such majestic
speeding is overwhelming, the smell of vegetation not enough to
convince the mind nor destiny to return to the even tenor of its
ordinariness, the earth. No wind could lift those thoughts. More
and more and more stars had gathered, obliterating distracted
observation. But Earth returned upon the memory in panic, when
suddenly the silence of this lonely time was pierced by an exclama-
tion. A horse had neighed close behind.

Darned horses. Always somewhere to the north or south . . .
almost stagnant . . . and enervating now. The horse was seen
descending the hill, and the wearisome series commenced.

First the horse, of unimpeachable breed, overtook and passed
the hill. Then a light appeared at a distance that illumined the
grayness to a great extent. It was almost ominously quiet; one

might have expected that it were a sign of death. It seemed as if there was a fire lit, an altar burning on the prairie, a solitary flame frayed by the wind that freshened and faded.

The horse could not see it well enough to know. He continued on across the grass, looking confused. Then he stopped, staring. A mile away a troop of figures passed between him and the light. Then again. Wolves perhaps. The horse stood darkly against the sky. He saw vultures at their soaring whose wingspan so dwarfed all lesser birds. When they were gone—fierce wolves, ragening vultures—the softer horse's tramp then recommenced, and the fire grew larger.

It was a lone tree burning. A heraldic tree that the meteoric stones had left afire. By the time the horse was watching up close, the light of the fire sufficed to show the ghostly gathered husks around it: black leaves and drenched grass and fallen branches, and the dead animals scattered over the ground beside it. The leaves were shrivelled, moribund, blackened, furled tight like rolled umbrellas, while all about in that circle attended companies of lesser auxiliaries routed forth into the inordinate day, small owls that crouched silently and stood from foot to foot and beaded lizards with mouths black as a chowdog's and the little basilisks that jet blood from their eyes. Rattlesnakes were always lurking about like seemly gods, silent and the same. It was all hell, a constellation of ignited eyes that edged the ring of light all bound in a precarious truce before this torch whose brightness had set back the stars in their sockets.

Beyond the fire it was cold and the night was clear and the stars were falling. Trees glistened, and the green things on earth seemed to hum. In the dimness of the world, it all must have looked the same to the horse. But the prairie, the stars and the fireflies, everything had changed. The blossoms of the fire flames shot up and out, yellow and white and red and orange, and the heat was oppressive. It was not beautiful. It was an object of terror. This was the tree of death. Of itself, it was neither poisonous nor cruel, but the fire was ominous, a new omen, connected only with the time to come.

4

YOU WOULDN'T THINK THE NIGHT COULD BRING SUCH A change, but it did. No good. The horse was watching, out there past the tree. Left hind foot was flexed and resting on the toe, the way horses did when they had to stand in one place for a long time. And the horse stood, watching in the wind.

Before dawn the horse began to toss its head, and soon it quivered and stepped and raised the flues of its nose to the wind. The tree was no more. Around the charred core, where the bark had peeled away, the smoldering skeleton of a blackened scrog. All the creatures that had been at vigil with him in the night were gone.

As the sky grew less gloomy, indeed, began to grow a little genial, the mood faded into blue hazes and dull early light as far as the eye could see. The horse went by slowly through the groves of sunflower stalks left over from better years, and it was then he saw a hummingbird swinging his head from side to side. And hummingbirds, as everyone knows—unlike those scoundrel hustling crows that have no redeeming value—are an omen of true love. There was a peaceful silence beneath the sounds of the wind, the bird of joy flapping overhead in the early grayness.

Soon the light of dawn was a little sharper. The sky was a pale pearly color, waiting for the warm gold of the rising sun. Where the grass was thick and green, a cool earth-smelling breeze lifted into the sky. And while the wind blew across miles of prairie land, you could hear the stalks crackling in the dewy, heavy-odoured fields and the hum of insects. The horse grazed nearby on the good grass.

As the dawn came on, the darkness didn't last. The light was just coming. A redness grew up out of the eastern horizon, and on the ground, birds began to chirp sharply. The dawn in the east looked like the light from some great fire that was burning under the edge of the world. The color was reflected in the globules of dew that sheathed the grass. The sun was beginning to glare.

In an instant, a long fan of light ran out from the east and the rising sun swelled blood red along the horizon. Look yonder: sunlight, a singing bird. The rim of the prairie red, as if a line of coals had been spread along it. The feathered stalks stood so juicy and pure and bright. As the rim of the blinding sun came up over the horizon, water sparkled on the grass blades. Two red chickens on the ground flamed with reflected light. The prairie rolled out of its sleep into a sunlight grandly announced, proclaimed throughout heaven.

All around, shadows were moving over the waving grasses. Light and warmth flowed in ripples across the field. A few meadow larks were springing straight up from the billows of grass into the high, clear sky, singing as they went. Over yonder, the buffalo-peas were blooming in pink and purple masses, and the larks, perched on sunflower stalks, were singing straight at the sun, their heads thrown back and their yellow breasts a-quiver.

The sun was over the horizon when, in all that space of land and sky, more birds, now hundreds of meadow larks, were rising from the prairie, singing higher and higher in the air. Their songs came down from the great, clear sky like a rain of music. And all over the land, where the grasses waved and murmured under the wind, thousands of little dickie-birds clung with their tiny claws to the blossoming weeds and sang their thousands of little songs on and on.

In the brilliant sunlight, gophers were popping up and down, uttering their cheerful tweets in harmonious relation with the birds. Gopher count? Dozen or so. These little creatures looked soft as velvet. They had bright round eyes and crinkling noses and wee paws. They popped out of holes in the ground and stood up. Their hind legs folded under their haunches, their little paws folded tight to their chests, and they looked exactly like bits of dead wood sticking out of the ground, only their bright eyes glittered in the morning sun.

Just beside them the horse stood watching the east, where there was nothing but those birds and grassy prairie spreading to the edge of the sky. Quite near, to the north, the creek bottoms lay below the prairie. Some darker green tree-tops showed, and beyond them bits of the rim of earthen bluffs held up the prairie's grasses. Far away to the east, a broken line of different greens lay on the prairie, and that was the river, but the horse could not see the river through the trees. The horse turned and looked out across the blowing grass where the cows fed and a herd of wild horses stood and quietly trotted on toward the low hills, over the broad prairie, and past the mounds of trees and earth and sky, then picked up speed. He started racing without effort, flying across the sloping meadows, meadow-hills, patches of all colours and fragrance of flowers, past the dark rocks, forward into the light.

5

THERE IS SOMETHING FRANK AND JOYOUS AND YOUNG IN the open face of the country. It gives itself ungrudgingly to the moods of the season, holding nothing back. It seems to rise a little to meet the sun. The air and the earth are curiously mated and intermingled, as if the one were the breath of the other. In the atmosphere, the same tonic, puissant quality that is in the ground, the same strength and resoluteness that brings good fortune.

Yes, looking at the glowing, beautiful land was a shock to the senses. So beautiful, so perfect, so unsullied. Far across the plains, the horizon was lost in the radiance of the sun hanging above it, and the flood of golden glory which formed a glittering halo around the sun spilled out, like water on the earth.

As soon as the sun got high enough to be warm, the land and the sky seemed too large, and the country seemed endless. It seemed as if the grass was the country, as the water is the sea. The grass made all the great prairie the colour of certain seaweeds when they are first washed up. And there was so much motion in it; the whole country seemed, somehow, to be running in the fresh, easy-blowing morning wind, and in the earth itself, as if the shaggy grass were a sort of loose hide, and underneath it herds of wild buffalo were galloping, galloping . . .

Out across the blowing grass, it was high season for summer flowers. The summer rains had been so many and opportune that all sorts of weeds and herbs and flowers had grown up there: splotches of wild larkspur, pale green-and-white spikes of hoarhound, tangles of foxtail and wild wheat. South of the apricot trees, cornering on the wheat, was alfalfa, where myriads of white and yellow butterflies were always fluttering above the purple blossoms. Farther away, out in a sea of grass, the pink bee-bush stood tall, and the cone-flowers and rose mallow grew everywhere. The flimsy faces of pansies blazed, and the wild prairie roses in the ditches bloomed an innocent pink.

Rabbits were everywhere on the grass, and thousands of prairie chickens. All the wild things on the prairie ran and flew and hopped and crawled. Sometimes there'd be a great gray rabbit, so still in the lights and shadows of a grass clump. His round eyes stared without meaning anything. His nose wiggled, and sunlight was rosy through his long ears, which had delicate veins in them and the softest short fur on their outsides. The rest of his fur was so thick and soft—soft and almost translucent, like a piece of Turkish delight; as if you could suck off his fur like sugar. Then he was gone in a flash, and the place where he had been sitting was hollowed and smooth and still warm from his warm behind.

All the time, of course, horses grazed in the grass. The tiny dickie-birds were everywhere, and their tiny nests were in the tall weeds. On the grass, with the sky above, it was easy. Then, coming over a little rise in the ground, two big hawks were skimming the surface of the prairie, not far away. The birds came flying over, and a rabbit cautiously hopped and looked. Huge rabbits bounded away before them; the tiny dickie-birds fluttered up and settled again. The tawny hawks sailed over, making slow shadows through the grass, past the horses and toward the river. Grass knee high over there.

This river was the last of an ancient ocean, miles deep, that once had covered the land—a broad, muddy river curving down from the north. The river curved east, across the plains, but when the river curved south, there it was—a narrow, straight river, swift but not deep, shallow and warm. The farther north, the colder and swifter the river. Farther south through the open grassland, though running freely, the river was shallow and evidently boggy. Somewhere the river branched, went out into the endless prairie.

The subject of rivers was becoming more pronounced. A flock of cranes came in and disappeared behind the brush along the river. A horse neighed over the trees. One of the huge grey cranes flew low over the rippling grass. He flew on his strong wings, and in the sunshine and wind. Some small birds ran off into the trees. A big rabbit bounded right over the riverbank. The heavy beat of wings dipped off the slope, down into a rocky river.

At the bottom of the shallow draw was mud. Here cranes and other aquatic birds had congregated. Coming along the river, the horses stepped archly among the shadows, that green enclosure where the sunlight flickered so bright through the leaves. The horses stood in the marshy grass and sucked quietly at the water, ignoring the strings of ducks that swam nearby, the cranes standing solemnly in the shadows. The horses raised their dripping mouths from the water one and then the other and blew and leaned and drank again.

The river is very shallow at that time of year, and the bottom was half exposed and braided like water. There were sandbars right across, the bigger ones small jungles of weedy vegetation weedily in bloom, with butterflies and dragonflies attending on them like spirits. And the sun was shining as well as it could onto that shadowy river, a good part of the shine being caught in the trees. And the cicadas were chanting, and the willows were straggling their tresses in the water, and the cottonwood and the ash were making that summer hush, that susurrus.

Upstream the wooded shore was unvarying in its features. The same greenness throughout, the same dogwood bushes, all overgrown with wild grapevines. The roots of trees brown and bark smelling, cold. Down a hill toward the wide spot in the river, a great chunk of the shore had been bitten out by some spring freshet, and the scar was masked by elder bushes, growing down to the water in flowery terraces. There was no sound but the high, singsong buzz of wild bees and the sunny gurgle of the water underneath. Over the edge of the bank the little stream made the noise; it flowed along perfectly clear over the sand and gravel, cut off from the muddy main current by a long sandbar.

The scene was rural and picturesque, very peaceful. The water was the color of clay and roily. The sandbar below was thickly grown with sedge and willow, and the bluffs on the far side were stained and cavepocked and traversed by a constant myriad of swallows. Beyond that, the river was uneventful. Now and then a rabbit. Or geese or mergansers that would beat away over the water. Down river was the same, the sky was the same, the same thicket. The horses drank, squirrels chattering in the trees. But when the big white bird flew suddenly up among the glossy leaves, something spooked the horses. The horses were stepping forward and back, snorting up the crumbling side of a clay bank.

6

THEY HAD LEFT THE WINDINGS OF THE RIVER. THEY CAME
up out of the river breaks and climbed into a meadow where the
grass was tall, looking off at the gentle, humplike rises to the north.

The sun fell like a warm hand. To the west a mile away ran a
rolling country covered with grass and wild daisies. And beyond
that a small band of antelope grazing on the rolling prairie.
Everywhere, as far as the eye could reach, there was nothing but
shaggy grasses and flowers waving in the wind. Far overhead, a few
white puffs of cloud sailed in the thin blue air.

Between that earth and that sky, yes, the breeze was freshening, the winds and the meadow larks and the shadows fleeing
always over the hilltops. The wind, running over the flower heads,
peeped in at the little brown buds and bounded off again gladly,
through the grass, past the horses, over the hills, and far away—
the wind often blows from one week's end to another across that
high, active, resolute stretch of country.

In the dunelike hills of grass, the horses were grazing. Two
horses were standing up top of one of the bluffs. Twelve young
colts were galloping in a drove. Several horses could be seen snaking through the grasslands across the plain to the south. They were
beautiful little horses. They were not really ponies; they were western mustangs—strong as mules and gentle as kittens. They had
large, soft, gentle eyes, and long manes and tails, and slender legs
and feet much smaller and quicker than the feet of horses in the
Big Woods.

One horse was the elected leader of vast herds of wild horses,
the White Steed of the Prairies; a magnificent milk-white charger,
large-eyed, small-headed, bluff-chested. The flashing cascade of his

mane, the curving comet of his tail, invested him with housings more resplendent than gold and silver. A most imperial and arch-angelical apparition, the stallion would come prancing and pound-ing the ground and arching its neck with the dignity of a thousand monarchs.

Whether marching amid his aides and marshals in the van of countless cohorts that endlessly streamed over the plains, or whether with his circumambient subjects browsing all around at the horizon, the White Steed gallopingly reviewed them with warm nostrils reddening through his cool milkiness. And that day, as the herd wound through these great stretches, the stallion went forward, shaking its white fetlocks and looking up at the little clouds that, like ravelled skeins of glossy white silk, were drifting across the hollowed turquoise of the summer sky.

The herd, working slowly and quietly, followed him out across the prairie to the west, through never-ending miles of grain and grass and bright-flowered pastures, trotting and walking and trot-ting again. Sometimes, when the wind was coming in off the grassy plains, the young colts ran with their dams and trampled down the flowers in a haze of pollen that hung in the sun like pow-dered gold and they ran the young mares and fillies over the plain where their rich bay and their rich chestnut colors shone in the sun and the ground resounded under their running hooves and they flowed and changed and ran and their manes and tails blew off of them like spume and there was nothing else at all in that high world and they moved all of them in a resonance that was like a music among them and they were none of them afraid horse nor colt nor mare and they ran in that resonance which is the world itself and which cannot be spoken but only praised.

7

FOR A LONG TIME THEY WENT ON, ACROSS THE PRAIRIE. THE sky got bigger and the country emptier. There was nothing to see but grass and sky. Sometimes a big jack rabbit bounded in big bounds over the blowing grass and the prairie hens came walking. It seemed as if the grass were about to run over them. The grass had, indeed, grown back over everything, hiding even small trees.

The day had become hot. The temperature had risen since early morning, and it was past noon when waves of heat shimmered over the grass. As the herd and the stallion went forward, there was the smell of hot dirt and dry hills, wild azalea and the sweet cloy of lupin and horse sweat.

The country had begun to flatten out, brown in the distance, the prairie grass waving in the breeze. Two miles away, across the green and brown and yellow, on dry land, the hooves of the horses beat the ground, the dirt crust broke, and dust rose over the relatively flat blanket of grass. The hot sun blazed and the hot winds blew, and the horses kept moving westward.

Edging further into the distance, scattering stones and snorting, they watched as the beauty of the prairies, the abundance of high grass, grew bleaker, no longer as luxuriant as it had been. Overhead the sky was that indescribable blue, bright and shadowless, hard as enamel. All about stretched drying fields of pale-gold colour, bare on the high places, the long plain shimmering with mirages.

The prairie had changed. The wind wailed in the tan grass, and it whispered sadly across the curly, short buffalo grass. There the wind had been blowing for days and days and had made the short grass very brittle, and the surface below as hot as in a desert.

For many miles around, the vicinage presented a single determinate fact: the grass grew weakly and sickly from the surface. And the grass heads were heavy with oat beards to catch on a dog's coat, and foxtails to tangle in a horse's fetlocks, and clover burrs to fasten in sheep's wool; sleeping life waiting to be spread and dispersed, every seed armed with an appliance of dispersal, twisting darts and parachutes for the wind, little spears and balls of tiny thorns, and all waiting for animals and for the wind, all passive but armed with appliances of activity, still, but each possessed of the anlage of movement.

An hour or perhaps two hours passed. Water was scarce and the terrific sun beat fiercely. The horses trod and broke the dirt. They were on a plain of grass so huge that it was hard to imagine there was a world beyond it. The herd, themselves, were like a dot, surrounded by endless grass, no trees or bushes. And distance, toward the horizon, was tan to invisibility.

Looking out at the country to the west, the yellowing, dusty, afternoon light put a golden color on the land. There was a brightness, a beauty. You might get the idea that there was some sort of vitality about the place. But it was parched and sun-stricken. It was hard to imagine the grass had ever been green. Everywhere little grasshoppers would fly up by score, making that snap they do, like striking a match. In the shade under the grass the insects moved, ants and ant lions to set traps for them, sow bugs like little armadillos plodding restlessly on many tender feet. Queer little red bugs came out and moved in slow squadrons.

As the horses passed, there were also birds and other animals, the larger ones, roaming from east to west and north to south. A flight of swallows swooped overhead toward some waterhole. A land turtle crawled, turning aside for nothing, dragging his high-domed shell over the grass. Occasionally, black crows flew overhead, cawing their rough, sharp caws. Once, far in the distance, there was nothing in the empty prairie except a darkish strip that looked like the shadow of a cloud. Turned out to be two buffalo, standing on the prairie as if they were lost.

But the buffalo cloud wasn't much different than other animals that are commonly found in the vicinity of this prairie; the sun was so hot, the space was so empty, that it was hard to imagine that wild animals lived without being afraid. This was midsummer. The wind was hot. As if it came out of an oven. Twelve o'clock noon. 106°. Three o'clock. 107°. The parched fields frowned. From time to time there were sudden explosions of southeast wind, and the devil's breath charred the sparse grass and blew the fields away. Even the weeds were faded and dry. The dust and heat, the burning wind, reminded of many things: stimulating extremes of climate, burning summers when the plants strove against the sun, the color and smell of strong weeds under the great bowl of the sky.

And yet there, the wild animals wandered and fed as though they were in a pasture that stretched all around them, to the very edge of the world. The sun had baked the land into a dry and dusty mass, with little cracks running through it. The sun had burned the tops of the grass blades until they were the same color to be seen everywhere. In all directions. And they went on, grazing the dry grass in a Prairie of desperate Immensity . . .*

Now the passage of time becomes incomprehensible. Between the arrival of the hot day and now, the heat had not lessened, time slowly revolving. Crimson and gold horses trotted along, crossing the plain in heat and a sense of loneliness far more intense than anywhere else in the world.

The plain now was empty, not a creature moved on it beside the horses. There was such a sound of wind rattling that dry grass, but the noises of hot grass—of crickets, the hum of flies—were a

---

* There, in the continental trough, is the hardest weather in the world. In winter there are blizzards, which come bearing hail and sleet and snow and ice. Hot tornadic winds, heavy clouds, torrential rains arise in the spring, and in summer the prairie is an anvil's edge. Loneliness is there as an aspect of the land. Loneliness and silence and memory. Yes, all things in the plain are isolate; there is no confusion of objects in the eye, but one hill or one tree. To look upon that landscape is to lose the sense of proportion. Your imagination comes to life, and this, you think, is where Creation was begun.

tone that was close to silence. Whenever the sound of the wind died away, it was like the air itself had caved in. Nothing moved. Not a leaf. No birds sang. No sound. But everywhere the sky and earth were listening, and everything was so still that nature's repetition overtook the empty land without hope of anything, simply going on because there was nothing but anonymous stretches of prairie. There was just the stillness and the silence and the sound of the horses breathing and the sound of their hooves clopping.

And on across the lonely fields, through the tough prairie grass, the horses trod. In a perfect circle, the sky curved down to the level land, and they loped along in the circle's exact middle. An hour passed, and then another, and they couldn't get out of the middle of that circle. The horses began to strain and rear, but there was nothing to do but plod on. There was no water. Nothing new to look at. There was no sound, not any. There was only the enormous, empty prairie. And on the whole enormous prairie there were no signs of biological life-forms except the hawks and buzzards circling in the blue sky. There wasn't so much as a grasshopper on the plains. A few of the horses tried to stop and graze, but there was nothing left to graze on. No grass. There was only the enormous, empty prairie. There was the feeling of a weight of light—pressing the rough country. Three or four miles away the sun shone in much the same fashion. And miles farther the same thing. The wind blew through, the smell of burned dust was in the air, and the air was dry so that the light air about told that the world ended here, only the ground and sun and sky were left, and if one went a little farther there would be only sun and sky, and one would float into them, like the tawny hawks which sailed over, making slow shadows on the dirt.

8

IT MUST HAVE BEEN THE SCARCITY OF DETAIL IN THAT tawny landscape that made detail so precious. Nothing happened under the sun. The land was level, and there were no trees. No grass. But there was a hot breath coming from the south.

While the hours passed, the sun moved on in its course and the shadow of the afternoon moved out, lumbering away and behind, the mustang herd strung out across the prairie. Now that the sun was on the wane, some of the impact was gone, and while the air was hot, the hammering rays were weaker. Still, when there was nothing to see around but a few horses, the horses were nervous.

In the late afternoon, the country began to change slightly for the better. The grass improved, and occasionally sunflowers grew; some of them were as big as little trees, with great rough leaves and many branches which bore dozens of blossoms. Occasionally one of the horses would tear off with his teeth a plant full of blossoms and walk along munching it, the flowers nodding in time to his bites as he ate down toward them. Over the gently curving land, antelopes became more common, and now and then a rabbit bounded away. Sometimes a prairie hen with her brood of prairie chicks scuttled out of sight in the grass.

As the herd galloped out of the barren plain, it seemed to all of them that they were leaving behind not only heat and drought but ugliness and danger too. Green appeared. And water and deep shade. Occasionally there were clumps of trees and bushes. The herd found good grass, grazing when there was anything to graze on, swishing their tails back and forth with pleasure.

The prairie had changed again, and the grass was thick as a carpet there. Thistles were blowing across the uplands. Through the grass, past the horses, the ground sloped westward: prairie dogs watched flocks of little prairie chickens running and pecking around their anxiously clucking, smooth brown mothers. The dogs were out, dozens of them, sitting up on their hind legs over the doors of their homes. They barked and shook their tails and scurried underground.

The prairie-dog-town was spread out over perhaps ten acres. The grass had been nibbled short and even, so this stretch was not shaggy like the surrounding country, but velvety. The holes were several yards apart and were disposed with a good deal of regularity, almost as if the town had been laid out in streets and avenues. One felt that an orderly and very sociable kind of life was going on there. Before the mouths of the holes were little patches of sand and gravel, scratched up from a long way below the surface. Here and there in the town came larger gravel patches, several yards away from any hole.

It was on one of these gravel beds that suddenly the dogs started up from the dust and listened. Something was wrong. The prairie hens were jumping up and down in a state of great ferment. Suddenly, a mass of snakes streamed across the ground, rippling between the grass stems or lying so still that only their tiny flickering tongues and glittering eyes showed that they were alive. The prairie hens ran silently, their necks outstretched and their wings spread. The dogs scurried underground. The floor was dusty from use, like a little highway over which much travel went.

Now, as the snakes crawled down a path which they had often used before, the procession was constant. Snakes, rattlesnakes, glided in their most brilliant blue and yellow guise. And there, on one of those dry gravel beds, was the biggest snake ever seen. He was sunning himself, lying in long loose waves, like a letter "W."

The serpent in the grass was sex.* He was not merely a big

---

* It may also be disclosed that the snake is just a husk of doves; when the snake dies, great clouds of seminal-gray doves will flutter out and bring tidings of peace around the world.

snake—he was a circus monstrosity. His abominable muscular-
ity, his loathsome, fluid motion, somehow made his ugly head
look like a king-sized roll of steel wool. In the trees the squirrels
gazed at him, all together, for a moment, before returning to their
feeding. A great black bird was flapping and hopping a little way
behind the serpent and watched. The snake whispered, remained
motionless except for the black, delicate tongue which flickered in
and out from time to time, for several lifetimes.

9

IT WAS A LONG, LONG TIME BEFORE THE SNAKES CRAWLED out of the bottoms and the prairie hens came walking again; it was almost sunset. The sun had lowered until it threw long shadows on the ground. Small birds come to feed in the evening cool of the open country flushed and flared away over the grasstops, and the hawks in silhouette waited in the upper limbs of a tree for them to pass.

Upcountry, the horses stepped slowly through the pasture where cows and calves stood. Miles of grass were drenched in sunlight that was stronger than at any other time of the day. The fields were red gold, the cows chewed and threw long shadows. And in the manada were mares who took a great interest in what they saw, and some would look back at the cows chewing in enormous fields, lying and standing. Those of them that were spotted with white reflected the sunshine in dazzling brilliancy, and the polished brass knobs of their horns glittered with something of military display.

The sun slowly sank. All around the edge of the prairie the sky flushed pink. That hour always had the exultation of victory, of triumphant ending. It was a sudden transfiguration, a lifting-up of day—how many an afternoon had passed along the prairie under that magnificence! Across the fields, the sun dropped and lay like a great golden globe in the low west. While it hung there, the moon rose in the east, as big as a cart-wheel, pale silver and streaked with rose colour, thin as a bubble or a ghost-moon.* For five, perhaps

---

* Who would have thought that the moon could dazzle and flame like that? The moon looks wonderful in this warm evening light, just as a candle flame looks beautiful in the light of morning. Light within light. It seems like a metaphor for something. So much does.

ten minutes, the two luminaries confronted each other across the level land, resting on opposite edges of the world.

In that singular light, every little tree and shock of wheat, every sunflower stalk and clump of snow-on-the-mountain, drew itself up high and pointed; the very clods of the fields seemed to stand up sharply, felt the old pull of the earth, the solemn magic that comes out of those fields at nightfall. The curly grass was on fire now. The bark of the oaks turned red as copper, and the light trembled in the thickets as if little flames were leaping among them. The breeze sank to stillness. A ringdove mourned plaintively, and somewhere off in the bushes an owl hooted.

Presently there were no clouds. The sun was going down in a limpid, gold-washed sky. Just as the lower edge of the red disk rested on the high fields against the horizon, a great black figure suddenly appeared on the face of the sun: the big elm tree standing in the field. The sun was sinking just behind it. Magnified across the distance by the horizontal light, it stood out against the sun, was exactly contained within the circle of the disk. There it was, heroic in size, a picture writing on the sun.

Through the long red sunset, the sun burned forever and stayed balanced on the horizon for an age. So it seemed that time stopped; time hung unchanging, or with no more visible change than a slow reddening of poison oak leaves, an imperceptible darkening of the golden hills. Then the ball dropped and dropped until the red tip went beneath the earth. A shadow came over the prairie just then, and the last remnants of sunlight were being driven toward the low hills to the south. Though the sky was bright yellow with afterglow, the mounds ahead did have a bluish electric look, almost as if blue lightning had condensed over their tops. The fields below were dark, and that elm tree had sunk back to its own littleness somewhere on the prairie.

The light was going gradually. Where the sun had gone down, the sky was turquoise blue, like a lake, with gold light throbbing in it. Higher up, in the utter clarity of the west, the evening star hung like a lamp suspended by silver chains, like the lamp engraved upon the title page of old Latin texts, which is always appearing in new heavens. As the sky darkened, more stars were coming, more, more, flickering like lighted lamps, growing steadier and more golden. A few tough zinnias and marigolds and a row of scarlet sage bore witness.

There, after sundown, the last color was fading from the enormous sky and all the level land was shadowy. Nighthawks were chasing insects in the dark air. Bullfrogs were croaking in the creek bottoms.* A bird called, "Whip! Whip! Whip-poor-Will!" "Who? Whoo?" said an owl. Far away, a cold wind blew. The birds hushed. The sky bent to listen. Everything seemed to grow blacker, except for the fireflies whose tiny pulsing lights drew arcs through the dark summer air. On off . . . on off . . . on off . . . on off.

---

* The bullfrogs a-cluttering the quietude of night, serenading one another across the water. The three frogs croaking, Krak!, Krek!, and Krik!, at one, nine, seventeen, twenty-five, etc., and at one, six, eleven, sixteen, etc., and at one, four, seven, ten, etc., respectively: Krak!   —   —   —   —

```
—        —        —      Krek!      —        —        —        —      Krek!
—        —      Krik!      —        —      Krik!      —        —      Krik!
—      Krak!      —        —        —        —        —        —        —
—      Krek!      —        —        —        —      Krek!      —      Krik!
—        —      Krik!      —        —      Krik!    Krak!      —        —
—        —        —        —        —        —        —        —      Krek!
—        —        —        —        —      Krik!      —        —      Krik!
—        —      Krak!      —        —        —        —        —        —
—      Krek!      —        —        —        —      Krek!      —      Krik!
```

10

IT WAS A STILL, DEEP-BREATHING SUMMER NIGHT, FULL OF the smell of fields, the night air. Somehow the hum and heat of the day seemed far in the past, and now the wind was right. The world seemed reversed here. Horses rested from their exertion. The crickets and the meadowlarks, the rabbits and the flies slept on the dim and purple vastness of the plains. There were stars by the millions, birds flyin across the moon. Geese maybe. The large star winked.

As the hours passed, the full moon rose high into the sky, lighting the land. A faint breeze stirred and cooled sensationally, significantly, consistently. Midnight came and passed silently, for there was nothing to announce it. Around the middle of the night, the moon was well over in the west, and the plains were very dark. Anything could come out of the darkness—coyotes, snakes. But here there was no sound, not any. The horses were silent, the crickets, the locusts, the owls. There was only the sound of the wind rustling the grass.

At some point during the night, the first gray of daylight began in the sky, and a dark moving mass came over the western hill, a dark figure outlined by a gray blur of faint light that seemed to come from all quarters of the horizon at once. Sometimes it made a sound. The sound was comforting and reminded of a cow or a bull in a spring meadow. And, in fact, it was a moocow coming down along the grass. It brought a story of the passing hours to the fields and trees.

See, once upon a time and a very good time it was this moocow that was coming down along the grass met a nicens little pond, with rusty willow bushes growing about it. The cow was a little spotted calf. And the little calf curved round this little pond, beyond which it began to climb the hill, and lowed through the fields, crushing the silent grass, pounding the silent ground. The little calf wandered about the fields under the star-sprinkled sky, rambled into the rich scenery and luxuriant meadows, till morning put out the fireflies and the stars, until the sun leapt above the prairie, and, in the grass about the calf, all the small creatures of day began to tune their tiny instruments. Birds and insects without number began to chirp, to twitter, to snap and whistle, to make all manner of fresh shrill noises.

The sun had come up brilliantly. The ground was flooded with light; every clump of ironweed and snow-on-the-mountain threw a long shadow, and the golden light seemed to be rippling through the curly grass like the tide racing in. All about giant grasshoppers were doing acrobatic feats. The gophers scurried up and down. The earth was warm. The air was cool enough to make the warm sun pleasant and so clear that the eye could follow a hawk up and up, into the blazing blue depths of the sky.

Over gently curving land the sun just shone and the mulberry tree just glistened in the long grass. At a pond nearby—a big pond, where so many birds come—meadow larks hopped here and there while the long-billed snipe flickered round in great circles. The ducks were floating with their heads deep in the water as though they searched the bottom for food.

Here, into this pond, wild birds come from all quarters of the horizon. It is a part of life in their jolly way across the plains. They fly all the way from the ocean or mountains, or any natural features of the terrain. They must have water to drink and to bathe in before they can go on their journey, so they go looking for an area with water. They look this way and that, and far below them they see something shining, like a piece of glass set in the earth. They come to it and are not disturbed. There was a crane last week. She spent one night and came back the next evening. The following day another bird arrived, sat for a few minutes on the fallen log by the pond, and flew on almost immediately.

This morning a big white bird with long wings and pink feet

came and kept flying about the pond and screaming until dark. She was in trouble of some sort. She was going over to the other ocean, maybe, and did not know how far it was. She was afraid of never getting there. She was more mournful than the other birds here; she cried in the night. Next morning, when the sun rose, she flew up into the sky and went on her way, disappeared over the rim of the prairie.

II

WHEN THE BIG WHITE BIRD FLEW, THE GREEN PLAINS stretched past in a leisurely flow, the empty, flat country wheeling by like a great turntable. Some places had lots of trees, some did not; some fields were green, some were not, and the hills in the distance were like the hills in every distance. Twenty-two miles ahead, the grass was short and gray. Thirty miles away, grazing peacefully on the great plains, were pale herds of antelope, and near by the demure prairie-dogs sat up.

The country rolled away toward the plains of woods and hills where the winds were always blowing and the grasses seemed to sing and whisper and laugh. To the north were sandy slopes where grass only grew in tufts. West and south, across the earthy-smelling plains, across the rolling land of the creek bottoms, masses of trees covered some of the low, rounded hills, and some of them were grassy, open spaces, and they went on for twenty miles.

In the far distance, the roll of the plains got longer; the heat shimmers gave way to cool air. The skies seemed deeper than the skies in the lower plains. Their depth and blueness robbed even the sun of its harsh force—it seemed smaller, in the vastness, and the whole sky no longer turned white at noon as it had.

Farther and farther into the vast prairie the big white bird flew, mile after mile, hour after hour, past weeds growing green, past fields of wheat, past flocks of crows that flapped heavily to the ground, past herds of nondescript cattle with cowbirds sitting on their hipbones. Always, somewhere to the north, there was a swath of blueness, with white clouds floating in it like petals in a pond. The beauty of the high prairies stretched across an enormous emptiness, the interminable plains.

The big white bird drifted through the wild afternoon in a beautiful motion. The sun was well up in the sky, and it threw a brilliant pattern of light across the land. Now the distant view was thinned with haze, and the eye traveled for fifty miles before haze and a gradually ascending tableland blurred on the horizon.

About the middle of that afternoon, the bird suddenly noticed an unusually heavy gust of wind sweep eastward across the prairie, with the promise of more wind behind it. The air was cold and smelled of wet stone. The big white bird continued on across the grass until . . . Wait! To the west, at a great distance, emerged a faint, jagged blue line, low on the horizon. The shadowy outline was a mysterious sheet of shade until it rose miraculously out of the land: faint as a watermark on pale blue paper was the tracery of mountains, tenuous and far-off, but today accessible.

Toward the mountains the country was rolling and grassy, serene and cool. The land rolled like great stationary ground swells. But the slow succession of rise and fall in the plain changed and shortened. The earth's surface became lumpy, rising into mounds and knotted systems of steep small hills cut apart by staring gashes of sand, where water poured in the spring from the melting snow. After a time, the most startling visions were the mountains, their ragged peaks towering above in great sepulchral forms, filling alternatively with a feeling of romance or adventure.

Never halting the rhythmic advance that the mountains themselves intended, the bird was driven by deep inner compulsion, and it flew on and on. The ridges of hills kept moving closer, as if the plains were being folded into pleats. The flat stone shelves were advancing, and the distant reaches of the sky were shrinking into waves of bluish mountains. Far ahead, these mountains covered an extensive land area, and the air surrounding them was so pure that from a distance, it was impossible to calculate how far away they were. Of course, the air was just as pure around ranges to the north, but they were not faced by flat plains, so the phenomena did not apply to them. The good part was that close up, these splendid ranges were just as impressive as they had been at a distance. They dominated the plains and served as a backdrop to extraordinary beauty.

To the west, one could see range after range of blue mountains, and at last the snowy range, with its white, windy peaks. The mountains, the magnificent, uncountable mountains, were "papier-mâché," rocky forms so unusual they seemed to have been placed in position by an artist. Without foothills, though with curving approaches which spread some distance out upon the ground and then up at the hills, the mountains raised a magnificent barricade against the sky, the highest jagged crests floating in mist 8,000 feet above: up and up, granite rocks and stunted pines; stone accumulated in flat layers, one above the other like sheaves of paper in a pile; hills so steep that no horse could climb them. They were of innumerable, indefinable rock colors—grayish yellows, dull olives, old rose, elusive purples, and browns as rich as prairie soil. And over the whole area hung a smoky pall of energy, sometimes hiding trees, sometimes breaking into separated clouds between peaks.

Closer to the mountain range there was a little more wind in the sky than there had been. Now the wind grew strong and the bird dipped, made a quick drop, slanting down on back-swept wings. Down here, below, there were gentle hills and open sunny places. Here grew the tall trees whose tops the bird had seen from above. Shady groves were scattered on the rolling meadows, and in the groves, deer were lying down, hardly to be seen among the shadows. As the bird flew past, the deer turned their heads, and curious fawns stood up to see it more clearly.

The bird flew through the grass a long way, in the midst of great beauty, complex, almost chaotic beauty, such as the Mountains often display. For a while, the high, bare cliffs stood up, the ring of the mountains growing higher. But sometimes when the wind was coming and the trees stood upright against the sky, the mountains were almost hidden behind the hills and trees. The bird went higher in the air, and those strange cliffs rose up again. Then the mountains sheering up before the bird were very real and solid.

In a little while, that sweep of flat land shrunk beneath the high, abrupt thrust of the mountains. The peaks of the mountains came closer together in the sky, purpling in the shadows, the rock glowing golden red far back on the faces of the inner peaks. Where the sun came through it reached the margin of the crevices, then, trickling down the granite sides, cut violent shadows on the ledges and brought the mountains into the jiving finality of a form.

The bird that never alights flew on and on toward higher land. But in the place where an entrance should have been there was none. No crack. No stream that made a kind of gulch between the rocks. No mouth of a canyon. Perhaps the bird had flown for nothing, nothing, nothing. All the time it held its flight, but there was no real sense of motion. All that happened was that the steep thrust of the mountains grew higher and higher, until it was a jagged, absolute border to the world. As the bird went farther, the illusion became more instead of less convincing: the granite barrier was rising.

12

IT SEEMED THE BIRD WAS TRYING TO BREAK FROM THE
closed room of prairie and sky into the vastness of these mountains. Round and round it flew, under the old red walls like a
heron, milk white with a long black bill. It flew as a heron does,
legs trailing, with a down-curved, powerful wingbeat. It soared up
into the sun around the cliff, then down to a riverside clearing at
the foot of a grassy knoll.

The bird looked up, and everything fell into place. There in
the shallows, in the deep light of the fading afternoon, the mountains parted, flaring open like two wings—one wing green, made
of vertical needles, with whole pines serving as the pile of a solid
carpet, the other reddish-brown, made of naked rock, ploughed
with steep channels, broken with jutting knobs. Into those mountains, through broken light and shadow, the cordilleras rose and
sank. Distant mountains. Near mountains. More mountains.
Bluish beauties never attainable, or ever turning into hill after
hill. Southeastern ranges, altitudinal failures as alps go. To the
west heart and sky-piercing snow-veined colossi of stone, relentless
peaks appearing from nowhere, the clouds caught here and there
on their spurs.

After drinking from the river, the big white bird flew suddenly up and wheeled into the mountain range, second highest
on the earth. The bird was actually in the mountains, no goofing
around. Sheer rock faces rose all around, so high you could barely
see their tops. Into the northward loop of the river, through the
river trees, the sun touched and missed and touched again. Again
and again, the eye couldn't fix on a place. Things swam into sight
and out again, the pine trees rising still and tall, the river winding,

the mountains shouldering up to the timberline. The plains were shut out from sight here by design.

Well into the mountains, the distance heaved with stony ridges, needles, pyramids in whose shadowed cirques the snow curved smoothly. The imagination seemed to spring to full life in the clear air, beyond the rein of reason, and to look was to help-lessly see fresh clumps of rapidly moving fluff clouds over the dark beauty of the mountain-tops. It was a scene of high and wild excitement: towering mountains watching over a long oceanic roll of ridges and peaks, a forested valley stretching southward, a peak like an ear on its side.

Some twenty kilometers into the mountains, the jagged peaks were much bigger, wrought with illimitable joy in achievement by the Maker of Worlds. Over the distant mountains to the west and south—who knew how far?—an even taller mountain reared into the sky, its jagged tip only a silhouette that was now nimbused by the sun, which was beginning its decline. The distant peak was a noble peak of itself and would have been outstanding even if it had no significant features, but up its eastern flank crawled a granite beaver. It was really the oddest thing, but from a vantage point, this master-mountain, a thing of obvious majesty, moved like some animated mountain; up its side with immortal persistence climbed the little stone beaver.*

Along the precipice the sun was a long time descending, redden-ing where it deepened and flared over the west. Majestic! Majestic! The mountains and valleys and more mountains blasted with light. Long thin clouds of flamingo red, with edges like the edges of curled ostrich feathers, lay up and down the sky at different altitudes. Distant flocks looked no more than bits of string against the raucous red of the sky, and they were far too distant to be heard.

---

* This peak should have been called Beaver Mountain. Other peaks had poetic names—one with a perpetual mark of snow in its crisscrossed ravines had an alliterative ring—but the best mountain of them all, with a little beaver crawl-ing up its flank, was given the drabbest name of all . . .

As the sun turned red, the rock of the mountains to the west looked like a brewery at dusk, yellow and old. Far up in the purple shades of rock, the mountains rose in such splendor that when the sun was sinking in a fiery glory—deep laminar red—the sunset held the back mountains and higher places, and their fantastic shapes exhibited Nature in her most sublime and striking attitudes. Here her vast magnificence elevated the mind of the beholder to enthusiasm. Fancy caught the thrilling sensation, and at her touch the towering steeps became shaded with unreal glooms; the caves more darkly frowned; the projecting cliffs assumed a more terrific aspect. The romantic beauty of the surrounding scenery invited reverential awe, and thoughts involuntarily rose, "from Nature up to Nature's God."

It was at sunset that the mountains came into their own. On some days clouds would rest over them like a light blanket and reflect the dying sun. Then the mountains would be bathed in splendor, gold and red and soft radiant browns and deep blues would color the underside of the clouds and frame the mountains in a celestial light, a setting so grand that it seemed to have been ordained solely for stupefaction. The loveliest moment came, however, when the sun had set and its flamboyant coloring had faded. Then, for about twenty minutes, the softest colors of the spectrum played about the crests of the mountains, and the little stone beaver crawled toward the summit to sleep.

While the sun sank and the west wind moved along the peaks, presently, a change had come over the mountains, as if they were robbed of their earthly substance and composed merely of intense blue mist. The near ones blue as eyes or jay feathers, the further ones fading to cloudy purple, the ghosts of mountains. The last dying gleams of day tinted the rocks, and the red sun that burned in the broad gap of the mountains sloughed out of its form and was slowly sucked away to light all the sky in a deep red afterflash, throwing into black relief the broken skyline.

Pretty soon the redness turned purple. As light began to fade and vast streaks of color shot out from the mountains, the sunset left bright streaks in the snow on the upper peaks. Under the shadow of those peaks, things dim and dimming. The drowsy river. The quiet hills. Dark canyons cutting into the slopes. Trees, trees, millions of trees, massive, immense, running up high, the dark foliage spreading a pensive gloom around, offered a scene congenial to the present temper while night was beginning to rise from the earth into the sky.

13

THE MOUNTAINS AT NIGHT APPEARED FAR DIFFERENT THAN in the daytime. In the daytime they were silent, but at night they seemed to stir and rouse themselves. A little after sunset the mountains rose sheer from every side, heaving their gigantic crests far up into the night, the black peaks crowding together, and looking now less like beasts than like a company of cowled giants.

As the night advanced, the moon rose in the east, and very high and very faint one could hear the noises that the mountains made in their living—their immensity, their enormous power, crude and blind, was heard, rising now and then to a noble requiem. The wind's motion, the calls of birds, and the surging sound of the river were now a crescendo upon the air, and o'er the scene, from the cañon, from the crowding crests, from the whole immense landscape, there rose a steady and prolonged sound, coming from all sides at once. It was that incessant and muffled roar which disengages itself from all vast bodies, from oceans, from forests, and which is like the breathing of an infinitely great monster, alive, palpitating. Louder and higher and lower and wider the sound and motion spread, mounting, sinking, darking. The trees blew steadfastly one way as the hollow sounding wind swept by; the river continually rolled along with its deep, resounding murmurs. The sounds and the breeze would last all night, as the stars moved across the sky and the moon followed. The next morning having little or no wind, however, all these sounds made a great, warm, happy silence. The wind had died down completely and the sky began to lighten.

It was gray dawn. The stars had dimmed out and the dark shapes of the mountains stood along the sky. From the transparent

green of ice, the sky melted into pale gold, and the gold spread into
a floral yellow. Then the sun flung a long shaft over the mountain, and another, like a long-legged insect bracing itself out of its
chrysalis, and then it showed above the black crest, bristly and red
and improbable, the color of that forgotten morning which was the
first seen on earth.

As the great sun rose from the east, the country shaped itself
out of the darkness. A few spindled clouds smoldered and glowed
a most unfiery pink. Papier-mâché mountains grew red. The light
leaned on these eastward-facing mountains, gilding the ridges
southward and making a moiré of the varying leaf-faces in the
gulches.

Toward the rising sun the whole valley floor was spread out,
steep ranges and forests walled in on all four sides, almost without a break. There were trees, a thick cluster of spruce, a clump of
twinkling, sunny aspen down the slope, and below, a dense forest
of soft maple. In the sunny open spaces the grass grew thin (deer
had cropped it short), and the columbines were pure and tall and
white, sometimes a space of half an acre solidly white with them.
Farther up, around the flank of this mountain and its ravines, the
columbines were not so large, not so tall, but their petals were
touched with the palest blue and pink, like the blush of blood
through a transparent skin.

In the very picturesque valley, the hills came down into the
river on the north like three folds in a blanket. To the east the
mountains were eclipsed. To the west they stood in balmy light.
Along the south side rose great masses of granite, looking like ships
or sulking prehistoric animals, beyond which, disappearing finally
in a gauzy blue, were the highest mountains of all, which seemed
as far away as the end of the world. And here, lying below, the valley was now much more pleasant than it had been. Phoebe-birds
called from the woods. There was some white tail deer, and a right
smart o' jack rabbits, and up and up a rocky shelf in the mountain's
side two goats lived in subtle and long-approved harmony.

One of the goats was more like seeing two black wings up and nothing in between—two black wings thin and raised and barely moving, and then two spots as dark as coal, two spots like eyes under wings like horns. The smaller animal, another goat high on a ledge, sat down on its tail like a dog, its long face dull and curious under the spiked horns, the hair hanging in a beard from its chin, hanging in an apron across its front.

Imagine this animal. It had the dignity and dimensions of a canon. It had the sculptured look of naked mountains. It wasn't a goat. It wasn't a creature at all. It was something grown out of these rocks; it was something a crazy mind made up; it was an old spirit from the top of the world.

As the animal breathed, flies buzzed in a great peace. The breeze had risen steadily and there was a faint scent, a faint noise of bees, a wonderful quickness of happy morning. The valley was full of a calm and dry-eyed practicality. Even so, the goat sensed danger. Its head lifted and its oars came up and its black eyes shone with looking. It didn't raise its gaze. It kept it lower, on the rim and cup of the valley, as if enemies always came from below.

Away down below now, a little animal twittering somewhere near by made a small frightened cheep like a field mouse. The goat sat back farther on its tail, a look of slow surprise on its face, for there, dizzyingly far down below the ridge, there was a little glade with a flat rock in the center like a table. Beside the flat rock, a mountain lion.

She was about as big as a good-sized dog and she looked for all the world like an overgrown house cat. She was honey-coloured all over save for her face, which was darker, a sort of yellow-brown. And the sun illuminated her so clearly that it was as if the goat saw her close up: the mountain lion standing still, feeding on a jackrabbit. She delicately moved the rabbit with her paw and then savagely ripped it with her teeth.

14

THE SILENCE AT THE MOMENT OF EXECUTION AND FOR A moment or two continuing thereafter was pure. Nothing interfered. The cat crouched back, chewed and swallowed, and the entrails hung from its mouth.

The silence was horrible. No rustling of the leaves—no bird's note in the wood—no cry of water-fowl from the pools of the hidden lake. It chewed and swallowed, and the silence deepened.

After a few minutes passed, this emphasized silence was gradually disturbed by a sound not easily to be verbally rendered: a sound in the chokecherry bushes beyond. The mountain lion lifted her heavy head for only a few seconds, her long tail twitching, and then she bounded across the place where the columbines grew and disappeared among the trees.

The lion had peril in her, under her tawny hide, in the way her tail had moved, in the way she streaked across the flat land. She might now have climbed a tree like a tame cat and might be sitting there observing with large green eyes. In the glade where she had been, she had left her food, too startled to carry it off. A half-eaten jackrabbit lay beside a tree stump, its entrails chewed but its silly head intact and twisted to a sheepish angle. It had been mauled and slobbered on and its grizzled hair was clotted.

It was a unique and horrific situation, a highly distressing sight. The slaughterous red elevated the mind of the beholder to the awful meaning of such an event. But it was not so much the violence of this wilderness death that made the sight sinister; there was something disturbing about all death in the definite green of the world. Everywhere the imminent threat of death was only a question of time. Death was marching in relentless order across

the world, crushing, obliterating, destroying everything—all those
dead fish in the sea, yes! Thousands! Millions! All the storm-tossed
dead trees standing stark and white. Rotten stumps. Dead branches.
Then there were the barren lands full of tall dead weeds. A dead
colt in a field, the poor form stretched in tainted grass, eyeless and
naked. God was not always forgiving—especially in the streams,
lakes, and fields of these mountains.

It was a cruel land. They were beautiful mountains, but they
were hard; the mountains did not forgive many mistakes. Nature
might hurl a big thunderstorm, a big case o' lightnin' and thunder.
A hail storm might come up. Occasional catastrophes like earth-
quakes or floods might compress into one convulsion the losses for
an average millennium; a flood might carve away deposits which
had required ten million years to accumulate. Death was in the
sky, in the bone light. Death was coursing through the valley. It
might be a rabbit; it might be a mole; might see the ruins of a por-
cupine, teeth here, tail there; two bucks charging one another and
then, by lunatic accident, being joined as one, toppling into a river
to drown, still struggling to get free—the escaping current might
carry them down the stream, rushing like the buffalo over cliffs to
certain disaster.

This hyeh is a mighty cruel country. Mountain is an ugly
word—for animals, that is. Think of it! Animals lead lives of compulsion and necessity within an unforgiving social hierarchy, in
an environment where the supply of fear is high and the supply
of food low, and where territory must constantly be defended and
parasites forever endured. Animals are, in practice, free neither
in space nor in time, nor in their personal relations. The smallest changes can upset them. They want things to be just so, day
after day, month after month. Surprises are highly disagreeable to
them. You see this in their spatial relations. An animal inhabits
its space in the same way chess pieces move about a chessboard—
significantly. There is no more happenstance, no more "freedom,"
involved in the whereabouts of a lizard or a bear or a deer than in
the location of a knight on a chessboard. Both speak of pattern

and purpose. In the wild, animals stick to the same paths for the same pressing reasons, season after season.

Animals are territorial. That is the key to their minds. Only a familiar territory will allow them to fulfill the two relentless imperatives of the wild: the avoidance of enemies and the getting of food and water. Across the mountains, rabbits and field mice and all other small, hunted squirrel-like animals that feel safer in the concealing light crept and hopped and crawled and froze to resemble stones or small bushes when ear or nose suspected danger. Yes, and there were animals that bleached themselves over the eons, like a bird or a once-brown mouse that color-matched itself to escape the gaze of predators. The predators were working, too—the long weasels like waves of brown light; the cobby wildcats crouching near to the ground, almost invisible except when their yellow eyes caught light and flashed for a second; the foxes, sniffling with pointed up-raised noses for a warm-blooded supper; the raccoons padding near still water; talking frogs.

The sour smell of the bones was everywhere across the mountains. The wind in low and melancholy whispering sighed. The elms bent to one another, like giants who were whispering secrets, stories of hundreds of miles of wild timberland, hundreds of thousands of caribou, hundreds of millions of salmon in suicidal dashes up the rivers; of woods full of bear and deer and otter and fox and wolverine and mink at war with one another; and the bushes and the wild flowers and weeds, all ravening for earth and light. That cunt of a mountain range was composed in part of rock, but it was all wall. All these animals, and others, had fallen prey to predators with long, murderous teeth that protruded noticeably from their mouths. Let us hope that what wildlife remains can survive in what is left of the natural world. For heaven's sake, let us hope that it would finally be morning in the mountains, true to form, none of this gloom. Let us sing of purple mountain majesties: *oh beautiful, for spacious skies, for amber waves of grain, for purple mountain majesties, and penury, and pain . . .*

15

AMID THESE THOUGHTS THE SKY HAD BY NOW GROWN murky. A terrible cold world of death had replaced the living world of the dawn. The ragged clouds were both a part of and apart from the grayness, unintentionally mimicking the grim silence which held these mountains.*

In the glade, the flies had found the little piles of rabbit entrails on the ground. The scent of blood was all around. Little darts of purple, that were running quail, crossed the glade. And a plaintive peeping came from the coverts.

The wind was blowing harder now. The pines groaned. Shrubs waved to the gale in deeper murmurs. In the distant west appeared a female eagle flying lazily in the sky. The eagle, soaring amidst the clouds, watched as a herd of mustangs followed the windings of a brook. The eagle watched with unconcern as the great beasts moved out in a single file. But as the mustangs moved north, she noticed that at a certain spot each animal shied to the left, and this was worth inspecting, so she hovered for some minutes to confirm her observation then flew in lazy circles till the herd passed.

As soon as the last straggler had come to this spot, looked down, and veered, she dropped like an arrow from aloft, keeping her eye on the spot and noticing with pleasure that her deduction had been right. Below her, in the dust beside a rock, was food.

Increasing her speed, she swooped to earth. At the last moment she extended her talons and grabbed at the object which had attracted her, an enormous rattlesnake some five feet long and very

---

* Overcasts enhance the mood.

thick in the middle. Instantly she leaped upon it, catching it squarely in the middle so that her claws dug all the way through that part of the snake's body. With a flap of her extended wings she soared into the air.

It was an awful, holy sight, full of magic and meaning. The eagle flew in wide circles, searching for an area of jagged rocks on which to drop the rattler. She flew with her eyes into the wind to assure herself that it was not strong enough to blow the snake off target when she dropped him. Locating what she wanted, she flapped her wings and rose to a great height and shook the snake free, watching with satisfaction as it crashed onto the rocks, impaling itself in a score of places.

The bird flapped its great wings slowly, lowering itself until its curved talons could catch the serpent again, and flew up into the air. Then another eagle came sailing through the trees. During two or three minutes, together they rose and swung across the skyline. They were golden eagles, a male and a female. They were cavorting, spinning and spiraling on the cold, clear columns of air, and they were beautiful. They swooped and hovered, leaning on the air, and swung close together, feinting and screaming with delight.

The female was full-grown, and the span of her broad wings was greater than any other bird's. There was a fine flourish to her motion; she was deceptively, incredibly fast, and her pivots and wheels were wide and full-blown. But her great weight was streamlined and perfectly controlled. She carried the snake; it hung shining from her feet, limp and curving out in the trail of her flight.

Suddenly her wings and tail fanned, catching full on the wind, and for an instant she was still, widespread and spectral, while her mate flared past and away, turning around in the distance to look for her. Then she began to beat upward until she was small in the sky, and she let go of the snake.

It fell slowly, writhing and rolling, floating out like a bit of silver thread against the wide backdrop of the land and clouds. While the female held still above, buoyed up on the cold current, the male swerved and sailed. He was younger than she and a little more than half as large. He was quicker, tighter in his moves. He let the carrion drift by, then suddenly he gathered himself and stooped, sliding down in a blur of motion to the strike. He hit the snake in the head, with not the slightest deflection of his course or speed, cracking its long body like a whip. Then he rolled and swung upward in a great pendulum arc, riding out his momentum.

At the top of his glide he let go of the snake in turn, but the female did not go for it. Instead she soared out over the valley, nearly out of sight, like a mote receding into the haze of the far mountain. The male followed. The rattlesnake lay motionless a long time.

16

THE SCENE ASSUMED A SOLEMN OBSCURITY. FOR SOME TIME that day, the smudge in the sky seemed to be swaying in waves across the valley, but now a tragic thing happened—another animal perished here. Most other animals now hid away in the brush or elsewhere. The warren rabbits didn't show themselves (they needed to think what was best to be done). Down at the river, the trout hid in its cold shallows, and high above were the thin feathers of white birds fleeing in clamourous confusion into the clouds.

At such times—under an abated sun and clouds dipping low and trailing across the crests of the mountains—the center of the valley was confronted on every side by indifference or hostility. It was as though all terrestrial things, all that nature, the fields, the waters, went into the trees and thickets to hide. The light was cold, and the full flush of summer was over, and the wind was then much higher.

The valley of humiliation remained a lead or slate colour all afternoon. Not a single object could be seen above the trees, because halfway down the mountains, long billows of vapour were frequently seen rolling. It was an ominous, suffocating fog, now wholly excluding the country, and now opening, and partially revealing its features, the mountain peaks above like islands in an ocean of fog.

The blind whiteness of the fog be'aved pretty contrary at times. Fog was creeping, twisting and looping, losing the valley sometimes and then finding it again. At times the fog was conspicuous from all directions, but what was significant about it was hidden. The mountains were at once remote and oppressively confining.

No birds were flying overhead. No living creature was visible or audible. The fog was as dense as cotton waste, an increasing growth of surrounding wool.

This continued in perfect silence. Nothing moved in that high wilderness save the wind. Nothing new to look at. The clouds were not dropping; they stood congealed on the edge of the earth and above. The cradle of fog and fog-bred pestilence seemed as if it would go on for ever . . .

The next day was no better. The skies were like iron. The light was still too faint. At dawn, there was no wind. Nothing moved. A faint breeze stirred in an hour or two, but it was still quiet, it was still gray. Another sad and melancholy day.

Around noon the wind began to rise. It came rushing from far heights, trying to clear a way through the clouds. At last the mist which hangs upon these three pages opened a small round hole in itself, lifting its corner. Through this opening, there appeared a strange optical effect: a valley cupped in the rocks, a canyon running back into the mountains. Then the wind changed and blew the mass of fog to swallow the earth.

After a few minutes passed, the wind rose up again. Inspirited by this wind of promise, for a moment some more powerful influence acted upon the distant land: the blanket was torn open, and through the hole, the floor of the valley seemed more clearly visible. A field, a forest, a river came slowly from the void, and for a long stretch of time, as the mist thinned, the tops of the spruces were like stains in the fog.

Then the fog was lifting. The clouds hung low and heavy overhead, but in the foreground and beyond, in all directions, there were only a few wispy thumbs of fog. The lineaments below were seen as through the suffusion of vapour. And if you knew where to look, you could see it, sometimes almost imperceptible: cougars strolled through a field of columbine and moved along the rock and down the slope to where the river widened. A veiled sunlight lit up faintly the grey sheet of water where the animals drank. In the distance, along the course of the slow-flowing river, it was as if other animals, in their animal ardour, jostled to get a nearer view of the water.

Presently, as the land came back out of the fog, the whole appearance of this moderately high mountain valley was different—wide, level, and very green. Everywhere the tall spruce trees showed coloring, from powdery blue to indigo. But it was still the river which fascinated the eye. The water was so clear that you could see the pebbles at the bottom of the shallow part. Blue and white and striped red. Very pretty even in the dim light. Its stream of water ran the length of the valley before joining the other river, the wandering river that connects these high regions, high mountains, to new landscapes, new places.

Not far from where it joined the big river down there, there came a quick gurgle. The channel was gorged and overflowed by this new river on top of the old. Some eighth of a mile further down hill, away from that valley, it made a different sound. As it flowed broadly by, the sound swelled with only a slight curve, but continuing downward, the margin of the river went into a crack between those earthen walls, a notch cut as sharply as a wedge out of a pie. The canyon walls opened out and back, went up steeply high and high and high. The river went howling through the narrows like a train.

17

THE RIVER SLID AND TWINED ITS GREAT VOLUME. AS IT wound its way, down, down, through miles of rocks, there was nothing else to be seen but the river winding, looping in wide meanders between the clumps of skinny trees and the seamed and cracked cliffs, shallowing to brief rapids, deepening along the cutbanks in the bends. But from time to time throughout this story of the river, the steep mud banks changed abruptly into low mud walls and turned and followed the line of the river, which ran straight, flowing smoothly without gravel shallows. Then the river would rouse itself, winding bright through the break in the walls again. There, sure enough, the river continually twisted and wound like a snake, and beyond, the windings were larger and less perceptible, and it went on for miles like this.

Every once in a while promising features would appear in the distance: the sunlight breaking suddenly through the clouds; the clouds grinding white against the sun. The buttery yellow light turned the sky and clouds into a fantastic world of sombre masses with lakelike spaces. The paler blue of the sky was as blue as just-washed café crockery.

Farther downstream the clouds were still giving off light, but the sky was blue—bluer than before, and pleasanter—the air was warm, and the land was level. For miles and miles the canyon and hill had gradually grayed and flattened the progress of the winding, and now looked like remnants of a broken dam, or like the broken lip of an iron pot, just at a simmer, endlessly distilling water into light. The river, which throughout most of its course was deep and rapid, had expanded to more than twice its customary width, and the rippling of its waters made a quiet, busy murmur, as if it were talking to itself of things seen upcountry. A soft liquid joy like the noise of many waters flowed over all the land.

Soon it was mid-afternoon. The sun was shining with a brightness that seemed almost supernatural despite those giant high steep canyon walls . . . It became hotter. On level ground, the river now was a sleepy, slow stream, twisted back and forth in its broad bed of gray sand, and the water was not milky with silt but clear and pleasant. The willows that grow in the river bed were well leafed, and the wild blackberry vines were thrusting their spiky new shoots along the ground. Here and there a patch of green was spread like a gay table-cloth over the sand.

The water looked like liquid crystal, absolutely colourless, without the slight brownish or greenish tint that water nearly always has. It threw off the sunlight like a diamond, reflecting the clouds and the green willows and deep hay grass and brilliant wild flowers on its banks. As it flowed, the kite wind blew steadily from the south and turned up the silver undersides of the leaves, and leaves were falling in the river, willow and cottonwood, coiling and turning in the current. Their shadows where they skated over the river stones looked like writing.

It was a beautiful place. The sun shone on the sand and the river and the leaves of the tree, and waves of heat shimmered from the stones. The scalloped canyon walls rippled in the heat like drapery folds. Everywhere were pungent, aromatic smells. The vast, moveless heat seemed to distill countless odors from the brush— odors of warm sap and of tar-weed, and above all the medicinal odor of witch hazel. As far as one could look, uncounted trees and manzanita bushes were quietly and motionlessly growing, growing, growing.

About a hundred yards downriver, the river and the great rocks that stood in the gorge looked much the same. The only difference? The sky was filled with flights of waterfowl circling and dropping in to the river. Perhaps a mile, perhaps a league distant, the canyon walls stopped; the river widened, came out into a great amphitheater into which jutted huge towering corners of a confluence of intersecting canyons. This wild cross-cut of huge stone gullies was wider and loftier and, in the shade, more resolutely blue than a thousand others. All about was ridgy roll of wind-smoothed, rain-washed rock and scrub, studded here and there with trees.

The course of running water in crossing this amphitheater went by the mouths of five canyons. Little streams flowed into the larger one under overhanging walls. A little way further on, the main stream ran down the arroyo over a white rock bottom, and into a narrow box canyon. It must be a mile away, but this narrow turned and twisted and opened into a valley that was beautiful and mysterious, gold-shot with looming wonder.

18

THE VALLEY WAS A GOLDEN, SUNLIT WORLD. ALL THINGS
seemed to converge there: canyons with springs, the fragrance of
hot sun and sage-brush, a wind that seemed to be sitting in the
heart of a world made of dusty earth and moving air. This sand,
this stone, these trees and cactuses, led off toward a mountain
range many miles away.

A kind of desert country began here. Here, across the low plain
rose great rock mesas, generally Gothic in outline, resembling vast
cathedrals. They were not crowded together in disorder but placed
in wide spaces, long vistas between. This plain might once have
been an enormous city, all the smaller quarters destroyed by time,
only the public buildings left—piles of architecture that were like
mountains; steep bare slopes and towers.

For miles under the piercing sun and all the rest of that
impressive spectacle, every mesa was duplicated by a cloud mesa,
like a reflection, which lay motionless above it or moved slowly
up from behind it. Sometimes they were flat terraces, ledges of
vapour; sometimes they were dome-shaped, or fantastic, like the
tops of silvery pagodas, rising one above another, as if a city lay
directly behind the rock. The great tables of granite set down in
an empty plain were inconceivable without their attendant clouds,
which were a part of them, as the smoke is part of the censer, or
the foam of the wave.

That afternoon there was always activity overhead, clouds forming and moving, sun pouring through. The desert and mesas were
continually re-formed and re-coloured by the cloud shadows. Now
and then, in the vastness of those plains, a shimmering heat distorted objects at a distance and made curving rivers seem covered

with tinfoil glinting under the sun. And as sometimes happens when a cloud falls, the land would move into shadow, the rivers sometimes breaking into separated, intense blue shadows. The whole country seemed fluid to the eye under this constant change of accent, this ever-varying distribution of light.

Here was also an infinite number of little lizards and beetles and other lowly things that crawled about. Lady bugs. Butterflies. Anything. Even a big lizard rustling in the brush. The scratch-scratch of unseen animals as they grouped and skittered could be heard behind the wind, but except for a panting lizard here and there, or a dust-gray jack-rabbit, startled from its covert, most animals squatted off there in the shadows of the brush and the distant clump of cottonwoods and wonderful wind-worn cliffs to the south.

Yes, the long line of trees were the cottonwoods. They prospered and they grew near the place where the river widened at the base of a mesa, where the rabbits ran and the beautiful valley quail, as purple in color as the sage, ran fleetly along the ground into the trees, where the sun slanted, and where the trunks were limed white. The trees rose out of the ground at a slant, and forty or fifty feet above the earth, all these white, dry trunks changed their direction, grew back over their base line. Some split into great forks which arched down almost to the ground; some did not fork at all, but the main trunk dipped downward in a strong curve, as if drawn by a bow-string; and some terminated in a thick coruscation of growth, like a crooked palm tree. They were all living trees, yet they seemed to be of old, dead, dry wood, and had very scant foliage. High up in the forks, or at the end of a preposterous length of twisted bough, would burst a faint bouquet of delicate green leaves—out of all keeping with the great lengths of seasoned white trunk and branches. The grove looked like a winter wood of giant trees, with clusters of mistletoe growing among the bare boughs.

It was pleasant under the trees, in the gold-flecked shade, with the whistle of quail and a couple of rabbits dashing off down the draw as if they were playing a game of some kind. Among the trees by the river, a little gray brush rabbit sat quietly in the sun, drying his breast fur. The sun fell warm upon his face like a hand with a lovely touch. The rabbit stretched out one hind leg lazily, froze when there had been a rhythmic vibration in the ground audible through his paws. The rabbit's nose crinkled, and his ears slewed around, investigating small sounds that might possibly be charged with danger to a brush rabbit. Turned out to be a small, most peculiar deer-like creature, gazing down in the vigour and intentness of youth upon the river and the leaves on the ground. Then again—now on that sand on the far side of the river—there had been sounds of interest but not of danger: a troop of small gazelle-like creatures—a small band of antelope—had come to drink, lifting and lowering graceful horned heads. No odor of fear came to the rabbit, for there was no conflict of interest between them. Like most animals that did not compete for the same food, they merely kept out of each other's way. In their splendid harmony, a full-grown antelope was lying, looking calmly and majestically over the river; the rabbit with tipped ears lay back in the hot sand and looked up at the blue sky.

In any direction from here, the animal would have had in view a beautiful object. Every disposition of the ground was good, and the river was low but pretty. There were the cottonwoods, close in front of the broken glitter of the river. And on the other side of the river, through atoms of grey-blue air, the sun struck at the mesa. It was no longer a blue, featureless lump, as it had been from a distance. Its sky-line was like the profile of a big beast lying down. The flanks around which the river curved were marvelous, sheer cliffs that fell from the summit to the plain, more than a thousand feet.

All the way round were the same precipitous cliffs of hard rock, but in places it was mixed with a much softer stone. In these soft streaks there were deep, dry watercourses, like a mouse track winding into a big cheese, but nowhere did they reach to the top of the mesa. The top seemed to be one great slab of very hard rock, lying on the mixed mass of the base like the top of an old-fashioned marble table. The channels worn out by water ran for hundreds of feet up the cliffs but always stopped under this great rim-rock, which projected out over the erosions like a granite shelf.

Evidently, it was because of this unbroken top layer that these animals, where they stood, would never see the sun or the moon or the stars from the top of the mesa.* Down here, below, there were gentle hills and open sunny places. The air was still and hot, and the cottonwoods and bushes along the river bed were all things in earth and heaven for the rabbits and antelope.

---

* But the birds and lizards were to be found there, moving and passing through. On top of the mesa, the rays of sunlight fell as red as a daylight fire. And there was not a tree or a blade of green upon it, not a handful of soil. And the air, God, what air!—it was like breathing the sun, breathing the colour of the sky, a sky so blue and bewildering that the gazer was rendered speechless with amaze-ment. And over the wide plain below, out over the great plain spotted with mesas and glittering rocks & scrub oak/cactus, there were hills that resembled rubble heaps. The land seemed to be in open formation, harsh and scarred, and you could almost read upheaval and convergence. It looked like dinosaur country.

19

AS THE DAY ENDED, ANTELOPE BECAME MORE COMMON around the mesa. The antelope stepped and nodded among the bushy scrub, but upstream the animals drank and rested. Other animals had gathered in the northeast where the river bends.

Around sunset, from then on, everything became softly amorphous. The soft eye of the antelope and the lovely rabbits in the dusty floor. The mesa and the light that overshot the plain. The slanting light turning the desert a dazzling orange-gold. As the sun sank lower and lower, all sounds gathered in the dimming sky. The wind sighed, and the running water murmured down its stone-bedded channel. Birds were coming down out of the half darkness upcountry and shearing away off the edge of the mesa, and the antelope moved like phantoms when they faded from swimming gold to rose, from rose to purple.

Soon the sun was going down behind the scrub hills northwest to bury its red curve under the dark horizon. Across the valley slumbering, fading purple fire burned over the undulating sage ridges. Long streaks and bars and shafts and spears fringed the far western slope. Drifting, golden veils mingled with low, purple shadows. Colors and shades changed in slow, wondrous transformation.

Night was coming down. At the foot of the mesa, the grey sage-brush and the blue-grey rock were already in shadow, the towering cottonwoods were thick and dark, but high above, the rocky walls were dyed flame-colour. The mesa was like a vast altar, shimmering purple in the royal sunset. In a few minutes it, too, was grey, and only the rim rock at the top held the red light. When that was gone, the mesa was like one great ink-black rock against a sky on fire. Abroad in the plain, the scattered mesa tops, red with the afterglow, one by one lost their light, like candles going out.

Night came there quickly after the sinking of the sun. The dark drew down around all about, and stars peeped out to brighten and grow. Soon the moon came forth and, flooding the landscape, shone through the huge, windy, eastern heave of sage. Blanched in moonlight, the sage yet seemed to hold its hue of purple and was infinitely more wild. The moon smiled from crater to crater.

All night a cold wind blew over the desert. All that land lay still and blue, and the whole sky moved across the ceiling, stars and constellations and misty blue clouds. The baby moon. What else? The shadows of the brush and the dust; they are part of life too. Gray thorn bushes. Cactus outlined in the moonlight.

It was after midnight when in the desert, on the mesa, alone under the stars and under the moon's white eye, the landscape was still. Hills, rocks, rivers seemed locked in sleep. The moonbeams dreamt upon the ground; stars slept in the glittering sky; clouds hung motionless in the sky. The moon was full, hanging directly over the mesa, which had never looked so solemn and silent. It was a wonderful sight to see the full moon looking down on the ruins of centuries, an appearance of great antiquity and of incompleteness.

20

THE DESERT LANDSCAPE IS ALWAYS AT ITS BEST IN THE half-light of dawn or dusk. The sense of distance lacks: a ridge nearby can be a far-off mountain range, each small detail can take on the importance of a major variant on the countryside's repetitious theme. The coming of day promises a change; it is only when the day has fully arrived that the eye divines—from sudden shifts of colour and then from other signs for which there are no words, nor even thoughts—it is the same day returned once again. The same place. The mesas and the cactus. The clouds and the earth. A remote landscape of nostalgia.

When dawn finally came, the moon had gone down, and only a few stars still blinked in the west. The sun had not yet risen, but as soon as it was light enough to see, birds began to call and the world to appear again once more, expanding bits of the scene: the nearby rock forms, the shadowy depths beneath, the pure sky, the bushes, the pebbles. It was still dark along the ground and among the trees, but when the sun rose, a frail luminous glow pushed out between the edges of horizon and clouds.

Just as the sun was splitting the sky, the stars sank at last to ash. To the west the cloudy yellow sandstone was still smoky blue, and only a faint hint of yellow light touched the highest point of the mesa. As the sun rose, the blueness diminished, and the cliffs of the mesa radiated the sun's warmth. The power of each day spilled over the hills in great silence, gathering all things together—the rocks and the sky, the clouds, and the winds—celebrating this coming. Sunrise.

With the new day, the light that overshot the plain crossed to the rocks and the mesa and threw long shadows. The whole mesa was absolutely naked and glowed like serrated pillars of gold. The country beyond it spread out in all directions. To the east was dry and thirsty land. Westward, beyond the mesa's edge, the horizon lay flat and true as a spirit level for millions of acres.

The world was waking slowly. In all directions, strange plants, trees, birds, and other animals were beginning to light up. An occasional antelope. Now and then a rabbit. Doves and quail. Blackbirds swarmed above; their noise increased with the dawn light and they fluttered and circled their roosting places restlessly. And now, the same searching eye made out a blur on the horizon to the northward, caught sight of something moving out in the desert. The blur concentrated itself to a speck; the speck grew by steady degrees to a spot, slowly moving, a note of dull colour, barely darker than the land, but an inky black silhouette as it topped a low rise of ground and stood for a moment outlined against the pale blue of the sky.

Not far from the river there was a horse staring out upon the desert floor. The horse stood stock still, stretched in a kind of start. It was a massive, magnificent stallion, rigid with pent-up power. Its neck was arched and terrible, like a sickle, its flanks were pressed back, rigid with power.

The horse stood darkly against the sky and was watching the colour of the wind that was blowing across the hill. There the wild herbs and the dust blew up over the rocky terrain and past the low hills to the west. The horse turned and sniffed. It saw something at a great distance. Surface water? A cottonwood? Such vastness makes for illusion. Soon the horse diverged from the river and ran out through a broad reach of desert, past the rock buttes and mesas and brilliant sweep of purple sage.

21

THE STALLION WENT FORWARD. ALMOST EVERY MILE, THE country began to change. At first the golden light seemed rising higher and higher in the sky, and sky was beginning to shimmer and swim. Then the ground was drier, and the herbage had, in consequence, been less luxuriant: the grasses, sere and yellow, snapped like glass filament; the hillside was sandy and covered with tall clumps of deer-horn cactus and thorny shrubs; then, farther out, the short grass always seemed sparse, and the low sage-shrubs rather dingy, with streaks of bright yellow rabbit-brush and greasewood. The mesa landscape had disappeared.

The sun rose higher. The hours passed, the miles slipped behind, and the heat grew intense, pulsing through the air in waves into the deep blue skies. Sometimes when the wind was coming in off the desert, the raw smell of hot dust was in the air. The wind felt over the earth, loosened the dust, and carried it away like sluggish smoke. Then the wind grew stronger; the dust fluffed up and spread out and did not settle back to earth now but whisked under stones, carried up straws and old leaves and even little clods, marking its course as it sailed across the fields with the horse, the dust cloud moving on, enclosing the horse with not threat exactly but maybe warning, bland, almost friendly, warning, as if to say: Come on if you like. But I will get there first; accumulating ahead of you I will arrive first, lifting, sloping gently upward under hooves so that you will find no destination but will merely abrupt gently onto a plateau and a panorama of loneliness called a desert and there will be nothing for you to do but return and so I would advise you not to go, to turn back now and let what is, be.

The animal did not stop, and when the agitation of the blinding wind grew stronger, the dustcloud in which the horse moved appeared like a cloud passing over the sun. Make that a storm. Though there is no storm. No clouds. Only the indistinct sense of a flat space, broiling sky, distances, and dust. Especially dust to choke up ears and nostrils and set one's teeth on edge with grit.

The horse shook its head and, hoofs moving with broad thuds, the panicked animal tried to dash out of the dust. But the dust, not blowing away, continued to push upward, instantaneous and eternal, cubic foot for cubic foot of dust to cubic foot for cubic foot of horse. Sometimes the wind whipped the dust away from him for a moment before returning. Sometimes the tiniest breezes blew an opening where the country seemed to descend, ending in a serenity of still and exquisite, firm-seated mountains—the southern peaks were thin blue and skeletal in the great distance. But the dust came in, obscured the distance, veiled it from view.

This continued for hours. It was not until late afternoon, when the wind died down to little puffs, that the cloud passed from the dreary scene, and—and in short, red dust, dust as fire, settled back around on the dirt. The horse had broken down not far from the river which ran N. or N. by E. at the foot of the mountains. The wall of rock loomed in the fore, a huge scarred and cracked bulk. It frowned down in a different order and color of rock, a stained yellow cliff of cracks and caves and seamed crags.* And straight before was a scene less striking but more significant: A river glinted like a crudely bent wire. Brown and gold earth was veined with crevasses. Precipices rose like islands, cracked from the sun's heat.

---

* Any number of caves up there yawned, quite suddenly and wonderfully above. Cave after cave opened out of the cliff; now a large one (a cavern so immense), now a small one (a zone of shade), the greatest of which was a real cave, hollowed out right under the Rocks. Apparently, it was very ancient. The curved roof, stained by ages of leakage, with buff and black and rust-colored streaks, swept up and loomed higher and seemed to soar to the rim of the cliff. Here bats flew out on summer evenings. Tracks of wildcats and rabbits were everywhere in the dusty floor. But the cave was deep and dangerous and in places too narrow even for the cats. And then there was the yellow sandstone, so split

The horse rose and stood on trembling legs and walked over to the tender green tumbleweed shoots that grew along the river bluff. It stepped very carefully into the water and drank endlessly, the mountain behind it, and the hills close about it like two encircling arms.

and splintered, so overhanging with great sections of balancing rim, so impending with tremendous crumbling crags. Indeed, it seemed that these ruined cliffs were but awaiting a breath of wind to collapse and come tumbling down. Waiting avalanches of rock in that gigantic split. Yet how many years had they leaned there without falling! At the bottom of the cave was an immense heap of weathered sandstone all crumbling to dust, but there were no huge rocks as large as houses, such as rested so lightly and frightfully above, waiting patiently and inevitably to crash down.

22

THIS PART OF THE DESERT WAS BOUND TO BE DIFFICULT FOR any figure intruded upon it. The sun was an angry eye and looked down with disastrous results. Even a bird, a rat, or a snake feared the wind and the sun. Instead of trembling in its light, they were hiding in some bushes, holes, and burrows, and smooth unclimbable surfaces, puffing and panting. Yes, across the landscape, there were many burrows, and sometimes the rattlesnakes, caught far from the buttes in bad weather or when the sun was dangerously hot—for a snake, like the great reptiles of yore, would quickly perish if exposed too long to the direct rays—would crawl into the burrows, and even make them their home for extended periods. Life here was retired underground.

Horses were different from other animals. Where snakes could hide from ugliness, sheltering from the sun in the bowels of the earth, horses were in most cases far from any possible shelter. Many times the distance to water was eighty miles, the horses perishing if the sun were shining, if the wind blew rough. It made the desert at night a kind of hopefulness—stars shivered into it, like crystals dropped into perfectly clear water; the temperature dropped. But the day came too quickly, and the desert, all that land, was soon kindled by the warmth of the first light of the day, the blue gray streaked with red light like a belly opening under a knife.

It was the same almost every day. Early in the morning or late in the evening was a relief, after the constant battle with the mesquite and chaparral or the wind or the sun in the sky; every animal and insect waited collectively for the night—this was the predominant image. Then one day these two animals who had been voyaging across the deserts for many weeks appeared in the distance trotting easily, their heads high up, stupefying, suggestive of an infinite quiet, of a calm, complacent life.

It was still early when they arrived at this place. The sun had just cleared the valley's rim, and somewhere near by an unfamiliar bird was sweetly trilling. A pair of burros, mules, horses—there were several names for things—were standing upriver drinking from a riverbed pothole.

After drinking, the burro chewed the dry tufts of grass—it looked up and then lowered its head again into the river grass— but the mule stood alert, its milky staring eyes wide open, search- ing for an area of jagged rocks, the mouth of a canyon in an area so bleak and forbidding that only this animal had its eyes moving in search of new adventure.

In the morning light, they trotted along the river toward the distant mountain range, which on that day rose up against the sky like a graph of profit and loss. Following its course, they came abreast of the grand gateway to the valley, only in this instance it formed the Notch of a canyon. They looked up and twitched their ears and then lowered their heads to graze on the thin, bluish green leaves of salt bushes growing at the entrance to the canyon.

They were the same—the mule and burro. The burro moved its head as easily as a mule. The shapes of mule and burro chewed in varying forms with finite differences resulting similar to the whole. The animals were silent, each animal like an ancient sacred myth character, each of them so ordinary an animal as a white- tailed deer or a goat. After eating, the gray mule followed the burro without any trouble, holding its head alert and its jackrabbit ears forward, nostrils flaring wide. They moved over the sand about a hundred yards downriver, bodies disappearing and reappearing between dark, gleaming walls.

23

THERE WERE QUIET AND REST AND COOLNESS IN THIS CANyon. The river was up and muddy and there were many fords. They passed close under shady, bulging shelves of cliff, through patches of grass and sage and thicket and groves of slender trees, and over white, pebbly washes, and around masses of broken rock. The motion of the mule, swaying forward and backward with each stride, the burro's deliberate moves; the horses were sure not to go too fast and too far without water and grass.

Further in, the trees were larger. The canyon was full of a damp smell—pale cascades hung down the sheer mountain wall above them, blowing off of the high slick rock in wild vapors. The sun shone; the walls gleamed; the sage glistened. And then it seemed the sun vanished, the walls shaded, the sage paled. Shadows gathered under shelving cliffs. Then far ahead round, scrawled stone appeared to block the sky. They crossed and recrossed the river continually.

Presently they came to a dense thicket of slender trees, through which they passed to water. The canyon turned, brightened, opened. The shade under the walls gave place to sunlight, and the heat beat down. The canyon was wide at the water's edge, and though it corkscrewed back by abrupt turns, it preserved this open, roomy character with sloping sides, rugged and rocky, but well grassed.

There they passed, picking their way among the chattering grey stones, the bluish rock, and the sun-tanned grass that grew. Yet when a dry hot wind glided up and down the canyon restlessly, shaking the salt bushes, they looked away to the shade below the cliffs and the mouths of canyons, one of which surely was another gateway—a box canyon, very different in character. No gentle slope there. No trees, nothing but stillness. No ants, no bugs, no birds. But the shadows looked soft and cool and inviting. The walls were perpendicular where they weren't actually overhanging, and they were anywhere from eight hundred to a thousand feet high.

This canyon didn't break the solid outline of the intersecting canyons; it was only a continuation of the deep canyon orifice. The floor of it was a mass of huge boulders, great pieces of rock that had fallen from above ages back and had been worn round and smooth as pebbles. Many of them were as big as haystacks, yet they lay piled on one another like a load of gravel. There was no footing among those smooth stones, so they looked for somewhere where there was some. There was all day to do it, but they soon came to an opening where the rocks broke—a hump of rock with a hole in it—and an opening showed a passage through the canyon and into the shade. And so the stale heat still remained, but this canyon seemed to waken these animals. They trotted tirelessly, wandered through the wild jumble of massed and broken fragments of cliff.

The canyon narrowed; the walls lifted their rugged rims higher; and the sun shone down hot from the center of the blue stream of sky above, leaving shallow pools of light here and there on the sand and rocks. The going downhill there was difficult. The earth grew uncertain, gravely canted and veering out through sharp angles and turnings. A few feet from a turning of the canyon, one of the animals briefly lost its footing on the narrow path. It was almost too narrow, and the Mule sent a stream of pebbles and small rocks rolling.

When the animals in question had gone down this canyon for a mile or so, threading the canyon's close pressed flanks—the dry white rocks of the dead river floor round and smooth as arcane eggs—the canyon, without tempering the heat, turned and widened at the foot of a narrow, steep, ascending chute. The sunlight grew stronger, whiter, then the monotony of the yellow walls broke in change of color and surface, and the rugged outline of rims grew craggy; long shadows scored the sides of the rimrock. Beyond the shade, splits appeared in deep breaks, and up on the rocks were gigantic, deadlylooking bayonet plants—small black and olive-colored shrubs blasted under the sun.

With the light and the waves of heat, a fierce wind arose, imperceptibly hotter than the one before it, but there was something forbidding in the sight of that sun and that wind. It seemed the sun was a hot cannon-ball, an evil thing, an omen. When the animals entered a new space, the passage lightened even more, hazardous rays pulsing from it. And here opened a narrow chasm, a ragged vent in yellow walls of stone, the threshold, the opening between this world and the Land of the Dead.

24

THERE WAS A LONG PAUSE. THE HORSES PANTED IRREGU-
larly, the sweat dripping from their heaving bellies. One hundred
feet away in the blazing sun, a rough wind was blowing and now
whistling around the ragged edge of this solid block of loneliness
called a desert.*

The view opened, framed in the V of the canyon—the broad
valley was filled with air like that of a kiln, and all the world was
a weird, unnatural tint, hard to name, never to be forgotten.
Everything was dry, prickly, sharp—bayonet, juniper, greasewood,
cactus—and save for scattered clumps of buckbrush and prickly-
pear and the little patches of twisted grass, the ground was bare,
and there were low mountains to the east and west along the valley, and they were bare too. At this hour of the day, the sun beat
down with a swarming sort of density, and there was so much sky,
more than at sea, more than anywhere else in the world. The plain
was there, but what one saw when one looked about was that brilliant blue world of stinging air. Even the mountains were mere ant-
hills under it. Elsewhere the sky is the roof of the world, but here
the earth was the floor of the sky.

As it was, the situation was approaching a stage, a kind of
crossroads, you know. The horses stood like roadside spectators
waiting an event. The lead mule, the one with a yellow eye, looked
out across the waste country, the wind in the pass filling the air

---

* It was too powerful an entity not to lend itself to personification. The desert—
its very silence was like a tacit admission of the half-conscious presence it har-
bored. And what did this mean, save that such things were the imagination's
simple way of interpreting that presence?

with such sounds as were even grating to the ears of an ass, and yet somehow in the face of nature's pranks, the grave and thoughtful animals did not resist, but they persisted. So they moved and stumbled into the sunlight for miserable adventures.

25

THE HORSES WALKED INTO THE TEETH OF THE WIND. IT WAS a restless, dry wind that felt as if it blew out of dusty thin years of the past. It smelled of emptiness and loss. Around the desert now, the sun burnt uncompromising, undeniable. It struck upon the hard sand, and the rocks became furnaces of red heat. It fell upon the arid waste of the desert and kept right on going into the cactus field.

A mile across the valley floor in that goddamn sea of cactus, one could find bits of brilliant stone, crystals and agates and onyx, and petrified wood as red as blood. Huge boulders rose up, their shapes like children's clay models. An elephant. A gas mask. A skull. Lizards lay with their leather chins flat to the rocks and fended off the world with thin smiles and eyes like cracked stone plates.

The mule and the burro were making their way across a plain of round rocks scattered with ocotillo and sage. Mile after mile, hour after hour, kicking up red clay dust, they were still going south, south into a land more hostile yet. It was like a country of dry ashes; no juniper, no rabbit brush, nothing but thickets of withered, dead-looking cactus and rocks and that heartless blue of the sky. There was, high and motionless in the blinding sky, a buzzard poised. Some two hundred feet below, long-tailed crows among the thorny branches creaked and whistled, choked and rattled, snored and grunted.

A dull thump of hooves did not stop. There was not a sound but the horses and the crows and, behind that sound, the biblical wind that carries sagebrush, sand, chalky dust, and tumbleweeds. The air was furnace-hot, oppressive, and exceedingly dry. It seemed to exhale from the land itself, a prolonged sigh as of deep fatigue.

By the time the animals were through regions of particolored stone, the wind didn't blow as hard, but the heat had not lessened. The sandy soil of the plain had a light sprinkling of cactus and desert scrub. Across the dry bistre land, the horses were blowing and smoking like steam engines, like burnt phantoms kicking up the spume that was not real, and they were lost in the sun and lost out upon that cooking world, and they shimmered and slurred together and separated again.

They began to come upon bones. The ribbed frames of dead cattle under their patches of dried hide lay like the ruins of primitive boats upturned upon that shoreless void, and they passed, lurid and austere, the black and desiccated shapes of horses and mules. They saw halfburied skeletons of mules with the bones so white and polished they seemed incandescent even in that blazing heat, and they saw a mule entire, the dried and blackened carcass hard as iron. These parched beasts had died with their necks stretched in agony in the sand, and now, upright and blind and lurching askew with scraps of blackened leather hanging from the fretwork of their ribs, they leaned with their long mouths howling after the endless tandem suns that passed above them.

Bone palings ruled the small and dusty purlieus here and death seemed the most prevalent feature of the landscape: the lower jawbone of an antelope, with the teeth still in place; dried toads and lizards; birds, decomposing more rapidly, left only feathered skeletons. A buzzard labored up from among bones with wings that went whoop whoop whoop like a child's toy swung on a string, and a low-flying buzzard that had just risen off the carcass of an armadillo circled, and hovered, and swooped around.*

The horses trudged sullenly the alien ground and through the

---

* What a great dull hard rock the world was! All nature was weary and seemed to sing a dirge to that effect. Well, by definition, all were weary, all but the sun and the buzzards. They preyed on every creature they could find. But the sun was so hot that even passing buzzards sought a momentary relief. The sun seemed to glory in his power, relentless and untiring, as he swung boldly in the sky, triumphantly leering down upon his helpless victims.

studded vegetation and bones and the dried carcasses of mules and out across that horrible desert. The heat progressed. The snakes were listening (writhing snakes, like intestines). When at last they stopped, the horses shifted, and out here on this desert, at the hour when the sun shone its hottest, when the winds died, they came within sight of an oasis.

It was a miracle. From this desert of barren gold, behind the thorny shrubs, sagehorn, and cacti in queer tortured shapes, the oasis of poesy had appeared on the horizon that day no more than a line of gray—a line which varied in thickness as the eye beheld it, moving like a slow-running liquid: a wide band, a long gray cliff, nothing at all, then once more the thin penciled border between the earth and the sky.

As the afternoon wore on, these two animals eyed the sun in its circus. The dark spot of the oasis grew and grew until a solitary thing detached itself from the undecided mass on the horizon, rising suddenly like a djinn into the air. A moment later it subsided, shortened, was merely a distant palm standing quite still on the desert floor.

The illusions merged and grew in volume as the mule and the burro moved southward. Quietly they continued another hour or so, until presently they were among the trees, and, after hours of waiting, the horses drank and rested and drank again.

26

THIS SCRAGGLY LITTLE OASIS WAS GLITTERING BLUE GLASS—
a hole of blinding light and a little bit of grass. A few trees and
bushes kept it from appearing bare. You might call it a nice little
place if only it weren't for the heat and the vultures seen cowering
round some cacti in the distance.

Out beyond the oasis, in a wasteland made gray by too much
light, the afternoon sun beat down hotly. Even now, when it would
be setting in a half hour or so, the sun burned, and the wind
roughly jostled the plants and other things. All nature was weary,
and seemed to sing a dirge to that effect. As the wind blew a scud
of dust across the landscape, a smoky red sunset came on slowly,
painfully, lingering. Whirlwinds and dust devils darkened the
horizon and the sun sank lower, its glare too strong.

A new ferocity pervaded the landscape now that night was
approaching. The sun to the west lay in a holocaust where there
rose a steady column of small desert bats, and along the trembling
perimeter of the world, dust was blowing down the void like the
smoke of distant armies. As the sun got lower, the desert was washing its robe in red, as if preparing for some nocturnal orgy. The
little desert wolves yapped. The western sky was the color of blood.

After the sun sank, the valley seemed veiled in purple fire and
smoke. The crumpled butcherpaper mountains lay in sharp shad-
owfold, erupting the baleful fire of the swallowed sun. In the deepening dusk these colors did not simply draw down power from the
sky or lift it from the landforms. They pushed and pulled. They
were in conflict with each other under the long blue dusk. But
soon the unvarying emptiness of the country began to change
slightly for the better. The dusk passed into dark, and the desert

stars came out in the soft sky, stars stabbing and sharp, with few points and rays to them, and the sky was velvet.

All this time, the heat changed. While the sun was up, it was a beating, flailing heat, but now the heat came from below, from the earth itself, and the ground was breathing. That was odd. The whole desert was slowly inhaling and exhaling. Every rock, every grain of sand, was pumping out all the heat it had taken in during the day. The cacti raised their arms up to heaven. A tremendous, immeasurable Life pushed steadily heavenward without a sound.

27

APART FROM THE STEADY HEAT AND THE NEARBY ROCK
forms and the plants, memories of this night are extremely hazy.
The water had turned a deep golden color, and then red, purple,
and finally black. The stars had thickened, and the moon had risen
with spots of red appearing as if they had been left by the wild
brush strokes of a painter. At some point, the burro had eaten a poison weed and died. The other animal whinnied and leaned against
the rocks and filth beneath. Toward midnight the wind was all but
silent. The emptiness of primeval desolation stretched leagues and
leagues upon either hand. The gigantic silence of the night lay close
over everything, like a muffling Titanic palm.

In that vast silence, the hours passed. Still there was no wind
but only the dark stillness and the stars. The water lay black and
motionless. Toward the morning there was no wind and no sound,
but by and by the edge of the eastern horizon began to grow
blacker and more distinct in out-line. An hour passed. Then two.
The stars winked out, and the dawn whitened. The air became
warmer. And soon everything looked different. There the whole east,
clean of clouds, flamed opalescent from horizon to zenith, crimson
at the base, where the earth blackened against it; at the top, fading
from pink to pale yellow, to green, to light blue, to the turquoise
iridescence of the desert sky.

The sun had not yet risen, but the east flushed pale streaks of
light and then a deeper run of color, like blood seeping up in sudden reaches flaring planewise, and where the earth drained up into
the sky at the edge of creation, the top of the sun rose out of nothing like the head of a great red phallus until it cleared the unseen
rim and sat squat and pulsing and malevolent. The shadows of the

smallest stones lay like pencil lines across the sand, and the shapes
of rocks advanced elongate before them like strands of the night,
like tentacles to bind them to the darkness yet to come. Sunrise
over the desert. Very tense.

Under the great split sky sat vultures, shoulder to shoulder, facing east to the sun, lifting one foot and then the other and holding
out their wings like cloaks. They saw the bones of one of the horses
dead with its shapeless head stretched in the mud. The other animal kept shaking its head sideways as if it had something in its ear.

For a short while the steel-yellow sun glittered distantly in the
sky, a serpent's eye above the bald and flyspecked mountains to
the east, and the mountains in their blue islands stood footless in
the void like floating temples. As the sun rose, water sparkled. The
long, thin shadows of the early hours drew backward like receding
serpents. The vultures now felt the distance and stillness of that
sprawled dawn like some endless sky waking.

Soon the mule was browsing, out there past the birds and all
their whistles and squeaks and quacks. The mule, starting and shying, paused and began blowing and snuffing as though in search of
feed. Then, for no reason, he shied again, and started off on a jog
trot, pushing boldly to the southward.

28

LET'S JUST SAY THE DESERT IS AN IMPULSE. IT'S THE SUR-round. It's the framing device. It's the four-part horizon. All distance. Hardpan and sky and a wafer trace of mountain, low and crouched out there, mountain or cloud, cat-shaped, catamount. That morning, the fifteenth day of the eighth moon, when the mule moved southward, the first stretch of the desert was crossed, as it were, in the womb of the desert sun. It was warm but pleasant, the dry wind being laden with a kind of sage. By nine o'clock the sun stood high in the sky, and the heat was intense; the atmosphere was thick and heavy with it.

The sun rose higher. Hour by hour, as the mule moved steadily on, the heat increased. The baked dry sand crackled into innumerable tiny flakes. The twigs of the sage-brush snapped like brittle pipestems. At eleven, the earth was like the surface of a furnace; all distant objects were visibly shimmering and palpitating. Another hour and the sun from ambush was threatening the world with red daggers. The rocks trembled and sleared. The very shadows shrank away, hiding under sage-bushes, retreating to the farthest nooks and crevices. All the world was one gigantic blinding glare. It was bad going for even a mule.

At a certain spot, the ground ahead faded away into a thankless dead landscape. You couldn't call it desert, really. It was waste ground. The region where even the sand and sage-brush begin to dwindle, giving place to white, powdered alkali. Nothing but barren desert for at least a hundred miles.

The mule paused there in the hot sun, put his nose in the air and blew once or twice through his nostrils. In the immediate foreground, the desert unrolled itself, white, naked, inhospitable, palpitating and shimmering under the sun. In the neuter austerity of that terrain, all phenomena were bequeathed a strange equality, and no one thing nor spider nor stone could put forth claim to precedence.*

The mule was hot and lathered. He looked back across the open country one more time and then pushed on toward the horizon. All across those reaches, the silence, vast, illimitable, enfolded him like an immeasurable tide. At long intervals, a faint breath of wind out of the south passed slowly over the levels of the baked and empty earth, accentuating the silence, marking off the stillness. Not a twig rattled, not an insect hummed, not a bird or beast invaded that huge solitude with call or cry. Everything as far as the eye could reach, to north, to south, to east, and west, lay inert, absolutely quiet and moveless under the merciless lash of the sun's rays.

At midday, it was no longer the sun alone that persecuted from above—the entire sky was like a metal dome grown white with heat. The merciless light pushed down from all directions; the sun was the whole sky, a vast red-hot coal floating in fire. But the mule moved on to the south.

---

* The very clarity of these articles belied their familiarity, for the eye predicates the whole on some feature or part, and here was nothing more luminous than another and nothing more enshadowed, and in the optical democracy of such landscapes, all preference is made whimsical, and an animal and a rock become endowed with unguessed kinships. The earth and the eye beholding it were one and the same as far as the eye could see.

29

AN HOUR PASSED, THEN ANOTHER, AND ANOTHER. THE sage-brush dwindled and at length ceased; the sand gave place to a fine powder, white as snow; and mule's hoofs were crisping and cracking the sun-baked flakes of alkali. From horizon to horizon it was a desert with no trace of sand, and it was a plain unbroken by so much as a rock or cactus stump, so flat that ball bearings were said to roll forever into the distance as if in perpetual motion.

Bravely the horse stepped over the scorching alkali and under the blazing sun where no life moved. Far behind him the hills were already but blue hummocks on the horizon. Before him, upon either side and to the south, stretched primordial desolation. League upon league, the infinite reaches of dazzling white alkali laid themselves out like an immeasurable scroll unrolled from horizon to horizon; not a bush, not a twig, relieved that horrible monotony. Even the sand of the desert would have been a welcome sight; a single clump of sage-brush would have fascinated the eye; but this was worse than the desert. It was abominable, this hideous sink of alkali. The great mountains had been merely indifferent, but this awful sink of alkali was openly and unreservedly iniquitous and malignant.

As the animal breathed, while the wind whipped the mule's thin tail between its hind legs, time ceased to be measured accurately. Events moved slowly in an unreal world of sultry heat, heat waves blurring the reality of the desolate scene, the air quivering and palpitating like that in the stoke-hold of a steamship. The mule trotted in some nameless distance until the heat was too intense to bear and then was crouched upon the ground, panting rapidly, with half-closed eyes.

Looking out over the great plain, miles across, there was no change in the character of the desert. Always the same measureless leagues of white-hot alkali stretched away toward the horizon on every hand. Here the heat-covered landscape was desert absolute, and it was devoid of feature altogether. The earth fell away on every side equally in its arcature, for miles and miles over its horrible desolation. No shade was in sight. Not a rock, not a stone, broke the monotony of the ground. There was nothing in sight because the sun was just too smoking hot. The blown-out white plane of a salt flat, almost too bright to look at. There was no water. No clouds. There was just stillness and waves of heat. There was the brazen sky and the leagues upon leagues of alkali, leper white. There was nothing more.

30

DEATH WAS ONLY A QUESTION OF TIME. THE SUN HAMMERED down, pounding on that goddamn desert, and the air was positively venomous-looking. Some act of God was possible, but unlikely. It was too late. The land was too huge. Water too far away. Animals were failing elsewhere and in a variety of scenes.

As the day ended, death became inevitable. The great luminary of the universe had become a sackcloth of hair, but the heat did not seem to decrease. To the east, the firmament was as a scroll rolled away. The stars of heaven were falling upon the earth. When the moon rose, the air was dead; not a breath stirred, and death was in the sky, in the bone light. Death was coursing through the barren lands of eternal monotony, all so gray and wide and solemn and silent under the endless sky. Death was now.

31

IN GAZING AT SUCH SCENES, IT IS ALL IN ALL WHAT MOOD you are in; if in a trance, the devils will occur to you; if in the act of expanding into grandeur, the archangels. For death—at that moment or any living thing dying back to nothingness anywhere in the world—is a part of life.

Ceaseless life and death. It is of the great facts of the world, like sunlight, or spring-time, or the reflection in dark waters of that silver face of the moon. It cannot be questioned. It has its divine right of sovereignty. It's part of the story, and it happened to the horses, but now and again to the birds, insects, frogs, fish, and other animals. The battle for life was taking place there on the desert to the immediate north, but also in the mountains and on the plains, in the forests and oceans and polar ice. Like an undulating wave of the sea itself, such living things as then existed rose and fell, but whereas the cycle of an ocean wave is apt to be a few minutes at the most, the cycle of the rising and falling of animals like deer, like horses, was of the nature of years.

Each animal, at any given moment of time, existed certainly and securely within that cycle: it was either rising toward birth and significance, or it was perishing. It was the same with every tree or bush or flower, lake or river. They were either rising in birth or falling in decay. And there was much pushing and shoving as new germination, new growth, burst upward to the light, as a bird hatched in the sun, or a river, in another instant there, burst from a lake. Now and again the lakes and the rivers were turbulent: it was the river which laid down new land; it was the river which took it away. The endless cycle of building up, tearing down, and rebuilding, using the same material over and over, was contributed to by

the river. It was the brawling, undisciplined, violent artery of life
and would always be.

The major characteristics of land and everything that grows
upon it, of all the birds, of all the horses and all the other beasts
everywhere, were these mystic gestures: limitless cycle, endless
change. Here, in this desert where so many mightier beasts had
passed away on panting plain or scorched summit, where the sun
had branded all the land with its mark, death was upon all things
that were beautiful. Life here was over for many horses, trees, and
plants. But life was continuing and expanding in a different place.
All over the world this was happening: taciturnity of winged creatures, emergence of nocturnal or crepuscular animals, persistence
of infernal light, obscurity of terrestrial waters and mountains,
woods and vales. On some distant island, the first birds were waking, the wind singing over a dawn sea colored like the breast of
a dove. Far to the south, the high and snowy mountains were
crossed and recrossed with the tracks of deer and other animals.
Elsewhere, the dear sun shone on the sand and the river and the
leaves of the tree; a distant forest far northwest was alive with
robins—great, plump, saucy fellows, strutting along—and with
grasshoppers whose husky noises on every side formed a whispered chorus.

It was very big to think about everything and everywhere.
Endless cycle, endless birth and death, endless becoming and disappearing. The Universe and all the world was one gigantic event.
To complete itself was to melt out into the darkness and sway there,
identified with the great Being more than anything. On earth, the
cycle of life, however, was still incomplete, limited, unfinished, like
an open flower under the sky. On the marshes, in the clouds, in
the light, in the darkness, in the wind, in the woods, in the sky
and the sea was endless expenditure of beauty and capacity, tireless
ebb and flow of light and shadow, life and death. How meaningless and yet how promising was this interplay of forces.

Life was certainly very interesting. Seen from a distance, the
world was a stallion rolling in the blue pasture of ether. Up close,

high on the highest peak or at the bottom of the unfathomable
ocean, the world was full of darkness and light and busy in all
the fullness of life. The world was really a wilderness: white rivers
and noble mountains; forests full of magic presences; sand full of
glittering grains; meadows, marshes, waters, and water-courses full
of sun and loveliness and a kind of invitation. But most lovely of
all was the hour of sunset, when the clouds cleared or glowed gold
in the evening light, when the sun relaxed and vivified the sea or
land, when light grew in strength and splendour as it neared death,
drawing long shadows and reflections.

That hour always had the exultation of victory, of triumphant
ending, of stars flashing, of cloud and sky brought purposely
together to assemble outwardly the scattered parts of the vision
within: there would be a slow suffusion of inutile loveliness; a low
sun in a platinum haze with a warm, peeled-peach tinge pervading the upper edge of a two-dimensional, dove-gray cloud, fusing
with the distant amorous mist. There might be a line of spaced
trees silhouetted against the horizon, and another cloud turned a
pale red, fashioned into illusion. Whatever the case, every time
the sun was low, minute objects and colours and different forms of
life grew wilder and denser, touching other sensibilities than those
which are stirred at any other time of the day. There was a real
joy in that—perhaps the most satisfying joy—but when the sun
dipped lower and lower, turning the western sky to flaming copper
and gold, it felt like spirits moving, the elements and time swirling
and spreading far across the plains, deserts, and seas. The past had
vanished and become nothing; the future was uncertain. As the
nightshades fell, the past refused to come back, as it did in dreams,
to be remade. The thin, dark line of sea or land disappeared. The
wind dropped and light vanished. There was nothing to be seen.
There was no sound. All that was left was the ceaselessly shrinking fragment of time called "now."

AFTERWORD

The Nature Book was inspired by *City of Nature* (2010), a seven-minute animated video by my friend artist Kota Ezawa. In the video, Ezawa collages and rotoscopes nature shots from feature-length movies: the rivers of *Fitzcarraldo* cut to the rivers of *Deliverance,* which cut to the rivers of *Rambo,* which flow to sea of *Swept Away,* which cuts to the sea of *The Old Man and The Sea,* and so on.

Before *City of Nature,* much of Ezawa's video work examined depictions of violence in American culture. Surprised by this seemingly tame new video—in *City of Nature* the only hint of danger is a cartoonish shark fin poking above the water for a few seconds—but finding clear echoes of Ezawa's past work in his rotoscope technique, I wondered if this video was pointing to something pernicious about the process of framing life and flattening it into images. I wondered what a similar literary procedure might reveal about writing, language, and our relationship to nature.

The Nature Book also takes a cue from the French avant-garde group the Oulipo, in its use of literary constraints. It was important to me that this book be both a narrative and an archive of how we think and write about nature and less about the inventive things that could be done with the found language. Constraints helped to limit my authorial whims and fancies and allowed for the narrative to be driven primarily by patterns I found in the source material.

As in a recipe or instruction manual, some constraints take the form of declarative statements. One such statement acted as the overarching constraint of this book and guided all the collaging and microconstraints in my process: "This book collects nature descriptions from English-language novels since the beginning of the novel form." Below, I've detailed the microconstraints I used to execute this overarching constraint. In a way, these microconstraints are the derivatives, elaborations on, and extensions of this simple statement, the tactics I used to complete this novel.

Sample Selection

While searching through novels for nature descriptions, I used these selection guides:

- *A nature description can be as long as a few paragraphs or as short as "a tall tree."*

- *A nature description ends where a human form or human-made object begins.* For instance, in the sentence, "The bird flew over the car, sped past the tree and into the window," the usable nature language would be "the bird flew over the" and "sped past the tree and into the."

- *A nature description may contain a reference to a human form or human-made object only if the form or object is used metaphorically.* In an early version of this book, I attempted to fully remove the human from the source material, going so far as to exclude words like "banks," as in the land bordering a river, because of their linguistic connection to financial institutions. I quickly found that this approach was not only a fool's errand, but it also ignored a significant trope: writers often project human characteristics onto nature, referencing people and human-made objects in their descriptions. Excluding phrases like "big elbows of Rock" or "cathedral-arching trees" would limit this book's capacity to examine the full breadth of how authors describe nature. So while direct references to human forms and objects do not appear in this book, pareidolia, or the tendency to see the human in nature, can be found throughout.

- *For nonvisual descriptions, "nature" is defined as anything that is not explicitly human or human-made and is commonly seen as "outside" of the human, such as distance, the passing of time, etc.* Nature also appears as emotional content in many novels. Since nature descriptions are always connected to human perception and feeling, I consider this emotive content to fall within the category of nature descriptions as well.

Pattern Arrangement

With a corpus of nature descriptions in hand, I gave myself additional microconstraints to ensure the book remained more of an archive of how authors have written about nature and less of a display of my own inventiveness:

- *The book must display and exhaust patterns found while gathering source material—as many of them as possible.* Writing the first draft, I quickly found that nature descriptions fall into two categories, macropatterns and micropatterns. The macropatterns deal with season and setting: the four seasons, oceans, islands, jungle islands, jungles, outer space, prairies or grasslands, mountain ranges, and deserts. (You'll notice that this is the basic structure of the book.) Micropatterns exist inside of each of these seasons or geographies and deal with the minutiae of life: different times of day, different weather patterns (jolly, sunny language; gloomy, rainy language; raging stormy language, etc.), different animals specific to each macropattern, etc.

  With a lot of table space while I was in residence at the Bemis Center for Contemporary Arts in Omaha, Nebraska, one summer, I printed out my three-thousand-page corpus, cut it up, and separated each macropattern onto a different table. There was a winter table, a desert table, an outer space table, etc. Then I went through each table/macropattern and sorted the language into smaller piles/micropatterns. With each pattern laid out, I went to work grouping language from each table into a separate narrative. Once all micropatterns were used up and each macropattern seemed exhausted, I then worked to connect these separate narratives into a novel-length story.

Through the writing process, I discovered another kind of pattern: nanopatterns, or commonalities that appear across multiple books but not as frequently as macropatterns and micropatterns. Some examples of nanopatterns include descriptions that compare islands and aquatic life to different forms of punctuation (see part two, chapter twelve), or dense jungle foliage to weaving (part two, chapter fourteen). Sometimes a nanopattern would appear independent of a macropattern, like the trees and clouds described as warring armies that appear in the autumn section (part one, chapter five); these descriptions were not necessarily connected to autumn in the novels in which I found them but appear there because their tone resonated with that section. Some nanopatterns, like language that compares nature to photographs, postcards, or theatrical backdrops, are scattered throughout the book as refrains.

- *In combining macro, micro, and nanopatterns, all efforts are made to create a smooth flow between patterns and to exhibit the similarities and differences between them.* Examples of this can be found in storm build-ups, where different intensities of stormy language line up one after another.

- *All efforts are made to use a description no more than once.* Some repetition appears in order to create textual rhythm or thematic echoes throughout the book.

Novelization

Outside of patternmaking, a number of other constraints were added in the service of maintaining the book's archival qualities while also creating a readable novel:

- *No words of my own may be added anywhere in the novel.*
- *The only modifications to the found language may be changes to capitalization, punctuation, and paragraph breaks.* These modifications

were used sparingly. As a result, you'll find inconsistencies in punctuation and in American, British, and antiquated spellings.

- *Descriptions may overlap in order to keep the narrative moving.* Sometimes the only way I could meet my constraints was to connect two fragments via an overlapping word or phrase. For instance, these two fragments: "starved for color, for life. The new sense of" (Jhumpa Lahiri, *The Lowland*) and "sense of coolness in the air" (Frank Norris, *The Octopus*) become ". . . starved for color, for life. The new sense of coolness in the air . . ."

- *If all else fails in attempting to smoothly connect micro- and nanopatterns, short fragments of found language may be used that are not exactly nature descriptions but were gathered incidentally in the sample selection process (i.e., copy and paste).* This caveat, or clinamen as the Oulipo would call it, is used far more sparingly than the punctuation modification mentioned above.

- *The text must adopt traditional modes of novelistic narrative, incorporating common fiction devices like narrative arc, rising action, falling action, and cliff hangers to shape these patterns into readable threads.* The goal was to write a novel, after all.

SOURCES

When I set out to write this book, I focused only on English-language novels, because, along with being a native speaker, I wanted to work directly with the original material of the authors. I saw translations, with their inherent interpretations and reformulations, as introducing a remove from the language I wanted to investigate. This decision limited the scope of the natural world and perspectives that the book would cover, but it also enabled *The Nature Book* to not only comment on the words of the authors but the English language itself, with all of its hang-ups and imaginative limits.

With English-language books in mind, I started with canonical novels to get a fuller picture of the history of writing in English. I studied well-known lists like the appendices to Harold Bloom's *The Western Canon* and the Modern Library's "100 Best Novels," but, unsurprisingly, found them too limited. These lists are known to skew conservative and focus heavily on white, cis, male authors. They're also dated—both were published in the nineties—and, at least in the English-language sections of *The Western Canon,* are temperate-climate centric, focusing largely on novels set in the British Isles and the northeast of the United States. In order to actually see the history of the English-language novel in all of its geographical, ethnic, and aesthetic diversity, I looked to additional canon lists and authorities such as University of Nebraska at Lincoln's "Encyclopedia of the Great Plains"; online lists of best novels written by women and writers of color as well as best novels of a particular geography, season, or genre from sites like BookRiot, LitHub, and Goodreads; the *New York Times*'s "What Is the Best Work of American Fiction of the Last 25 Years?";

TheGreatestBooks.org, a synthesis of 130 "best of" book lists; winners or nominees of major awards such as the Booker, Pulitzer, and Nobel prizes; and UCLA PhD oral-exam reading lists. In some cases, if a book from one of these lists proved to have little to no nature language, I would refer to another book by the same author.

Below is the full list of books that I source in this novel:

1984, George Orwell

2001: A Space Odyssey,
    Arthur C. Clarke

2312, Kim Stanley Robinson

Absalom, Absalom!,
    William Faulkner

The Adventures of Augie March,
    Saul Bellow

*The Adventures of Huckleberry
    Finn,* Mark Twain

*The Adventures of Mao on the
    Long March,* Frederic Tuten

Alaska, James Michener

Alice's Adventures in Wonderland,
    Lewis Carroll

Alphabetical Africa, Walter Abish

The American Claimant,
    Mark Twain

Angel, Elizabeth Taylor

All the Pretty Horses,
    Cormac McCarthy

And Then There Were None,
    Agatha Christie

Angle of Repose, Wallace Stegner

Anne of Green Gables,
    Lucy Maud Montgomery

Anne of the Island,
    Lucy Maud Montgomery

Another Country, James Baldwin

Artemis, Andy Weir

At Swim-Two-Birds,
    Flann O'Brien

Atlas Shrugged, Ayn Rand

The Autobiography of an Electron,
    Charles R. Gibson

Autumn, Ali Smith

The Awakening, Kate Chopin

Banjo, Claude McKay

Bear, Marian Engel

The Bell Jar, Sylvia Plath

Beloved, Toni Morrison

A Bend in the River,
    V. S. Naipaul

The Big Rock Candy Mountain,
    Wallace Stegner

The Big Sky, A. B. Guthrie Jr.

Big Sur, Jack Kerouac

Billy Budd, Herman Melville

The Birchbark House,
    Louise Erdrich

The Bird in the Tree,
    Elizabeth Goudge

Black Beauty, Anna Sewell

Bless Me, Ultima, Rudolfo Anaya

Blood and Guts in High School,
    Kathy Acker

Blood Meridian,
    Cormac McCarthy

Blue Remembered Earth,
    Alastair Reynolds
The Book of Khalid,
    Ameen Rihani
Brideshead Revisited,
    Evelyn Waugh
The Brief Wondrous Life of
    Oscar Wao, Junot Díaz
The Call of the Wild,
    Jack London
Camilla, Fanny Burney
Cane, Jean Toomer
Captain Blood, Rafael Sabatini
The Castle of Otranto,
    Horace Walpole
Catch-22, Joseph Heller
The Catcher in the Rye,
    J.D. Salinger
Centennial, James Michener
Ceremony, Leslie Marmon Silko
The Cider House Rules,
    John Irving
Cities of the Plain,
    Cormac McCarthy
Childhood's End,
    Arthur C. Clarke
Chronic City, Jonathan Lethem
City of Illusions,
    Ursula K. Le Guin
The Clan of the Cave Bear,
    Jean M. Auel
Clarissa, Samuel Richardson
The Code of the Woosters,
    P. G. Wodehouse
The Conquest, Oscar Micheaux
Contact, Carl Sagan
The Crossing, Cormac McCarthy

The Custom of the Country,
    Edith Wharton
The Daughter of Time,
    Josephine Tey
David Copperfield,
    Charles Dickens
Dawn, Octavia Butler
Death Comes for the Archbishop,
    Willa Cather
The Desert of Wheat,
    Zane Grey
Dhalgren, Samuel R. Delany
Dracula, Bram Stoker
The Dragon in the Sea,
    Frank Herbert
Dragon's Egg, Robert Forward
East of Eden, John Steinbeck
The Einstein Intersection,
    Samuel R. Delany
The English Patient,
    Michael Ondaatje
Ethan Frome, Edith Wharton
A Fall of Moondust,
    Arthur C. Clarke
Fanshawe, Nathaniel Hawthorne
Far from the Madding Crowd,
    Thomas Hardy
Farewell Summer, Ray Bradbury
Fear and Loathing in Las Vegas,
    Hunter S. Thompson
The Fifth Horseman,
    José Antonio Villarreal
Finnegans Wake, James Joyce
The Flamethrowers,
    Rachel Kushner
Flatland, Edwin Abbott Abbott
Frankenstein, Mary Shelley

The Friends of Eddie Coyle,
　　George V. Higgins
A Fringe of Leaves, Patrick White
Galápagos, Kurt Vonnegut
The Garden of Eden,
　　Ernest Hemingway
Gilead, Marilynne Robinson
Glitz, Elmore Leonard
Go Tell it on the Mountain,
　　James Baldwin
The God of Small Things,
　　Arundhati Roy
The Gods Themselves,Isaac Asimov
Gods Without Men, Hari Kunzru
The Grapes of Wrath,
　　John Steinbeck
Gravity's Rainbow,
　　Thomas Pynchon
Great Expectations,
　　Charles Dickens
The Great Gatsby,
　　F. Scott Fitzgerald
The Guide, R. K. Narayan
Gulliver's Travels, Jonathan Swift
Hawaii, James Michener
The Heart Is a Lonely Hunter,
　　Carson McCullers
Heart of Darkness,
　　Joseph Conrad
Heat and Dust,
　　Ruth Prawer Jhabvala
The History of Tom Jones, a
　　Foundling, Henry Fielding
The Hitchhiker's Guide to the
　　Galaxy, Douglas Adams
The Homesteader,
　　Oscar Micheaux

A House for Mr. Biswas,
　　V. S. Naipaul
House of Leaves,
　　Mark Z. Danielewski
The House of Mirth,
　　Edith Wharton
House Made of Dawn,
　　N. Scott Momaday
Housekeeping,
　　Marilynne Robinson
The Human Stain, Philip Roth
I Love Dick, Chris Kraus
Ice, Anna Kavan
Infinite Jest,
　　David Foster Wallace
The Interpreters, Wole Soyinka
Invisible Man, Ralph Ellison
The Island, Aldous Huxley
The Island, Robert Creeley
The Island of Dr. Moreau,
　　H. G. Wells
Ivanhoe, Sir Walter Scott
Jane Eyre, Charlotte Brontë
Jaws, Peter Benchley
Jonathan Livingston Seagull,
　　Richard Bach
The Joy Luck Club, Amy Tan
Jude the Obscure, Thomas Hardy
The Jungle, Upton Sinclair
Jurassic Park, Michael Crichton
Lady Chatterley's Lover,
　　D. H. Lawrence
Last and First Men,
　　Olaf Stapledon
The Last Samurai, Helen DeWitt
Last Stand at Saber River,
　　Elmore Leonard

*The Life, Adventures and Piracies
    of the Famous Captain
    Singleton,* Daniel Defoe
*The Life and Opinions of Tristram
    Shandy, Gentleman,*
    Laurence Sterne
Life of Pi, Yann Martel
Little House on the Prairie,
    Laura Ingalls Wilder
Little Women, Louisa May Alcott
Lolita, Vladimir Nabokov
Lonesome Dove, Larry McMurtry
Lonesome Land, B. M. Bower
Loon Lake, E. L. Doctorow
Lord Jim, Joseph Conrad
Lord of the Flies,
    William Golding
Love Medicine, Louise Erdrich
The Lowland, Jhumpa Lahiri
Lucky Jim, Kingsley Amis
The Magic of Oz,
    L. Frank Baum
The Magus, John Fowles
Main Street, Sinclair Lewis
The Making of Americans,
    Gertrude Stein
Malone Dies, Samuel Beckett
Mason and Dixon,
    Thomas Pynchon
Master and Commander,
    Patrick O'Brian
A Maze of Death, Philip K. Dick
McTeague, Frank Norris
Middlemarch, George Eliot/
    Mary Ann Evans
Midnight's Children,
    Salman Rushdie

The Mill on the Floss, George
    Eliot/Mary Ann Evans
Moby-Dick, Herman Melville
Molloy, Samuel Beckett
The Monk, Matthew Lewis
Motherless Brooklyn,
    Jonathan Lethem
The Mountain Lion, Jean Stafford
Mr. Midshipman Hornblower,
    C. S. Forester
Mumbo Jumbo, Ishmael Reed
My Ántonia, Willa Cather
My Brilliant Career,
    Miles Franklin
The Mysteries of Udolpho,
    Ann Radcliffe
Naked Lunch,
    William S. Burroughs
The Namesake, Jhumpa Lahiri
*The Narrative of Arthur Gordon
    Pym of Nantucket,*
    Edgar Allan Poe
Nemesis, Isaac Asimov
Neuromancer, William Gibson
Night and Day, Virginia Woolf
North and South,
    Elizabeth Gaskell
Not Without Laughter,
    Langston Hughes
O Pioneers!, Willa Cather
The Octopus, Frank Norris
Of One Blood, Pauline Hopkins
The Old Man and the Sea,
    Ernest Hemingway
Oroonoko, Aphra Behn
On Beauty, Zadie Smith
On the Beach, Nevil Shute

On the Road, Jack Kerouac

Oryx and Crake,
     Margaret Atwood

A Pale View of Hills,
     Kazuo Ishiguro

The People in the Trees,
     Hanya Yanagihara

Persuasion, Jane Austen

The Picture of Dorian Gray,
     Oscar Wilde

The Pirate, Sir Walter Scott

Plainsong, Kent Haruf

Pnin, Vladimir Nabokov

Pointed Roofs,
     Dorothy M. Richardson

The Poisonwood Bible,
     Barbara Kingsolver

*A Portrait of the Artist as a
     Young Man*, James Joyce

Possession, A. S. Byatt

The Prairie,
     James Fenimore Cooper

The Precipice,
     Elia Wilkinson Peattie

Pride and Prejudice, Jane Austen

The Prime of Miss Jean Brodie,
     Muriel Spark

The Professor's House,
     Willa Cather

Purity, Jonathan Franzen

The Rainbow, D. H. Lawrence

Rebecca, Daphne du Maurier

Remainder, Tom McCarthy

The Remains of the Day,
     Kazuo Ishiguro

Rendezvous with Rama,
     Arthur C. Clarke

Reservation Blues, Sherman Alexie

The Return of the Native,
     Thomas Hardy

Revelation Space,
     Alastair Reynolds

The Revolt of the Cockroach People,
     Oscar Zeta Acosta

The Riddle of the Sands,
     Erskine Childers

Ride the Dark Trail,
     Louis L'Amour

Riders of the Purple Sage,
     Zane Grey

The Robber Bridegroom,
     Eudora Welty

Robinson Crusoe, Daniel Defoe

The Romance of the Forest,
     Ann Radcliffe

A Room with a View,
     E. M. Forster

The Round House, Louise Erdrich

The Rules of Attraction,
     Bret Easton Ellis

The Scarlet Letter,
     Nathaniel Hawthorne

The Scarlet Pimpernel,
     Baroness Orczy

Sea of Poppies, Amitav Ghosh

The Sea, the Sea, Iris Murdoch

The Sea Wolf, Jack London

The Secret Garden,
     Frances Hodgson Burnett

The Secret History, Donna Tartt

The Secret of the Storm Country,
     Gracie Miller White

Shark Dialogues, Kiana Davenport

The Sheltering Sky, Paul Bowles

The Shining, Stephen King
The Shipping News, Annie Proulx
A Sicilian Romance, Ann Radcliffe
The Sirens of Titan,
      Kurt Vonnegut
Slaughterhouse-Five,
      Kurt Vonnegut
So Far from God, Ana Castillo
Sometimes a Great Notion,
      Ken Kesey
Song of Solomon, Toni Morrison
Song of the Lark, Willa Cather
Sons and Lovers, D. H. Lawrence
The Sound and The Fury,
      William Faulkner
Sphere, Michael Crichton
St. Irvyne, Percy Bysshe Shelley
The Stand, Stephen King
Star Maker, Olaf Stapledon
State of Wonder, Ann Patchett
The Stone Angel,
      Margaret Laurence
The Stone Diaries, Carol Shields
Strangers on a Train,
      Patricia Highsmith
Strong Poison, Dorothy L. Sayers
Surfacing, Margaret Atwood
The Surrounded,
      D'Arcy McNickle
A Tale for the Time Being,
      Ruth Ozeki
Tarzan of the Apes,
      Edgar Rice Burroughs
The Tenant of Wildfell Hall,
      Anne Brontë
Tender is the Night,
      F. Scott Fitzgerald

Tess of the D'Urbervilles,
      Thomas Hardy
Their Eyes Were Watching God,
      Zora Neale Hurston
Things Fall Apart,
      Chinua Achebe
The Third Policeman,
      Flann O'Brien
This Side of Paradise,
      F. Scott Fitzgerald
Three Lives, Gertrude Stein
Through the Arc of the Rain Forest,
      Karen Tei Yamashita
Through the Looking-Glass,
      Lewis Carroll
The Time Machine, H. G. Wells
To Kill a Mockingbird,
      Harper Lee
To the Lighthouse,
      Virginia Woolf
Treasure Island,
      Robert Louis Stevenson
A Tree Grows in Brooklyn,
      Betty Smith
Ulysses, James Joyce
Underworld, Don DeLillo
The U. P. Trail, Zane Grey
Victory, Joseph Conrad
Villette, Charlotte Brontë
The Virginian, Owen Wister
A Visit from the Goon Squad,
      Jennifer Egan
The Voyage Out, Virginia Woolf
Walk Me to the Distance,
      Percival Everett
Watership Down,
      Richard Adams

Waverly, Sir Walter Scott
The Waves, Virginia Woolf
The Way of All Flesh,
    Samuel Butler
We Have Always Lived in the
    Castle, Shirley Jackson
White Fang, Jack London
White Noise, Don DeLillo
The White Peacock, D. H.
    Lawrence
Wide Sargasso Sea, Jean Rhys
The Wind in the Willows,
    Kenneth Grahame
Wings of the Dove, Henry James

Winter in the Blood, James Welch
Wives and Daughters,
    Elizabeth Gaskell
The Wizard of Oz,
    L. Frank Baum
The Woman in White,
    Wilkie Collins
Women in Love, D. H. Lawrence
Wuthering Heights, Emily Brontë
Yellow Back Radio Broke-Down,
    Ishmael Reed
Yonnondio, Tillie Olsen
Zastrozzi, Percy Bysshe Shelley
Zone One, Colson Whitehead

ACKNOWLEDGMENTS

Endless thanks to my brilliant editor Lizzie Davis for believing in this book, and to the incredible team at Coffee House, particularly Anitra Budd, Daphne DiFazio, Daley Farr, Chris Fischbach, Kellie Hultgren, Abbie Phelps, Courtney Rust, Marit Swanson, and Carla Valadez.

I am grateful for the support of the staff and my fellow residents at the Bemis Center for Contemporary Arts. Thank you to Rachel Adams, Chris Cook, Ellina Kevorkian, Holly Kranker, and the rest of the team. Special thanks to Rebekah Wetzel for taking the deep dive into this project and helping me sort through thousands of paper scraps. Thank you to Kelly Lynn Jones and Little Paper Planes for the residency where I polished the autumn and winter sections, and to the Foundation for Contemporary Arts for helping me publicly present this work for the first time.

I am deeply indebted to my friends and early readers Natasha Boyd, Ben Segal, Suzanne Stein, and Aaron Winslow for their insight and generosity. Many thanks to Kenneth Kunkle for his Fair Use advice, and to George Yabra for his virtuoso coding skills. Thank you to Mariah Stovall, my agent, whose support made all the difference.

A mountain of thanks to the friends and mentors who encouraged and challenged me throughout the years: Einat Amir, Brian Ang, Hayden Bennett, Samantha Boudrot, Ashley Brim, Jez Burrows, Jessamyn Cuneo, Sara Davis, Jonathan Durham, Craig Dworkin, Kota Ezawa, Zach Fabri, J. Gordon Faylor, Emily Gastineau, Ivy Johnson, Josef Kaplan, Kevin Killian, Jarett Kobek, Jonathan Lethem, Carey Lin, Daniel Levin Becker, Elyse Mallouk, Gabriel Matthey Correa, Emily McVarish, Jonah Mixon-Webster, Joseph Mosconi, Billy Mullaney, Denise Newman, Alex Nichols, George

Pfau, Erika Recordon, Kate Robinson, Kathryn Scanlan, Melissa Seley, Anne Lesley Selcer, David Shields, Callie Siskel, Danny Snelson, Moheb Soliman, Emji Spero, Liza St. James, Zoe Tuck, and Jade Yumang. A special thank you and belly rub to my closest more-than-human friend through the writing process, Dora. I am eternally grateful for my family: Carolyn and Tom Comitta; Anne and Gary Ragusin; and Elena and Ilya Ocher.

My thanks for the partnership and support of Medaya Ocher are hard to put into words. Without her there would be no *Nature Book*. Daya was my guide and best friend throughout this process and taught me much of what I know about the novel form. This book is also dedicated to our child Simone, who arrived during the proofing process. If you stumble upon these pages one day, I hope they bring you joy.

Coffee House Press began as a small letterpress operation in 1972 and has grown into an internationally renowned nonprofit publisher of literary fiction, essay, poetry, and other work that doesn't fit neatly into genre categories.

Coffee House is both a publisher and an arts organization. Through our *Books in Action* program and publications, we've become interdisciplinary collaborators and incubators for new work and audience experiences. Our vision for the future is one where a publisher is a catalyst and connector.

LITERATURE
is not the same thing as
PUBLISHING

FUNDER ACKNOWLEDGMENTS

Coffee House Press is an internationally renowned independent book publisher and arts nonprofit based in Minneapolis, MN; through its literary publications and *Books in Action* program, Coffee House acts as a catalyst and connector—between authors and readers, ideas and resources, creativity and community, inspiration and action.

Coffee House Press books are made possible through the generous support of grants and donations from corporations, state and federal grant programs, family foundations, and the many individuals who believe in the transformational power of literature. This activity is made possible by the voters of Minnesota through a Minnesota State Arts Board Operating Support grant, thanks to the legislative appropriation from the Arts and Cultural Heritage Fund. Coffee House also receives major operating support from the Amazon Literary Partnership, Jerome Foundation, Literary Arts Emergency Fund, McKnight Foundation, and the National Endowment for the Arts (NEA). To find out more about how NEA grants impact individuals and communities, visit www.arts.gov.

Coffee House Press receives additional support from Bookmobile; Dorsey & Whitney LLP; Elmer L. & Eleanor J. Andersen Foundation; the Matching Grant Program Fund of the Minneapolis Foundation; Mr. Pancks' Fund in memory of Graham Kimpton; the Schwab Charitable Fund; and the U.S. Bank Foundation.

THE PUBLISHER'S CIRCLE OF COFFEE HOUSE PRESS

Publisher's Circle members make significant contributions to Coffee House Press's annual giving campaign. Understanding that a strong financial base is necessary for the press to meet the challenges and opportunities that arise each year, this group plays a crucial part in the success of Coffee House's mission.

Recent Publisher's Circle members include many anonymous donors, Patricia A. Beithon, Anitra Budd, Andrew Brantingham, Kelli & Dave Cloutier, Mary Ebert & Paul Stembler, Jocelyn Hale & Glenn Miller, the Rehael Fund-Roger Hale/Nor Hall of the Minneapolis Foundation, Randy Hartten & Ron Lotz, Dylan Hicks & Nina Hale, William Hardacker, Kenneth & Susan Kahn, the Kenneth Koch Literary Estate, Cinda Kornblum, Jennifer Kwon Dobbs & Stefan Liess, the Lenfestey Family Foundation, Sarah Lutman & Rob Rudolph, the Carol & Aaron Mack Charitable Fund of the Minneapolis Foundation, Gillian McCain, Mary & Malcolm McDermid, Daniel N. Smith III & Maureen Millea Smith, Enrique & Jennifer Olivarez, Robin Preble, Nan G. Swid, Grant Wood, and Margaret Wurtele.

For more information about the Publisher's Circle and other ways to support Coffee House Press books, authors, and activities, please visit www.coffeehousepress.org/pages/donate or contact us at info@coffeehousepress.org.

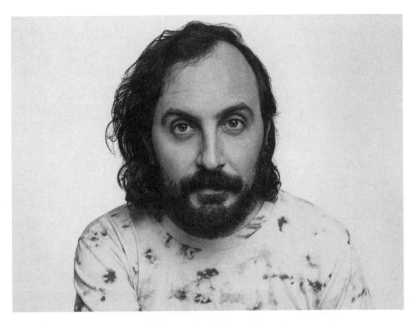

TOM COMITTA is the author of ◯, *Airport Novella*, and *First Thought Worst Thought: Collected Books 2011–2014*, a print and digital archive of forty "night novels," art books, and poetry collections. Comitta's fiction and essays have appeared in *WIRED, Lit Hub, Electric Literature,* the *Los Angeles Review of Books, The Kenyon Review, BOMB,* and *BAX: Best American Experimental Writing 2020.* They live in Brooklyn.

The Nature Book was designed by
Bookmobile Design & Digital Publisher Services.
Text is set in Adobe Garamond Pro.